The Darkest Assassin

Also From Gena Showalter

Gods of War:
Shadow and Ice
Frost and Flame

Lords of the Underworld:
The Darkest Warrior
The Darkest Promise
The Darkest Torment
The Darkest Touch
Burning Dawn
The Darkest Angel
The Darkest Craving
Beauty Awakened
Wicked Nights
The Darkest Seduction
The Darkest Surrender
The Darkest Secret
The Darkest Lie
The Darkest Passion
Into the Dark
The Darkest Whisper
The Darkest Pleasure
The Darkest Kiss
The Darkest Night
The Darkest Captive
The Darkest King

Original Heartbreakers:
Can't Get Enough
Can't Let Go
Can't Hardly Breathe
The Harder You Fall
The Hotter You Burn
The Closer You Come
The One You Want

Tales of an Extraordinary Girl:
Playing With Fire
Twice As Hot

The Darkest Assassin

A Lords of the Underworld Novella

By Gena Showalter

1001 Dark Nights

EVIL EYE
CONCEPTS

The Darkest Assassin
A Lords of the Underworld Novella
By Gena Showalter

1001 Dark Nights
Copyright 2019 Gena Showalter
ISBN: 978-1-970077-34-6

Foreword: Copyright 2014 M. J. Rose
Published by Evil Eye Concepts, Incorporated

Acknowledgments from the Author

A huge thank you to the wonderful ladies at 1001 Dark Nights: Liz Berry, MJ Rose, and Jillian Stein. Your friendship, support, kindnesses and business savvy make my heart happy!

Sign up for the 1001 Dark Nights Newsletter
and be entered to win a Tiffany Key necklace.

There's a contest every month!

Go to www.1001DarkNights.com to subscribe.

**As a bonus, all subscribers can download
FIVE FREE exclusive books!**

One Thousand and One Dark Nights

Once upon a time, in the future…

*I was a student fascinated with stories and learning.
I studied philosophy, poetry, history, the occult, and
the art and science of love and magic. I had a vast
library at my father's home and collected thousands
of volumes of fantastic tales.*

*I learned all about ancient races and bygone
times. About myths and legends and dreams of all
people through the millennium. And the more I read
the stronger my imagination grew until I discovered
that I was able to travel into the stories... to actually
become part of them.*

*I wish I could say that I listened to my teacher
and respected my gift, as I ought to have. If I had, I
would not be telling you this tale now.
But I was foolhardy and confused, showing off
with bravery.*

*One afternoon, curious about the myth of the
Arabian Nights, I traveled back to ancient Persia to
see for myself if it was true that every day Shahryar
(Persian: شهریار, "king") married a new virgin, and then
sent yesterday's wife to be beheaded. It was written
and I had read, that by the time he met Scheherazade,
the vizier's daughter, he'd killed one thousand
women.*

Something went wrong with my efforts. I arrived in the midst of the story and somehow exchanged places with Scheherazade — a phenomena that had never occurred before and that still to this day, I cannot explain.

Now I am trapped in that ancient past. I have taken on Scheherazade's life and the only way I can protect myself and stay alive is to do what she did to protect herself and stay alive.

Every night the King calls for me and listens as I spin tales. And when the evening ends and dawn breaks, I stop at a point that leaves him breathless and yearning for more. And so the King spares my life for one more day, so that he might hear the rest of my dark tale.

As soon as I finish a story... I begin a new one... like the one that you, dear reader, have before you now.

"I'm not afraid of the dark. I *am* the dark."
– Bjorn, the One True Dread

"The best way to navigate the dark? With a sword."
– Fox the Executioner

Chapter One

What have I done? What the hell have I done?

Vision blurry and ears ringing, Fox the Executioner stumbled around the ancient, crumbling temple. This was a warzone. She needed to focus but… *So dizzy.*

How many enemies waited nearby? Hoping to ward off an attack, she waved her short swords wildly, metal whistling. A cool wind blustered past the temple's pillars, the warm, wet blood that coated her hands and dripped down her arms chilling in an instant.

She had portaled here only minutes before and…and…she had gone into some kind of trance and murdered…she'd killed… A cry of distress parted her lips. She'd killed ten demon assassins known as Sent Ones. Immortals who'd been bound and utterly helpless.

Innocents.

Killing wasn't new to her. For centuries, people had paid her big bucks to slay their targets. As an equal opportunity assassin, she always welcomed a chance to take out liars, perverts, thieves, abusers, and cheaters. Even fellow exterminators. And she never failed to complete the job. No dead body meant no payment. No payment, no happiness.

Money was her source of life, and she always wanted more.

As a child, Fox had tasted the horrors of destitution. Without shelter, you were vulnerable to predators as much as the elements. Without food, you were rendered weak. Too weak to defend yourself. Without water and clean clothes, you were stripped of your humanity. *Never again.* She'd learned to save backup money for her backup money's backup money.

Today, however, she would earn no fee for her kills and derive no satisfaction from taking out bad men. The Sent Ones had been good. They had not deserved death. And yet, the moment she'd spotted them, something dark and insidious had overtaken her. She'd attacked.

Something? Like she really had to wonder where to cast the blame. Not too long ago, the demon of Distrust had possessed her, and she'd let him. Hell, she'd welcomed him. Her people lived to the ripe old age of five thousand, never any longer. As she'd neared the end, she'd sought true immortality.

That was her first mistake.

Her second? Considering herself too strong-minded to be influenced by her dark companion.

Now, crazed, gleeful laughter rumbled in the back of her mind, disrupting her thoughts.

Fox dropped her swords, a clang reverberating. Still stumbling about, she fisted her hands and punched her temples. Anything to make the hated laughter stop. But it didn't stop. It never would. Evil didn't play by any rules. It lied, cheated, stole, abused and murdered, the very things she'd spent centuries fighting against.

Worse than the laughter, the whispers. The demon enjoyed wafting his poison into her mind, little suspicions quickly ballooning into huge over-reactions.

She lies, kill her... He is setting you up for a fall, kill him... They cannot be trusted, kill them...

Today had been no different. *The Sent Ones hunt the demon-possessed, kill them...*

A shudder nearly rocked her off her feet. She should not have portaled here. But, she'd wanted to help her best friend and mentor, Galen, who'd hoped to save the woman he loved from a cloned god. Long story. The unarmed Sent Ones had occupied a far corner, as still as statues, locked in some sort of trance.

The next thing she'd known... she'd moved through their ranks, decapitating each and every warrior. No one had fought back or even ducked.

I can't be trusted anymore. If she were to inadvertently harm her friends, because of her demon's whispers...

Horror consumed her in an instant. *Won't risk their lives.* The time had come. After spending five thousand years with Galen, she needed to ditch him.

Ready to sob, she planted her heels, going still, then blinked to clear her vision. She would return home, pack a bag, and go. A hot tear trickled down her cheek. *I don't want to go.*

As she wrapped her arms around her middle, the temple crystalized. A bloodstained altar, and a golden throne. The tree that had grown through the marble floor. Where were her frien—

Firm hands settled on her shoulders and squeezed. An enemy?

Distrust did his thing, whispering, *Kill him before he kills you. Kill him now, now, now.*

No! Not again. Never *again.* Heart thudding, Fox wrenched free, but she didn't dart off. Not yet. Not until she knew the male's identity.

She pivoted, spying blond curls, baby blue eyes, and feathery white wings. Galen! Relief bombarded her. She loved the keeper of Jealousy and False Hope with all her heart.

He'd found her on the flagstone roads of Ancient Greece, mere days after the death of her mother. She'd been a child, and he'd saved her from a life on the streets. Not only had he cared and provided for her, he'd helped her anytime she'd encountered a problem.

With a sob, she launched into his strong, open arms. *Me? Sob?* Fox wasn't a crier. Except for that one…ten times she'd accidentally watched a Hallmark movie. In every other case, tears were reserved for kids and men with colds. But still she didn't stop snotting against Galen.

"Did you do a bad thing? Yes. Can we undo it? No," he told her, gently petting her hair.

"Are you strong enough to get through this? Hell, yes. I'll send in a crew to dispose of the bodies, though we both know word will spread anyway."

Oh, yes. Word would spread. They were in an immortal realm, where spirits could be hiding around every corner, watching and listening.

"You are my favorite protégé, and you can do anything," Galen said. "Even overcome a terrible mistake."

Heartbeat, heartbeat, heartbeat. "I…I'm your only protégé." He'd fired all the others. Literally! They'd died screaming as flames melted their flesh. What? They'd deserved it.

His soft chuckle ruffled strands of her hair. But, only seconds later, his amusement evaporated. "Other Sent Ones will come for you. They will want to end you, but it's going to be okay, babe. I swear it."

"Why didn't the Sent Ones defend themselves, Galen? *Why?*"

"I don't think they could. They were under some sort of enchantment. At least you made it quick and painless."

She recoiled, but he held tight, refusing to let her go. "You should cut ties with me. Otherwise, you'll be guilty by association and—"

"Don't be foolish. I will *never* cut ties with you."

A pang ripped through her chest. Most people considered Galen a villain, and they weren't wrong. Centuries ago, Fox and Galen had done terrible, awful things in the name of war. At the time, they'd entertained a single goal: do whatever proved necessary to gain more money and power. Only friends in their circle of trust had been safe. Therefore, *no one* had been safe, because they'd had no friends. But. In the past year, he had *built* a trust circle. Fox had not.

Fox still had Galen and only Galen, but he had Legion—his every waking hour revolved around her happiness—and a close-knit group of warrior confidants.

Would Fox ever find someone special? Or even a friend?

Don't want to. Better off on my own. According to previous "boyfriends"—her relationships never lasted past a few weeks—Fox didn't know how to love.

The foundation at her feet evaporated as Galen swept her up into his arms. The temple vanished next, her private bathroom appearing, complete with hundreds of tools, screws, and sheets of metal. In her spare time, Fox loved to build...anything. Her specialty happened to be robotics and weaponry.

Someone must have flashed them home, moving from one location to another with only a thought. She sucked in a familiar breath: machine oil, leather, and lavender.

When her friend set her on her feet, the ringing in her ears subsided. Her vision cleared. Legion, Galen's mate, stood at her side, a beauty with blond hair, dark eyes, and tanned skin. The opposite of dark-haired, hazel-eyed, pale-skinned Fox.

Their personalities were just as different. Legion was sugar, and Fox was spice. They'd never gotten along, and it was Fox's fault. She'd been rude as hell, too proud to admit she was jealous of the bond Legion shared with Galen.

Voice soft and sweet, Legion told her, "We're here for you, all right? Whatever you need, we will provide."

Guilt and shame coursed through her, torching her newfound calm. For weeks, she'd acted like a total bitch to this girl, hating every minute they spent together. "Thank you, Legion. I don't deserve your kindness, but...thank you," she repeated.

"Fox, you need to shower off the blood. It's not a good color for you," Galen said. "And I need to put distance between us. My demons are itching to attack you." Unlike Fox, he hosted *two* fiends. Jealousy and False Hope. Also, unlike Fox, he had not willingly welcomed his dark companions. He'd received punishment for convincing other warriors to steal and open Pandora's box, unleashing the demons trapped within…then he ratted them out to the king of the Greeks. Partly because his pride had been pricked, partly because he'd felt bad about the plan. "Legion?"

"I'll take care of her," Legion vowed.

Galen kissed Fox's brow, then Legion's lips. "Thank you, love," he told his future wife before stalking out of the room and shutting the door behind him. Fox sank onto the edge of the tub, head bowed.

Legion perched at her feet and took her hand, linking their fingers. "I'm sorry you were hurt today. You went to the temple to save me, and now… I'm sorry," she repeated.

"You did nothing wrong." The ragged response tripped from her tongue. Sent Ones were beyond powerful; they commanded armies of angels and lived to assassinate demons. They were physically unable to utter a lie, and they despised magical abilities…like portal opening. Once they decided to travel a particular path, they could not be budged until they reached the end. They delivered wrath better than any other species. "I plan to pack a bag and hit the road after I shower. I won't let you and Galen get injured in the crossfire—"

"No, no, no. I'm not worried about being pestered by an army of Sent Ones. You are a Gatekeeper. You can escape, overcome, and win anything."

True. Gatekeepers were extremely rare; they wielded the power to open a portal to any location at any time, as long as they knew the coordinates. No one could catch her, because no one could keep up with her. If anyone had a chance of success, however, it was a Sent One.

"But," Legion continued, "I *am* worried about your state of mind."

Another pang lanced Fox. "But why? I treated you terribly."

Legion waved in dismissal. "I was afraid of my own shadow, and you called me on my crap. How can I complain about any harsh words you uttered when I'm a thousand times stronger as a result? I mean, I got to decapitate Galen's greatest enemy today. Actually, I got to decapitate the bastard twice! I'm a new woman, and I've left the past in the past. I hope you do, too. You are a wonderful, secretly nerdy, closet do-gooder, and I love you."

"What's nerdy about loving fun things?" she asked as Legion patted her knee. "Trolling internet trolls. Playing Dungeons and Dragons, with *actual* dungeons and dragons. Bingeing reality TV shows. And, yeah, okay, I know a lot of my favorite shows have sucked this season, letting people break rules while pretending viewers are too stupid to notice."

Legion grinned, clearly proud that she'd distracted Fox from her pity party. "Maybe you're getting a wee bit worked up about your TV obsession?"

If there'd been a narrator for Fox's life, the bastard would have said, *"She* always *gets worked up."*

"Maybe," she agreed, only then realizing she'd sunk her nails into her thigh, drawing forth a bead of blood. "I usually ship and stan the so-called villains, and love to hate the supposed good guys. A couple of times, I've even portaled to places where live broadcasts are being filmed to cheer on my favorites." Once, she'd been a total conspiracy theorist. She'd loved coming up with scenarios and theorizing about possibilities. After Distrust, she just wanted to believe *something, anything* beyond a shadow of a doubt.

"Ship? Stan?" Legion asked. "You are speaking English, but I'm hearing Greek."

"To ship is to love someone so much, you want to sail away into the sunset together. A stan is a mashup of stalker and fan."

"See! Nerd." Legion pressed her lips together, an obvious attempt to smother her laugh. "I don't want you going on the run. I've been there, done that, and it's no way to live. I want you here, with us. I will marry Galen, and you'll become my stepdaughter. I'll have daily chores for you and stuff."

"And I'll have a magic apple for you to eat," Fox muttered.

Legion laughed. "I'm the stepmother. I get to give *you* a magic apple."

Patting the woman the way Legion had patted her, Fox said, "Maybe I don't deserve to run. Those Sent Ones were in some sort of trance and weaponless, yet I removed their heads." Free of charge! No. Wrong. She would be paying a terrible price. "Whatever fate their brethren deliver is justified." The guilt and shame returned and redoubled, overtaking Fox completely. Stupid tears scorched her stupid eyes. Her chin trembled, the salty droplets spilling down her cheeks.

"You need to ease up on yourself, Foxy. You are newly demon-possessed. You haven't learned to fight Distrust properly yet."

How did one properly fight a demon? Though the bastard had

quieted—appeased and sleeping at the moment—it was only a matter of days…hours…before he woke and began her torment anew. How did she silence his dark whispers? How did she ignore the constant paranoia?

"What's more," Legion continued, "those Sent Ones could have been the evilest, vilest Sent Ones in town, banished to the temple for terrible crimes."

Maybe, but probably not. Wait. She arched a brow and asked, "Foxy?"

Legion shrugged. "I'm trying out new nicknames. Just go with it."

"Sure thing…Mommy."

One corner of Legion's mouth twitched. "We aren't without resources. We have allies able to aid us in amazing ways. Harpies, and queens, and goddesses, oh my. We will all do everything in our power to protect you."

No way she would endanger Galen and Legion. No, Fox would rather be on her own, the only one at risk.

"Thank you for everything." For the first time in their acquaintance, Fox wrapped her arms around Galen's mate and hugged her. Her first female friend in…ever? Fox wasn't just cold. Her acerbic personality tended to prick tempers. "I'm sorry for the pain I caused you."

"I told you the past is in the past, and I meant it. No more apologies from you. I reminded you how wonderful you are, and I meant that, too. You are loyal to the ones you love. Do you know how rare that is? You are strong and cool, and I want to be more like you so bad!"

"No!" Fox blurted out, then repeated the denial at a lower volume. "Don't be like me." Mostly unfeeling, unwanted, and despised by others. Distrustful of everyone. "You are perfect, just the way you are."

"Dude. I just got a compliment out of you. This is a good news day!" Again, Legion patted her knee. Then she gave Fox another momma-bear-like hug and stood. "Shout if you need anything, all right? I'll be nearby." She padded to the door and paused. "Love is truly the only thing worth fighting for."

Not waiting for a reply, Legion closed the door, leaving Fox alone.

Love is the only thing worth fighting for.

Love. An emotion she had yet to experience.

Great! Her chin began trembling again. She stripped, her motions jerky, turned on the hot water and stepped into the stall. Crimson-tinged water rinsed from her and circled the drain. The blood of her victims.

Guilt and shame intensified, burning her throat and chest as if she'd drunk a gallon of acid. Her chin trembled, and her chest tightened. Emotions were garbage, she decided. They always shaved points off her IQ.

She needed to think of a way out of this situation, which meant she first needed to calm. So, Fox stuffed every emotion in a mental lockbox, the good and the bad. In seconds, she went cold, her preferred MO. No feelings equaled no problems.

Time to work through my troubles and find a solution. Ten dead Sent Ones, murdered by her hand. An assassin would be sent to her, Legion and Galen were right about that. Probably *ten* assassins. Like for like. Sent Ones couldn't flash or open portals, so they'd have a difficult time catching her.

What if she—?

A loud crash sounded. A sound she recognized. Someone had just kicked in the door.

Chapter Two

Heart racing, Fox pressed a series of tiles on the wall before rushing out of the shower stall. Ahead, a section of the wall popped open, revealing a sword hilt. As soon as she reached it, she grabbed that hilt, freeing the weapon. A little compartment she'd built for emergencies like this. She refused to open a portal to a new location. Her attacker(s) might or might not follow her through. If not, Galen and Legion would be vulnerable to ambush. No, Fox would stay, and she would fight.

As she rounded the corner, she spied golden feathers. Oh, yes. A Sent One had come for her. Though she'd locked up her emotions, a new one sparked. Awed terror. This wasn't just any Sent One. This was one of the Elite 7. The best of the best for allies, the worst of the worst for enemies.

Suddenly, she came face-to-face with the most beautiful male of all time. Dark hair, bronzed skin. Rainbow eyes. Wow, wow, wow. His irises contained hints of blue, green, gold, and red.

The terror faded, leaving only awe. He wore a long white robe and held a sword of flames. How he'd gotten past her friends, Fox didn't know. Surely, someone had heard his entrance.

If so, she had a minute, perhaps two, before that someone showed up to check on her. Unless the Sent One did something to prevent others from hearing what occurred in her room. Or killed those others.

Rage overwhelmed her. "Did you hurt my friends?" The question exploded from her.

"I did not."

The rage dulled, and their gazes met, awareness punching her dead center in the chest. Never in all the eons of her life had she experienced such a visceral reaction to another person.

As she struggled to take in air, he pursued her inch by inch. He liked what he saw, no doubt about it. An erection tented his robe an-n-nd damn! He couldn't be that large. Nope. No way. He must have smuggled in a package of tube socks filled with dildos. Either way, her nipples puckered and goose bumps spread over her limbs.

He swallowed. "You are Fox the Executioner." A statement, not a question, spoken in a delicious, gravelly voice.

New shivers hurried down her spine. "I am." Why deny it?

"Then you know why I'm here."

"I do." Again, there was no reason to deny it. "Nice hate-on, by the way."

A growl rumbled from him.

Excellent. She pushed back a little more. "Be honest. You're regretting your assignment now that you've seen me, yes? I mean, it's pretty obvious you gave my body a five-boner review." Despite the dire circumstances, Fox couldn't help but tease the big, bad warrior who'd come to slay her...a male who looked like sex on legs and sounded like the world's best-paid phone sex operator.

A blush painted twin circles of pink on his cheeks.

A blush? From an assassin? How adorable was that? Even still, she lifted her blade. As much as she'd struggled to survive her childhood, as fiercely as she'd fought to endure her demon, she would not go down without a fight. No matter how much she deserved the punishment.

"You are mistaken. I regret nothing," he told her. "An involuntary bodily reaction *changes* nothing."

"Or maybe it changes everything. Who are you, anyway?" And why hadn't he launched his first strike, if he had no regrets?

"I am Bjorn, the One True Dread."

Well, well. He'd actually answered. Now, her mind whirled. Bjorn... Fox kept mental files on every major species and player in the heavens, Earth, and the Underworld. He qualified. She knew Bjorn and two other Sent Ones had interacted with Galen a couple of times, and every meeting occurred while Galen interacted with the Lords of the Underworld. The men and women Galen had once convinced to steal and open Pandora's box. Every one of those warriors played host to a demon.

In fact, Distrust used to live inside a Lord named Baden. After

Baden had died—the first time—the demon had wandered the Earth for centuries, tormenting humans. Then, Galen had captured the fiend and forced him to possess Fox.

What else, what else? Bjorn's two friends were Thane of the Three and Xerxes, once known as the Cruel and Unusual until a monstrous immortal named Lazarus came along and did something crueler and more unusual, and Xerxes was redubbed the Terrible...and why did any of this matter right now? *Moving on.* The three owned and operated the Downfall, a popular nightclub in the heavens.

Other Sent Ones once considered Bjorn a bit of a playboy. Then he'd been held captive for months, by someone, somewhere, and emerged unpredictable and vengeful, more selective about his partners, preferring those who wanted rough and temporary. For the last year or so, he'd been linked to a grand total of zero women. Or men! Either he'd gotten better at hiding his liaisons, or he'd simply stopped having liaisons. She'd heard rumors about a crazy ex attacking anyone who caught his fancy, but those rumors had yet to be verified.

"Is the plan to beat and imprison me?" Fox asked, keeping her tone conversational. "Or to straight-up kill me?"

A muscle jumped beneath his eye. The fact that he continued to hold her stare, despite her nakedness and his erection, proved the strength of his willpower. "What you did to my brethren, I will do to you. This day, you *will* die by my hand."

Exactly as she'd suspected. "Did you hurt anyone on the way in?" If so, *she* would kill *him* this day.

"I did not. Unlike you, I do not slaughter innocents."

Ouch. Such a low blow. Accurate, but low. At least she didn't have to worry he'd lied. Sent Ones were only able to speak truths. "Would it help my cause if you knew I was under the influence of a demon I despise with every fiber of my being?"

His eyes narrowed to tiny slits. With zero hesitation, he told her, "You welcomed the demon and now complain about its influence? No. Nothing will help. The men you killed were beloved. They had families and friends eager for their return."

She flinched, a heavy weight settling on her shoulders. "You know I'll defend myself?"

"I do," he said with a slight incline of his chin.

For whatever reason, the action spurred him into dropping his gaze to her small but pert breasts...where it remained.

She arched a brow at him, not that he noticed, and fought a new wave of shivers, his stare more potent than a caress. "Let me know when you're done staring. Okay, sport?"

"I will." He shocked her. He didn't offer any more, and he didn't look away.

Was this a battle tactic meant to disarm her mentally and emotionally? Like she really cared about her nudity. She wasn't shy, or modest, and she maybe kinda sorta...liked the way he studied her, almost as if he'd never beheld anyone so fine. A trick, no doubt. Fox wasn't classically beautiful. Her features were too angular for such a claim. But she liked to think she had *presence*.

"Is this your first time seeing a girl?" Two could play this game. Anytime he stared, she would issue taunts.

Finally, Bjorn returned his attention to her face. For the second time, a blush pinkened his cheeks. "My apologies. You are lovely, and it has caught me off guard."

A compliment, from a Sent One? Fox reeled. She cleared her throat. "Shall we try to kill each other, then?"

Nod. "You may try. I will succeed."

Chapter Three

"Ohhhhh. I guess we've reached the trash talk portion of our evening," Fox the Executioner said.

Bjorn the One True Dread watched as she assumed a battle stance. Shoulders back, spine straight, one leg positioned in front of the other.

The woman had certainly earned her moniker. Where she went, people died.

He studied her more intently. Face it, the woman was emotionally cold but physically hot, and the juxtaposition intrigued him greatly. A phase, only a phase, and only because he'd gone a year without sex. Or maybe because she was so different from the females he'd once chosen, before his captivity. So hard and rough. Whatever the reason, it had nothing to do with her lithe yet strong body, with its perky breasts and small, pink nipples…flat stomach…tiny tuft of dark curls at the apex of her thighs…long legs made for wrapping around a man's waist.

As he imagined Fox's legs wrapped around his waist, every muscle in his body knotted with tension.

Enough! He'd meant what he'd said. Her loveliness had caught him off guard. There was no more to his attraction than that.

Immediately after receiving this assignment, Bjorn had visited the Hall of Records, where scribes tracked every human and immortal alive. Each scribe reviewed the thoughts, words and actions of a single being, and wrote them in a book. Only a select few received permission to read those books, and Bjorn wasn't one of them.

However, he *was* allowed to read what other Sent Ones wrote about her, and any interactions they'd had with her. Every detail confirmed a killer without a conscience. A true monster.

"This is getting embarrassing—for you," Fox said, exasperated. "Do you realize you're stroking yourself off?"

Damn it, he *was* stroking himself off. He'd done it without thought. Now, he froze.

Chagrinned, he dropped his arms to his sides and forced his attention elsewhere. The bathroom decor provided the perfect background for the woman, sleek and modern with gold facets, white tiles, and breasts.

Breasts? He cursed inside his head. He was staring again. *Not my fault. She is...unexpected.* Never had he seen such striking, arresting features. She possessed the kind of face that somehow suggested both incredible strength *and* staggering vulnerability. A face you never, ever forgot, with heavy-lidded bedroom eyes, spiky lashes, and red, pouty lips. A hint of rose complemented her pale, flawless skin.

She was so different from Alana. So—*enough! Do not think about her.* One Alana-centric thought would lead to another and another until he spiraled into a rabbit hole of shame and fury.

"If you'd prefer to battle me in a better location," he said, unsure why he continued to stall, "I will allow you to portal us—"

"You'll *allow* me?" she interjected. "How wonderful of you. But, no thanks. I can kill you here just as easily as elsewhere."

So confident. So foolish. *The same can be said of you.* Why else would he offer to let his target decide the location of their showdown? "Very well. We fight here." Close-quarter combat required a particular skill set. The bigger the combatant, the bigger the disadvantage. With two hundred and fifty pounds of muscle and a six-foot-five-inch frame, Bjorn fell into the *major* disadvantage category. Fox probably weighed a hundred and twenty-five pounds max, and topped out at five-nine.

So, she held an advantage at the moment? So what? He endured a lifetime of training, the best tool in any arsenal.

"Don't take this the wrong way," she said, "but are you sure you know how to fight? Hint. There are myriad ways, but standing there, doing nothing isn't one of them."

Ignore your fascination with her body. He had a job to do, so, he would do it. He would rather live with the memory of her death than his failure. "Goodbye, Fox. May you find peace in the hereafter." With a war cry, Bjorn tucked his wings into his sides and pushed off the balls of his feet.

Anticipating a strike, Fox raised her sword. Smart. He swung his. Metal met metal, their blades clanging together. As intense vibrations rushed up his arms, Fox attempted to stab him in the gut, using a dagger she'd hidden in her other hand.

He blocked at the last second, spun, and swung at her. Again, their blades clanged together, her reflexes faster than expected. A louder *clink* sounded, acting as a starting bell for round two.

Tension thickened the air as they danced around the bathroom, slamming into the trash can…the sink…the toilet. Toiletries dropped, the toothbrush holder shattering. On the walls, tiles cracked.

Throughout the eons of his life, he'd participated in countless battles. Some willingly, some unwillingly. This was the first time he'd challenged a naked female, but (hopefully) wouldn't be his last. The view could not be beat. Any move she made caused her breasts to bounce, and when she kicked up a leg, he received a straight-up money shot.

A strategy, perhaps. The sight always distracted him, blanking his mind and stopping him in his tracks, allowing her to land another blow— a heel to the kneecap. Pain shot through his entire leg and sickness churned in his stomach. Did he slow? Not even a little.

She fought well, her lithe body quick and flexible. She didn't hesitate to deliver harm. Didn't flinch when she failed to block an opponent's strike. Her true talent, however? Predicting his moves and reacting accordingly, never receiving more than a bruise or a surface cut.

But, her ability to predict his actions also proved to be her greatest weakness. As light as she was, she had to exert tremendous amounts of energy to remain upright each and every time she blocked his sword. Soon, she would tire out…

He swung once…twice…again and again, driving her backward. When the wall stopped her, he prepared to deliver the final blow. A water droplet dripped from her hair, landed on her collarbone, and sluiced to her nipple, where it hovered.

Beautiful nipple. The perfect bull's eye.

The next thing he knew, a sharp pain exploded through his abdomen. He blinked back into focus just in time to watch Fox twist the blade she'd sunk into his gut. Searing agony consumed every inch of him, stars winking through his vision. *Eyes off the nipples!* Right.

He slammed a fist into her forearm with all his might. The bone broke, maybe even shattered. A hiss parted her lips, but she refused to release the sword hilt. Impressive. Had any other opponent ever proven so stubborn?

Knowing she would use this newest distraction against him and go for a vital organ, Bjorn wrenched backward, sliding free of the blade. Blood and something as thick and black as motor oil gushed from the wound, pooling on the floor. Wonderful! She'd clipped his stomach.

Before she delivered the counterstrike, he shot out his wing, sweeping her off her feet. She toppled, the back of her head slamming into the sink. The porcelain cracked. He swung his sword once, twice, but she reeled to the left, blocked, then rolled past him and lurched to a stand, blocking again.

With a grunt, he drove her backward a second time. He would trap her in the stall. Except, the little vixen surprised him. The moment he stood upon the mat in front of the tub, she swooped down and pulled the wool out from under his feet.

As he fell, he kicked her ankles together. They crash-landed at the same time, air bursting from his lungs. Though his head swam, he leaped to his feet. She did the same. Panting, they circled each other.

Kill or be killed. Do your duty.

Voice ragged, she said, "You'd be a stellar opponent if you weren't so easily distracted."

"You might have killed me already if you had bigger breasts." He had to add "might" in order to turn the lie into a supposition. Her breasts were perfect; every inch of her was perfect. He hoped the trash talk prompted her to rage. When your emotions took the wheel, you made mistakes.

She grinned, propelling his heart rate to warp speed. *Lovely.* Beyond *lovely. Wicked, carnal.* If she hadn't murdered ten of his comrades, she would have tempted him to forget his vow of celibacy.

"If my breasts were bigger," she all but purred, "you'd have died of a heart attack the second you spotted me."

She wasn't wrong.

He opened his mouth to offer some kind of rebuttal, only to pause. His ears twitched, a pair of footsteps snagging his attention. At least two people approached the bedroom. Most likely Galen and Legion.

For a moment, Fox went still. "Galen's coming." A curse exploded from her. "Do not hurt him. Do not challenge him. He's done nothing wrong."

Such a volatile reaction. From his research, Bjorn knew Fox and Galen enjoyed a close relationship. Not romantically, he didn't think. Galen had an unwavering obsession for his girlfriend, a former demon minion turned immortal human. "You have my word. No harm will come to him this day. There is an invisible blockade around the entire room. No one, not human, immortal or god can enter in any way, shape or form. Not through a door, or a window, or a portal. Not even a flash." The Underworld's word for teleporting.

"How is that possible?" she demanded.

"A bloodline." Before Bjorn kicked his way into the bathroom, he'd poured a mixture of his blood and Water of Life around the bedroom's perimeter, creating a powerful force field.

"Why would—the demon," she said, answering her own question before she finished speaking it.

"Exactly right." Once Bjorn removed Fox's head, the demon would lose its host and have to be captured, then transported back to Hell.

As he began to swing his weapon, Fox dove to the floor, rolled past him and leaped to her feet to sprint out of the bathroom. At the same time, he fought to slow the momentum of his swing...and failed. The sword's flames singed a line of soot into the wall, the pungent scent of burnt plaster saturating the air.

At least she remained in his sights. The woman halted in the center of the chamber and attempted to open a portal. When she failed, courtesy of the bloodline, she belted out a curse.

Bjorn gave chase, releasing the hilt of his sword. In an instant, the flames died, and the weapon vanished. Despite an increase in pain, his wounds bleeding faster, he dove into Fox, tossing her to the floor. Instinct insisted he twist mid-air to absorb the worst of the impact.

An instinct he ignored.

This wasn't a usual situation, and she wasn't a usual target. Saving her from a bit of soreness would only hinder his cause; a concussion might knock her out and save him the hassle of subduing her. And he wouldn't feel guilty about it. He wouldn't!

Impact! A heavy thud as she landed. A heavier thud as he landed on top of her. She gasped and struggled to get free, bucking and throwing elbows. He remained on top of her, different parts of him pinning different parts of her. As quickly as possible, he caught her wrists and wound her arms behind her back, shackling her hands between their bodies.

His blood dripped all over her, smearing on her skin. An obscene sight he found distasteful, but he didn't know why. "Enough, female. You lost. Time to accept it."

She bucked with more force, her scent hitting his awareness. He went still. His veins heated, white-hot desire rushing to his groin. That fragrance…so incredibly sweet. Too sweet for a cold-blooded killer. It fogged his head, enveloping him in a sensual cloud.

"You have signed your death warrant, warrior," she said with gritted teeth.

"When I slay you, and I will, all the world shall hear your screams. Tell me. How will you deliver my death then, hmm?" The feel of her… Softer than he'd expected. Hotter, too.

I'll sport an erection for the rest of my life.

Suddenly, the bedroom door split down the middle. Galen marched through it, clutching two short swords. The second the male with wings of ivory hit the invisible wall of energy, he bounced back. More enraged by the minute, he used the sword to hack at the barrier, his navy gaze continually shifting to Fox. All the while, he shouted obscenities and threats.

Finally, Galen switched his gaze to Bjorn, watching as he held out his arm, palm open. The sword reappeared, flames quickly spreading over the blade. Fox slowed before stilling altogether.

Go on. Do it! His grip tightened on the hilt as he glared down at her. She lay on her stomach, panting, her head angled to the right, revealing her profile. There was a slight discoloration on her jaw, a bruise already forming. His chest tightened.

She bellowed, "What are you waiting for? Do it or release me. You have no other options."

Yasssss. Kill her! But…his chest tightened further, constricting his airways. Could he—should he?—do the deed in front of the male who loved her? Was he truly so cruel? Galen had done nothing to earn a punishment from the Sent Ones. Not recently, anyway.

No. Bjorn wasn't so cruel.

Gnashing his molars, he swung the sword. Instead of removing her head, he brushed his thumb over the bottom of the sword hilt, freeing a needle from confinement. Then he angled his wrist midway, ensuring the hilt and the needle laced with a temporary paralytic slammed into her temple.

Her entire body fell lax, her eyes closing.

Being an immortal, she healed faster than normal, so he must work fast. Ignoring Galen, who still beat at the wall, Bjorn rolled Fox to her back. He released the weapon, and it vanished once again. With his knees pressing into her shoulders, he freed the vial of powder that hung from a chain around his neck.

As he uncorked the top and poured the contents into his hand, the paralytic wore off. Her eyelids fluttered open, and their gazes met once again. His shaft *throbbed*.

She squirmed and bucked, desperate to unseat him. When she failed, she glared up at him and screamed, "Do it, then! Put me out of my misery." Her eyes widened as soon as the words registered; the command had surprised her. It had certainly surprised Bjorn. "I've been fighting to survive for so long," she said, her tone soft. "I'm tired."

The strangest urge hit him. To gently, tenderly brush back a lock of hair from her brow. He ground his molars, resisting with all his might. "You wish to die? Then you will live—for a little while. Until I tire of your suffering."

Leaning down, he blew the powder into her face. She coughed until her body fell limp once again, sagging against the floor.

He did not let himself look at her again. Not really. He wasn't sure how he'd react to seeing her lying motionless. But, he did keep his attention focused in her general direction as he stood and stalked to the closet, walking backward so he wouldn't have to turn his back. A compliment he only extended to the greatest of warriors.

When he reached his destination, he reached out, searching blindly, still unwilling to remove his attention from her. If she faked her unconsciousness…or if she hadn't, and she awoke, they would fight again. Could he win another round? Multiple wounds ached and bled profusely, making him hemorrhage strength at an alarming rate.

When he brushed against a buttery-soft garment, he yanked it from the hanger. A T-shirt. Excellent. He stalked to the dresser and selected socks and a pair of panties. Silk, in various colors. Lace.

Bjorn imagined Fox wearing every scrap of material he lifted, and his erection throbbed harder. In the end, he selected a gold one with flecks of green, because it matched her eyes.

This is ridiculous. He returned to Fox and tugged the shirt over her head, then fit her arms through the appropriate holes. Next, he closed his eyes and slid the panties up her legs. *Such silken skin.*

Ignore! He opened his eyes and hefted her over his shoulder, then met Galen's gaze.

The blond male stopped beating at the invisible wall at last, instead choosing to point an accusing finger at Bjorn. A warning.

Leaving the bloodline in place, Bjorn let himself, and thereby Fox, fade into spirit form. He spread his wings and leaped through the ceiling, flying to the heavens. Blood, still dripping… Strength, still waning…

His pain escalated. For some reason, the sweetness of her scent kept his mind awake and active, which kept him fighting to reach his friends at the Downfall. Once there, he would be patched up. Once patched up, he would regain his strength.

Then, he would kill Fox.

Chapter Four

Bjorn flew through the third level of the heavens. The first and second levels were located above this one, where the Most High, angels, and spirits of the dead resided. Night had fallen, the darkness thick and cloying.

He did his best to dodge the clouds, for Sent Ones lived inside them. Problem was, his eyelids seemed to gain a hundred pounds with every minute that passed. If he failed to reach his destination soon, he would pass out and fall from the sky. A crash-landing would end him, as well as Fox.

He tightened his hold on her. To distract himself from the pain and weakness, he hosted a one-way conversation with his baggage. "The order to slay you came directly from a leader of the Elite 7, Zacharel. He received his orders from the second-in-command of all Sent Ones, Clerici, who oversees the three types of Sent Ones. Messengers, who deliver heavenly missives between realms. Warriors, who hunt and kill demon minions. And the Elite 7, who fight the most powerful demons, the High Lords."

Finally, the Downfall entered his line of sight. *Praise the Most High!*

He flapped his wings with more force. The nightclub for immortals was a literal fortress perched atop a mossy cliff, both enveloped by a cloud Bjorn owned with his closest friends, Thane and Xerxes. Males he loved like brothers. No, more than brothers. They hadn't been born into the same family, but they'd chosen to stay together. That mattered.

Centuries ago, before they'd met, an Elite soldier had recruited them to help track and kill the demon High Lord of Perversion. Only, Bjorn was captured and imprisoned instead, along with Thane and Xerxes. After months of torture he couldn't relive without screaming, sobbing, or wanting to hurt himself and anyone around him, he'd changed. They had, too. Charismatic Thane grew morose. Energetic Xerxes turned sullen. Carefree Bjorn became broody. The only beauty to grow from the ashes of his torment? An unbreakable bond.

In the years since their escape, they'd discovered they worked better as a unit. He trusted the pair with his life. They guarded his back, no matter the situation, just as he defended theirs. To keep them safe, he would cross any line. He would even fall, losing his wings, his immortality, and his home.

The second his feet touched the roof, a wave of dizziness suffused his mind. His legs buckled, his knees too weak to bear his weight. He landed on his ass, somehow managing to maintain his hold on Fox, who bounced on his shoulder.

Careful. Fox the Executioner was as cunning as her named suggested. If she awoke and pretended to be asleep, he needed to know it. Bjorn readjusted her as gently—read: clumsily—as possible so that he cradled her against his chest. Her cheek rested on his shoulder, her warm breath fanning his neck. Now, at least, he would detect a flutter of her lashes, or a hitch in her breathing.

Unable to rally the strength to audibly shout for his friends, he was reduced to transmitting a telepathic SOS. A talent all Sent Ones possessed. *On roof. Injured. Need help.*

He had no doubt they'd stop whatever they were doing and…yes. His sensitive ears picked up the sound of hurried footsteps. Hinges squeaked, the only entrance/exit on the roof swinging open. The steps started up again, only faster. Then Bjorn saw them. Thane and Xerxes both wore concerned expressions.

His chest swelled with a calming mix of relief, love and confidence. Everything would be okay. His friends would rather die than lose him, just as he would rather die than lose them.

They sprinted to his side, and Xerxes attempted to take the girl.

Bjorn held fast, grating, "Mine." His assignment. His target. Strangely enough, one of his favorite memories. Nakedness should be a requirement for any form of combat.

Xerxes lifted his hands, a gesture of innocence before working with Thane to help Bjorn stand with Fox still cradled in his arms. It brought back memories of their imprisonment. How many times had these males patched him up while offering comfort and encouragement? Countless.

"Let us dispose of the body, my friend," Thane said, his tone tender.

With golden curls, blue eyes, and tanned skin, Thane resembled an angel. With long white hair, red eyes, and scarred white skin, Xerxes resembled a devil. Bjorn hovered somewhere in the middle, part angel, part devil.

Other Sent Ones considered their threesome amoral. They often slept around, got high on ambrosia, and killed anyone who wronged them. Well, Bjorn used to sleep around.

"She isn't dead," Bjorn admitted. "Just resting."

If any other Sent Ones were present, protests and criticism would have rung out. If those Sent Ones were prone to fits of temper, punches would have been thrown. And he would deserve all of it! Fox had murdered ten Sent Ones in cold blood. Perhaps she'd been paid to do it. Maybe she did it for grins and giggles. Or, what if the demon had dictated her actions? The reason didn't really matter. The ten had been innocents with families desperate for their return. Now, they were dead.

The reaction he received from his boys? Nods. They accepted what he'd done, or what he'd *not* done, and they trusted him to make it right.

"How can we help?" Xerxes asked. "Shall I kill her for you?"

"No!" The word burst from him with more force than he'd intended. "Want to keep her in the dungeon. Will kill her after I heal." Going against Clerici's orders was a crime. If they were found out, they would be punished. Yet, he knew neither friend would hesitate to offer aid.

"Of course," they said in unison.

"Whatever you need," Thane added.

"We will ensure no one knows," Xerxes vowed.

See! "Love you," he croaked, still hemorrhaging strength in great waves.

With the males acting as crutches, he hobbled past the doorway, entering the upper level of the building. A secluded haven inaccessible by patrons. The club itself consisted only of the two bottom floors. Thane, Xerxes and Bjorn kept private suites up here. Thane and his wife Elin occupied the biggest one. Xerxes selected the one with the best view, and Bjorn chose the one with a balcony. Staff members lived on the floor below, also inaccessible by patrons.

A wide hallway led to an equally wide elevator, both big enough for their wings. With every step, Bjorn's feet dragged a little more. Still, he pressed forward, riding the elevator down, down into the dank, musty dungeon. Or rather, Fox's new—and last—home.

* * * *

Fox awoke with a moan. Her head ached, and the rest of her smarted as if she'd been the gooey center in a seven-car pile-up. What the—?

Memory fragments trickled into her foggy mind...dead Sent Ones... Bjorn... Pain... Darkness. With a gasp, she jolted to an upright position. Ow, ow, ow. The aches worsened, and her stomach twisted.

Swallowing bile, she blinked rapidly, relieved when her vision cleared. The second she spied her surroundings, the relief fled, and horror took over. Mold and old blood decorated walls made of crumbling stone. No windows. The only light spilled from a single overhead bulb, highlighting a dirt floor, a bloodstained cot, and a broken toilet.

Moans of anguish echoed in a continuous stream. The smell of waste, urine and metal stung her nostrils. Beneath the pungent odor of filth, she detected a hint of Bjorn's scent—rainstorms and sultry summer nights. Fox breathed deeply, savoring. Shivering. Until she remembered she hated him and hoped to strangle him with his own intestines.

No sign of him nearby. Good thing. She might have killed him with her bare hands.

He thinks to torment me before he ends me? Fox fisted her hands.

She had researched Sent Ones. Knowledge was power, after all, and knowing an opponent's strengths and weaknesses could save your life in battle. What she knew now? Bjorn could not be swayed from an assigned task. No reason to try.

All she could do? Portal away, regroup, then battle Bjorn again. On her own terms next time.

Very well. Decision made. She would open a portal and return to Galen.

Fox spread and pressed her fingertips together. The ends heated, and she slowly separated her hands. An ember sparked between them. Then another and another until a portal burned through the atmosphere to create a doorway to another world. But, only a split second later, the almost-portal extinguished.

What. The. Hell? For only the fifth time ever—six now—she'd failed to open a portal. Thrice, she'd been too weak from blood loss.

Twice, she'd been drugged.

Must escape. Fox didn't have many fears. But this? Incarceration? This happened to be a big one. Locked up, she controlled no aspect of her life. No control meant no future. Not one worth living, anyway.

If she couldn't open a portal, a bloodline must be responsible. But how did she get rid of a bloodline? *Think, think.*

When several minutes passed without a single intelligent thought, she concluded her mind hadn't shaken off the effects of whatever powder Bjorn had blown into her face. She'd try again in a bit. Meanwhile…

Had her injuries healed? She glanced down her body and cringed. *You've got to be kidding me.* Fox never cared about fashion, but come on! She despised thongs, yet she now wore a pair Galen had given her as a joke, as well as a pink novelty T-shirt with his smiling face in the center, giving a thumb's up.

For this, I'll make Bjorn's death slow and torturous.

Out of habit, she reached for a dagger. Gah! Of course, Bjorn had refrained from loading her up with weapons before he sealed her inside this shithole. At least she was on the road to recovery, each of the cuts and gashes mended. Only a bump on her head remained.

Recalling how easily Bjorn had knocked her out, she alternated between rage…and awe. Few combatants had the skill to take her down so swiftly. But then, she'd arrived fresh from another battle, compromised emotionally, and bare-ass naked.

The taste of blood coated her tongue, and she realized she'd been biting the inside of her cheek. Okay, waiting for her mind to clear wasn't going to work for Fox. She needed action, and she needed it now.

She eased to her feet and shouted, "Bjorn! Show yourself, you coward."

"Coward?" He materialized just outside of her cell and stepped from a cluster of shadows.

How long had he been there? How had he hidden so well? And how did she feel about being secretly watched by him? *Not* excited, that was for sure. Nope. Definitely not.

"We fought," he said. "I won. I didn't kill you while you slept. Now, your every breath belongs to me."

Oh, man, he looked good. Really good. He'd showered and changed into a clean robe. On most Sent Ones, the fabric remained loose. On Bjorn, the fabric pulled taut over his chest and biceps. Golden wings arched over magnificently broad shoulders. Locks of bronzed hair stuck out in spikes, those rainbow eyes gleaming with smug satisfaction. The bastard had her right where he wanted her.

Grinding her teeth, she said, "You should have killed me when you had the chance. I won't give you another one."

He hiked up a shoulder, unconcerned. "I don't need you to give me anything. I can and will kill you any time of my choosing."

No, not good enough. "You've already made the decision to do it. So. Go ahead. Do it."

"First, I have questions for you."

His tone tightened at the end of his statement, a sign she wasn't going to like what he asked.

"I have questions for you, too." Feigning nonchalance, she eased onto the edge of the cot. Anything to bide her time and figure out a game plan. Like...draw him inside the cell, kill him with his own weapon and flee? *Done!*

More Sent Ones would come after her, of course, but at least she'd be free. But...

Part of her didn't want to harm the Sent One. Well. *That's new.* She had a rule: always kill the one trying to kill you. But Bjorn wasn't doing this for a payout or even revenge. Okay, he might be doing this for revenge. Mostly, he was following his leader's order to punish the one who'd devastated their species. So. Killing him would be Plan B. Fingers crossed she created a stellar Plan A. Because...

She didn't want to kill him. He was the first male to make her shiver in...ever.

I...desire him? Sexually?

In the past, when hungering for a man, she'd picked one. They'd share a couple of weeks together, and she'd moved on. She never slept with a potential target, and she never slept with an enemy.

To Fox, men were like toilet paper. Necessary for a moment, but happily discarded after use. Too many lied, stole or cheated. Who was she supposed to trust?

"Very well," Bjorn finally said, nodding for emphasis. "We will converse as comrades...for a bit. I ask, you answer. And in return, I'll do the same for you."

Ugh. Did he have to be so reasonable? "I also have statements for you," she said. "I'll start with this one. Galen will come for you and yours. One by one, you'll all die screaming."

Shrug. "He can come, but he won't be the one doing the killing."

Bjorn stepped closer and leaned against the bars, the sensuality of his movements mesmerizing.

Focus up. Ogle her captor—more than she already had? No, thanks. "Go ahead. Gentlemen first."

"Why did you murder the ten?" He pushed the words through teeth as gritted as her own. "At our first meeting, you eluded to the demon's dark influence, but I wish to hear a play-by-play of your thought process."

Knew he'd go there. She opted to tell him the truth. "The moment I spotted the ten, Distrust began whispering his poison, reminding me the warriors were demon assassins, telling me they'd come for me and my friends and if I wanted my loved ones to survive, I had to strike first. The next thing I knew, the Sent Ones were dead, their bodies piled around me."

Despite the savagery of her words, he did not alter his expression or evince a single emotion.

"And I know, I know," she said. "I can't blame Distrust, because I willingly welcomed the fiend inside me." A point she could not refute then, now, or ever. She—ow! She winced as a sharp pain sprang from her head wound.

Bjorn, being Bjorn, offered, "If you are in pain, we can postpone our conversation."

A kindness from him, his concern for an enemy commendable. But also, useful. Had she just found the way to lure him in? "I'm in pain, yes," she said. The truth, only exaggerated. Playing her part, she rubbed her temples.

"I'm glad you hurt," he grated, dashing her hopes.

She jolted as if he'd punched her. Sent Ones could not lie. He'd meant what he said. He wanted her to hurt. *Can you blame him?* Irritated with him, and herself, she gave up temple-rubbing and resettled on the cot, getting as comfortable as possible. "You can go now."

He dropped his chin to his sternum, those rainbow eyes growing more intense by the second. "Do you think you deserve punishment for your crimes?"

Ouch. No matter how she responded to that one, she would sound like a total bitch. "You'll believe me, whatever I say?"

"Yes." Offered without hesitation.

Why would—? Oh, right. Sent Ones could taste lies when others spoke them. "Why do you want to know? Will the answer change your mind about me?"

"No. You will die, no matter your opinion."

Yeah, exactly as she'd suspected. "I do believe I deserve punishment. What I did was reprehensible, and I regret it with every fiber of my being. But I'm still going to kill you and anyone else who comes after me."

He blinked, surprised, then pivoted on his heel and paced before the bars of her cell. "Any last words?"

Their gazes met. She unveiled a slow, wicked grin and stood, rising from the cot to assume a battle stance: shoulders back and legs braced apart, with one positioned slightly ahead of the other. "Come in here and get me, big boy."

To her shock, desire flared in his eyes, there and gone. The possibility sparked an equal reaction in her. First excitement she couldn't deny, then disappointment. The desire wasn't for her. Clearly, the man entertained a battle fetish and got turned on by any type of fight. Or did the reason go deeper?

No. No way Bjorn desired Fox, the one responsible for his pain. And he *was* in pain. He'd recently said goodbye to ten members of his family.

Now, her head bowed with shame. Thankfully, she rebounded quickly, stuffing the shame into the emotional lockbox, going cold once again. There. Much better. The cold was familiar, and as welcoming as a long-lost friend newly returned home.

"I do have a question," she rasped. "Why were you chosen as my assassin?"

"I am *always* chosen for this type of case, because I do not care why something was done, only that it was, in fact, done."

"Motive should matter. Intent, too."

"Why?"

The simplest and most complex question of all time. "Because…just because! Someone who doesn't intend to cause pain should not be lumped with the ones who do intend to cause pain."

He ran his tongue over his teeth. "You hope to convince me you did not mean to cause the ten pain? That will—" Suddenly, he went still, his muscles bulging with tension. The overhead bulb flickered, darkness chasing away light, then light chasing away darkness. Just outside her cell, a thick, black cloud rolled through the corridor.

The fine hairs on the back of her neck stood to attention, as if a great and terrible evil had just neared. A reaction usually reserved for a prince of darkness. "What's happening?"

Bjorn's tension redoubled, then redoubled again. His breaths turned shallow. Panic lit his eyes before he blanked his expression. "Stay silent, no matter what you behold, hear, or smell. Draw no attention to yourself."

Wait. Hold up. Did he radiate *fear*?

No. No way. This particular Sent One feared nothing. But, as minutes bled into each other, her curiosity intensified. Seriously, what the hell was going on?

He thinks to trick you somehow. Whatever he tells you to do, do the opposite!

And there was Distrust, ready to work her into a frenzy. Fox resisted the urge to obey, instead pressing her lips together and nodding at Bjorn.

Her ears twitched, the click-clack of high heels reverberating through the cell at a slow, steady pace. *Click. Clack. Click. Clack.* One after the other.

"Tsk, tsk, tsk, Bjorn." A woman's lilting voice reverberated through Fox's cell. "In the past hour, I've summoned you twice, yet here you are."

Summoned? What, the bitch had snapped her fingers? She must be his lover, then. But why would he act so weird about a girlfriend? And why were Fox's nails sharpening into claws at the thought of Bjorn with some nameless, faceless female? Foolish!

At last, the speaker strode into view, stopping directly in front of Bjorn. Fox stared, awed. *Beautiful.* Oddly magnetic. Angelic. On the short side and trim, wearing an ice-blue gown made from see-through scarves. Curly white-blond hair flowed to a trim waist, the perfect complement to her tanned skin and black-as-night eyes. Her nails were *blacker* than night, and as long and sharp as Fox's claws.

Bjorn didn't move, didn't speak. Then. In that moment, Fox realized the truth. He did fear this woman, but mostly he raged. Whoever she was, he hated her with the heat of a thousand suns.

The woman walked a circle around him, tracing one of those razor-sharp nails across his chest and back. Blood welled and dripped. Wow. She'd sliced his skin, and he'd let her. *Seriously, what the hell is going on?*

The intruder spared Fox a quick glance before dismissing her, as if she meant nothing.

That's right, sweetness. Pay this little filly no mind. I'm just a prisoner in a novelty tee and butt floss.

When the woman stood before Bjorn once again, she gripped his chin between her fingers and glared up at him. "I do not know how you gained the strength to resist my summons, but it stops now. When I call, you run. Otherwise, I'll come to you. That happens, and I'll kill one of your friends. Their life will be payment for my inconvenience. Do you understand?"

He jerked his head in a facsimile of a nod. "My complete disgust for you. That is how I now resist. That is also how I'm able to speak of you to others, when I could not utter a word about you before."

The intruder narrowed her eyes further. "Say it," she snapped.

A muscle jumped beneath his eye. "Yes, Alana. I understand," he grated, pink stains of humiliation spreading over his cheeks. "You call, I run."

"That's my good boy." Alana patted his stubbled cheek and stepped back, widening the distance between them. "You have one hour to finish this...whatever this is. Do not be late." The smoke enveloped her, and she vanished. Next, the remaining shadows vanished, too.

For a long while, Bjorn remained in position, panting, his hands fisted. Fox felt like a voyeur, witnessing a major life event she wasn't supposed to see.

"Who is she?" The words croaked from her.

He flexed his jaw. "She is...my wife."

Chapter Five

Bjorn stalked to his bedroom, careful to avoid crossing paths with Thane or Xerxes. If they knew Alana had summoned him, they would worry. They would also drown in guilt, blaming themselves for their inability to save him. *No one* could save him.

He remembered the day he'd met Alana. She'd come to the Downfall, looking like a wingless angel on the hunt for a husband. Not that he'd known it at the time. Her top three requirements? Strong, immortal, and damaged.

Bjorn had been in a bad place then. Needing to hurt someone, he'd approached Alana. They'd flirted, nothing more, and only for a short time. It hadn't taken long to notice the severity of her narcissism. He'd ditched her fast. But soon after, she'd returned…with a legion of shadow warriors.

A battle erupted, Bjorn's crew against hers. Thane and Xerxes had almost died. Innocents *had* died, slain by one of the world's greatest evils. Even now, the memory caused rage to sear his chest.

Alana had done it all to force Bjorn into a marriage bond. *Wed me, or more will die. The choice is yours.* The marriage bond had been her insurance policy, after all. With it, Bjorn and Alana were linked. When one died, the other followed. Now, his friends couldn't murder his tormentor without killing him, too.

The funny thing? Not ha-ha funny, but *how-is-this-my-life* funny. Bjorn had more reason to despise Fox than Alana, yet he wanted Fox. Badly. And yet, if Fox had visited the Downfall before their shower-time battle, he'd failed to notice her. He'd gravitated exclusively to the sweet-as-sugar, angelic-looking types. But, as many *sweet* females as he'd bedded before the start of his celibacy, he'd never walked away satisfied, or eager for a repeat.

Why hadn't he gone for the pale, Goth types? Fox's straightforward, no-bullshit manner left him panting for more. Plus, she looked ridiculously adorable in a stupid T-shirt and a G-string.

The corners of his mouth curled up, only to fall. He shouldn't crave Fox, and he would never want Alana, a bitch and a parasite. She increased her lifespan by morphing into dark mist, possessing his body, and stealing his soul or life-force.

Bjorn shut himself inside his bedroom. He pushed open the doors that led to his balcony and stepped to the rail-less edge. Wind whipped his robe around his ankles as he dove off. Falling...spreading and flapping his wings... He caught an air current and flew high...higher.

A secret of the Sent Ones: In the sky, there were thousands of invisible doorways hidden inside designated clouds, and they led to different parts of the world. Some even led to other worlds, realms and dimensions. Bjorn navigated the path without incident, reaching Alana's lair in less than half an hour. A dark, cavernous realm that made his skin crawl.

He entered the palace. A cavern comprised of black stone, rose-scented smoke and cloying darkness. The stone caused a reaction similar to poison ivy: brush against it, and you blister. The smoke burned his eyes and stung his nostrils. The darkness set his nerves on edge.

The only light came from two rows of torches. What held those torches? Men and women hanging from pikes. They formed a line on both his left and right sides, creating a path. Some victims moaned in agony. Some sobbed. All had a small stack of kindling piled around their feet.

If anyone dropped their torch, they would set that kindling ablaze, then slowly burn to death, regenerate, then burn to death again. One of the most torturous ends an immortal could experience.

Every victim projected a bombardment of pain and hopelessness, and yes, his skin crawled. With every atom of his being, Bjorn longed to put the immortals out of their misery. His nature demanded it; as a Sent One, his sole purpose was the eradication of evil. But...

On his first visit here, he'd given in to his urge to help and removed the prisoners from their pikes. For his efforts, Alana had given him a taste of the very punishment he'd fought against: twenty-four hours on a pike of his own.

Weeks had passed before he fully recovered.

His hands flexed around imaginary sword hilts. *Must help them.*

No! Must resist. He had a plan. One day, after he'd found a way to sever his bond with Alana and survive, he would return. He would free every prisoner and force Alana to taste the punishment before he killed her. Also, he needed to maintain his strength however possible today.

He quickened his steps, the tips of his wings collecting soot from the ground. Once he finished with Alana, he must deal with Fox once and for all.

Fox… Anticipation fizzed in his veins. He couldn't wait to breathe in her lusciously sweet fragrance, feel the sublime heat of her body, or gaze upon those arresting features. He even enjoyed conversing with her; the woman wielded a ready wit he found appealing. She also displayed a talent for masking her emotions, making him frantic to dig deep and discover the truth beneath the unconcerned veneer.

The fact that he'd hardened while speaking with the murderess didn't matter. His dick ached for the challenge she presented, but his mind had not—did not—and never would.

A foul taste coated his tongue, and he scowled. The bite of a lie. Had he just told himself an untruth? Possibly. Fine, definitely. Fox's standoffishness was so different from Alana's clinginess, *of course* he liked it.

Careful. Alana, Queen of Shadows, always sensed when Bjorn considered someone attractive…and mutilated their face. She believed she owned him, spirit, soul and body. In her mind, no one else should play with her toy, even though said toy did nothing to encourage her advances. Actually, he did the opposite. Anytime she'd invited him into her bed, he'd declined. Bjorn refused to pretend to crave someone he despised.

To his delight, each rejection had infuriated and embarrassed her. Eventually, she'd stopped asking.

An agonized scream echoed through the cavern, jolting Bjorn from his dark musings. He pressed his tongue to the roof of his mouth, irritated. Distraction was the number one killer of warriors.

Again, he quickened his pace. When he reached the end of the darkened corridor, he paused to blank his features and raised his chin. Then, he entered Alana's throne room. Ice-cold air enveloped him, breath misting in front of his face to create a dream-like veneer. Or a living nightmare. Different colored crystals dripped from the ceiling and glittered in the torchlight. Well, well. These torches hung from pikes, not people. Relief rained over him.

An army of Shadows lined the limestone walls. Surrounding the royal dais, a cenote filled with something akin to motor oil. And in the center of the platform, a throne of black mist.

Alana perched on it, her back ramrod straight and legs crossed. Impatient, she drummed her long, pointy nails against the chair arms.

She'd anchored her mass of silvery-white hair around a jagged ruby crown and changed into a more revealing scarf-dress the same shade as the rubies. A bejeweled ring adorned each of her fingers, and strings of diamonds ran down both of her legs, creating a skirt-like effect. Anytime she moved, the strands parted, showcasing more skin. On her feet, a pair of diamond slippers.

Beautiful on the outside, a hideous monster on the inside.

Xerxes would have loved the outfit, and maybe even the woman. The male went for cold-blooded, high-maintenance wenches he could tame. Yet Bjorn much preferred the silly T-shirt Fox had worn.

Spotting him, Alana grinned with smug satisfaction. "I must admit, your obedience is your best quality."

He stopped twenty feet from Alana's dais. Sent Ones were supposed to be beings of love, hating only demons, magic, evil words and actions, but not the person responsible for the magic, words or actions. But... *Hate her!*

One day, if the hatred continued to fester, Clerici would come to him and give him an ultimatum. Forgive and move on, or fall. And he would be right to do so.

A telepathic bond connected all Sent Ones. They were like a tree of life. Roots: the Most High. Trunk: Clerici. Branches: Elite 7, Warriors and Messengers. Infected branches had to be pruned, or the hate—the rot—would spread. The very reason Bjorn had contemplated falling, oh, about a thousand times.

The moment he fell, his wings would be ripped from his back. His ability to regenerate would end, and his connection to the Most High would fade. A huge price to pay to escape and hurt Alana. And it *would* hurt her. As a bonded pair, what happened to one, happened to the other. But. If Bjorn fell, Thane and Xerxes would fall, too. They would not let him suffer as a mortal alone.

Knowing he'd contributed to their deaths...

A consequence I will not survive. He would rather suffer.

"Take what you want from me, and let us part," he grated. The urge to return to Fox strengthened by the second.

Her eyes narrowed to tiny slits. "Is there somewhere you need to be, *husband*? Something you need to do, perhaps? Something more important than your wife?"

How he missed Fox's candor. She did not mince words or pretend to be anything other than what she was: a killer through and through. Perhaps, if he channeled her aggression in the proper direction, he wouldn't have to—

No! He had orders from the top—no mercy. So, next time they were together, he would kill her. No more asking questions or entertaining curiosity about her life. No more thinking about her body or all the ways he could pet and penetrate it. No more admiring different aspects of her personality.

"And now your mind has wandered," Alana snapped, shattering his musings.

Focus! Infuriate her, so she'll speed this along. Afterward, he would return home, as he always did. He wouldn't go to Fox right away, though. He wouldn't have the strength, and he did not want her to see him like that. Or anyone. She wasn't special. Thane and Xerxes would take care of him. And he would feel their upset each time they neared; when he hurt, they hurt.

"What do you expect, Alana? I did not choose you as my wife. I do not love you. I do not even like you. Being in your presence fills me with hatred and disgust." *Be crueler. Make her explode with rage.* "Every time we part, I scour off my skin to remove any hint of your stench. Did you know that? I consider our time together a hellish—"

"Silence!" Panting now, she uncrossed her legs, stood, and stalked toward him. Just before she reached the mote, black smoke seeped from her pores, her body suddenly intangible. Like a ghost, she glided over the oil, only to reform as soon as she reached the other side.

As she stalked closer to him, she exaggerated the roll of her hips. A sexually suggestive gait meant to drive a male wild. A sexually suggestive gait Bjorn found repulsive. He didn't try to hide his grimace, making her narrow her eyes once again.

She stopped mere inches away, the scent of roses and ash emanating from her. "You bait me because you do not fear me. You do not fear me, because I've always been gentle with you during our…sessions. The gentleness ends now. Today, I show you the way my people enjoy syphoning power from a host." With that, she stepped inside his body to drain his soul…

* * * *

Distrust hungered for a new victim. No longer content with whispering, he screamed accusations inside Fox's head. *You have been wiped of your portal-opening ability—your* only *ability. You will die in this cell. Galen will blame himself for your death and spiral. Legion will cry. Your fault. Your fault. Your fault.*

She sat on the cot, her legs crisscrossed as she rocked back and forth. First, she fisted hanks of hair. Then she tugged. *Then* she beat at her temples. The bastard continued to bellow hellish nothings. Soon, she doubted her own capabilities. And her sanity!

The doubts kept her in a state of misery, his favorite food. The more he fed, the stronger he became, until he indulged too much and passed out for days. An endless, toxic cycle.

Perhaps she could distract herself? She forced her thoughts toward...Bjorn. Yes! His beautiful face made her stupid. How many extra muscles did he smuggle underneath his robe? Did he have any tattoos? Scars from before he reached the age of perfection and froze into his immortality?

Did he like to make love or fuck?

Whoa! Where had *that* question come from? Bjorn had a wife. A beautiful blonde. A beautiful blonde he seemed to despise. But so what? A wife was a wife. And, yeah, okay, when the two spoke, disgust had crackled in his eyes and tone. Still. They were married. Mare-reed. She gnashed her molars. *Bjorn's future belongs to another...* She bit down harder, surprised her teeth weren't grinding into a fine powder. The bastard had a wife, which meant he'd had no business staring at Fox during their first meeting. She would *not* be entertaining any thoughts about his dick today. Or tomorrow. Not until his divorce.

Qualifiers? Seriously? Fine! She would resist forever, no matter what.

Did she have the strength to resist, though?

Gah! Get it together, woman. Escape before he returns. Yes, yes. Escape. She'd already searched the cell for anything she might be able to use as a weapon, and she'd found nothing. But. She was Fox the Executioner, and she did not simply await death.

Those thoughts angered the demon, and he shouted his anti-affirmations with more force. Tuning him out to the best of her ability, she jumped to her feet and rushed around, patting the walls, hoping to find a nail of some sort. If not, maybe she could pry a piece of jagged stone loose?

No nails. No stone. Until she flipped the cot upside down. Voila! Screws held the legs together. Fox eased to the ground, grains of dirt sticking to her legs. For one…two…three hours, she worked on loosening just one of those screws. Some of her fingernails ripped and bled, but eventually, she succeeded.

As she peered at the shard of ridged metal resting in her palm, a sense of triumph overtook her. She'd done it! She'd acquired a weapon. A small one, yes, but a weapon all the same.

Perfect timing. Shuffling footsteps sounded. She stood and hurried to right the cot. One leg would give the second she sat, so she'd have to remember to remain on her feet if Bjorn had returned for another chat. And why the hell was her heart racing at the thought of verbally sparring with him?

His scent reached her first. Rainstorms and sultry summer nights. Her head fogged. Her blood heated, and her nerve endings tingled. Finally, Bjorn came into view. Or rather, he stumbled into her line of sight, his feet dragging. He held onto the wall to remain upright, his fingers digging into the grout.

Horror punched her, leaving her gasping. He looked as if he'd lost fifty pounds! His cheeks were hollow now, his eyes bloodshot and sunken. No, not just bloodshot—bloody. Streaks of crimson dripped from his nose and ears. His sweat-soaked skin appeared two shades lighter than usual. Soot streaked his robe and dusted his wings.

Fox rushed closer and gripped the bars of her cell. "What happened?"

He offered no reply. His head remained bowed, seeming too heavy to hold up. He blinked way too rapidly, as if fighting to stay awake.

Was the wife responsible for this? Or were the pair ambushed?

In his weakened condition, Fox could take him, no problem. But…she had no desire to harm him further. Not even to gain her freedom. *What is wrong with me?*

When he stood directly in front of Fox, he stumbled to a halt and slowly lifted his gaze. The action, slight though it was, seemed to agonize him. Struggling to focus, he opened his mouth…

"Help," he croaked. Then, he collapsed.

Chapter Six

Worry consumed Fox. The fact that Bjorn requested aid from *her*, his greatest enemy...

He must be near death. Must be out of his ever-loving mind.

Great! Her worry amplified, rousing an undeniable need to avenge him. Although, there was a good chance the desire sprang from seeing such a strong, proud male in such a deplorable condition. But that made no sense! Bjorn intended to kill her. Thus, he had to die. If someone else did the dirty work, great, even better.

No. No! The easy route wasn't always the best route. Or the right one. *Patch him up,* then *fight him.* It wasn't the smart thing to do, but it was honorable.

So she'd never before cared about honor. So what? For whatever reason, different parts of her panicked at the thought of Bjorn's death. For her peace of mind, she *must* save him.

The decision solidified, and she nodded. Unable to do anything worthwhile, she performed the only task certain to make a difference. She shouted for his friends. "Hey! Someone! Anyone! Bjorn is in trouble. Heeeey! Do you want him to die?"

Nothing, no response. Not even an eruption of footsteps. "Or not make a difference," she muttered. The dungeon must be soundproof, ensuring no screams reached the main house...castle? Fortress?

Where was she? The heavens? Yeah. Probably. Rumors suggested Bjorn and his friends stored prisoners in the Downfall's dungeon on numerous occasions.

Let the warrior die, Distrust whispered. *As long as he lives, you are endangered.*

Bjorn moaned and writhed in pain.

Ignore the demon. He's still feeding. Frustrated with the situation, with the fiend, with anything and everything, she crouched in front of the Sent One. He'd landed on his side, facing her. A major blessing. She extended an arm through the bars, contorted this way and that, and…contact!

She patted his ice-cold throat, feeling for a pulse… There! A cool tide of relief washed over her nerves, soothing the worst of her distress. Though weak, his pulse remained steady.

His lips parted, another moan slipping out.

"What happened to you?" she asked again.

He fluttered open his eyelids, revealing glassy irises and blown pupils. Their gazes met, and a tide of compassion rose up, flooding Fox.

Compassion? For the man tasked with her murder? *That's a first.* Probably due to the lust she'd experienced earlier.

Lust for her captor. Another first.

Well, it *had* been years…centuries…since she'd slept with anyone or felt any kind of arousal. But why him, and why now? "What do you need?" she asked, using a soft tone. A lump grew in her throat. "How can I help you, Bjorn?"

"Help," he echoed.

"I'm trying!" A sense of desperation overshadowed every other emotion. *Think!* She couldn't remove his robe to check for injuries or signs of internal bleeding. She couldn't portal out of the cell, and wouldn't be heard even if she screamed until her vocal cords seized. She couldn't even lay beside him to warm him up. *Think harder.*

Distrust whispered, *He's faking.*

She stiffened. *Ignore the demon and check Bjorn's vitals.*

Vitals. Right. If he'd slipped away while she debated how to help…

Fox latched on to Bjorn's wrist, planted her feet against the bars, and pushed with her heels, tugging the warrior close…closer. Another pulse check. Just as weak, but still steady. Excellent.

He'd lost so much blood, his lips had taken on a blue tint. Blood. Yes. He needed to replace what he'd lost. Since no other volunteers stood nearby, the obligation fell to Fox. She reached out and cut her palm on a jagged piece of rock protruding from the wall. Blood welled— blood she poured down his throat.

Wait! She balled her hand into a fist, catching the blood before it trickled to his mouth.

Gatekeepers, like Sent Ones, rarely shared their blood with others. Blood was sacred to them both. Blood equaled life and power.

So…what were the pros and cons?

Con: She and Bjorn would feed off each other, similar to the way Distrust often fed off her.

Con: For a day or two, Bjorn would have temporary access to her portal-opening ability. He would also see into her mind for that length of time.

Pro:

Well. Okay, then. She gulped. Was Bjorn truly worth all the risk with little reward?

In her mother's days, Gatekeepers had shared their blood with each other on a daily basis, using the temporary bonds to increase their individual strengths. Often, they'd held hands, stood in a circle, and worked together to create entire realms and dimensions. But those bonds had led to multiple wars as secrets came to light. If Bjorn learned *her* secrets…

If she did nothing, he would surely die.

Inside, she recoiled. Screw it! She would save him now and deal with any fallout later.

Fox opened her palm, letting her blood drip into Bjorn's mouth.

* * * *

A scene played within Bjorn's mind, as vivid as a movie on a screen. He watched as a little girl with tangled dark hair and large hazel eyes stumbled down a narrow alley between two stone structures. Those structures reminded him of shops he'd seen in ancient Greece, while the girl reminded him of Fox.

His chest clenched. She wore what appeared to be a burlap sack. A *dirty* sack. Filth covered her from head to toe, and she was thin. *Too* thin, basically a skeleton with skin and hair. Her complexion was sallow.

She exited the alley and entered an over-crowded market, with vendors hawking meat pies, cheeses, jars of honey, horseshoes, glass, pottery, fish, metals, fabrics, and so much more. He reeled as voices rang out. He detected Latin, Ionic, and Attic Greek. The girl *was* in Ancient Greece.

A blacksmith glistened with sweat as he hammered a sword before a crackling fire pit. A cobbler measured a little boy's foot. Men were dressed in long wool tunics and cloaks with shoulder clasps. Women were similarly attired, the fabrics more colorful and elaborate as well as several inches longer. Buyers paid for their wares with silver coins or drachma.

Was he reliving a memory from his past? But…he did not recall the girl in any way, shape or form.

Whenever people caught sight of her, they reacted in one of two ways. A grimace, or a glare. Far too many openly stared, their features etched with distaste. His chest clenched again, only harder, a sharp pang lancing his heart. The little darling knew these people despised her, but she refused to cower, keeping her head high and her shoulders back. Pride stamped every inch of her being. The same pride he'd witnessed when they'd faced off in her bathroom.

Pang, pang. This *must* be Fox. But how and why would he receive a glimpse into her past? Unless his imagination was responsible. But why would his mind craft a fake, sympathetic backstory for someone on his hit list? It wouldn't. Had to be a memory, as originally suspected.

When Fox came upon the vendor selling meat pies, she paused. A bit of drool leaked from the corner of her mouth, and she wiped it away with the back of her hand. Once again, his pangs worsened. This time, Bjorn longed to claw out his heart and lay it at her feet.

Noticing the girl's fixation, the seller scowled, pulled a pebble from a satchel tied to his waist—as if he'd been waiting for this moment—and launched it at her. The rock slammed into her forehead, breaking the skin. With a cry of pain, she stumbled back. A streak of crimson trickled between her eyes and dripped from the tip of her nose.

Too weak to catch herself, she bumped into a big brute who wore a bronzed cuirass and a pair of greaves. He carried a shield in one hand and a spear in the other. A foot soldier.

Cursing, the soldier hooked the shield to his back, then grabbed little Fox by the hair and dragged her off. Though she screamed for help, kicked and punched, he did not release her. Most people turned away, unconcerned. Others watched, curious. Only a few appeared sympathetic to her plight, but no one stepped in.

The soldier pivoted, hauling her down a shadowed, abandoned alley. In the darkest spot, he rested his spear against the wall, then pushed her beside it. A hand wrapped around her throat, holding her in place. The other ripped at her clothes.

A rage-roar barreled out of Bjorn's mouth. The soldier would die!

Fox fought with all her might but—

His mind blanked, erasing the memory, and Bjorn released another roar. Had Fox escaped before…before…? The urge to commit violence bombarded him. He would rather endure rounds of demon-torture than harm a child. Any child.

The soldier had been human, which meant he'd died centuries ago. *I will learn his identity and destroy his family line, wiping any trace of him from the planet!*

The thought shocked him. Savage. Brutal. Un-Sent-One-like. Those family members were innocent of the male's crime. Still, Bjorn did not calm. What other horrors had little Fox survived?

As a thick cloud of shadows rolled through his mind, Bjorn fought to awaken. He kicked and clawed with all his might. In the end, the shadows won. Just before he drifted off, a final thought seared his brain: *How can I execute a woman whose past is as riddled with as much abuse as my own?*

* * * *

When Bjorn finally ceased moaning and writhing in pain, a semblance of peace returned to his features. Fox exhaled a relieved breath. Sharing her blood had worked! At last, he'd begun to heal.

She expected threats from the demon but—Fox gasped. Miracle of miracles, Distrust went quiet, as if the fiend feared the assassin would speak up. Score one for her temporary link to Bjorn.

As best she could, she patted down Bjorn, searching for a key to the cell, weapons of any kind, or anything she could use to her advantage. Once she gained her freedom, she would hunt for a spot to portal, then alert Bjorn's friends about his condition. They would take care of him, and she would go…somewhere. Not home. Fox would not endanger Galen and Legion. Maybe a sub-dimension Galen owned: the Realm of the Forgotten. Whoever lived in the realm was forgotten by the rest of the world(s).

"What did you do to him?" a masculine voice demanded, breaking into her thoughts. The sharp tone reminded her of a cat o' nine tails. Treacherous, lethal, and agonizing—a weapon that kept on giving.

She flipped her gaze up, spying two other Sent Ones. They hurried toward the cell. Like Bjorn, they had wings of gold, but all similarities ended there. The slightly shorter one had blond curls, tanned skin and blue eyes—the infamous Thane. Not that six-foot-three-ish was short. The taller one had white hair, scarred white skin, and red eyes—the much-feared Xerxes.

Together, they projected the most savage air of violence she'd ever encountered. Clearly, they valued Bjorn.

"You're going to be okay," she whispered to Bjorn, patting his forearm.

Xerxes reached them first. When he noticed the placement of her hand, he growled—growled!—and stomped on her wrist once, twice. The bones cracked and shattered in seconds. Blistering pain raced up her arm, while her stomach turned inside out, bile spilling out.

Thane scooped Bjorn into his muscular arms, then the group hurried away.

Xerxes paused in the exit to glare over his shoulder and snap, "If he dies, you'll die, too. I promise, you will scream and beg for death."

"Sorry, sugar, but he was broken before I took him out of his box," Fox said before going quiet. No reason to exert precious energy trying to make him believe the Executioner only wished to help.

After what she'd done to the ten, the Sent Ones should not trust her. Ever. Actually, after what she'd done *her entire life.* No matter the circumstances, Fox only looked out for number one. And, yeah, okay, she'd looked out for number two, as well. But no one else.

Mental note: *Don't forget to tell Galen you likened him to a bowel movement.*

"—not even listening to me." Xerxes snapped his teeth at her before exiting fully.

Only after his footsteps faded did Fox dig the screw out of her pocket. But though she searched, she could not find a lock anywhere on the cell bars. What if there *wasn't* a door? That would mean Bjorn had morphed them both into mist to put her inside.

Yeah, that made sense. No door, no way out for non-misters like Fox. Gah! That left only one option for escape—infuriating Bjorn's friends so much, they took her out of the cell to punish her. Then, she could incapacitate them both and run.

Distrust gave the barest whimper, making it clear he had plenty to say about her plan, and none of it good. But…he continued to keep his doubts to himself.

I might need to consider turning my temporary blood-bond with Bjorn into something permanent. She shouted, "Hey, Zerk. Or do you prefer to be called Scars?" Why not get started on her plan now? "Guess what? I hope the Sent One dies." Xerxes wouldn't hear a lie in her tone, because she didn't state *who* she meant. In this case, "the Sent One" referenced a collection of warriors who hurt women, children, minorities, and animals.

Fox wasn't a fan of people, no matter their sex or species, but she loved animals. In fact, that was how she'd gotten her name. One summer, she'd saved a baby fox from a snare. She'd played with the critter every day after for weeks, even fed and watered him until he was old enough to make it on his own. Eventually, her mother began calling her Fox.

Later, as an adult, Fox found a beautiful Siamese cat she'd named Tawny. But it wasn't long before her enemies snatched and tortured the little darling, depositing the remains in her bed. She'd barely survived the loss. *Can't go through that again.* One day, though, she would retire from war, find a quiet place to live, and become a crazy cat lady. The best future anyone could have.

"Hey," she called at a higher volume. "If Bjorn dies, I call dibs on his wings. Sew on some straps, and I can cosplay a Sent One at the next Comic-Con. And someone bring me a big-screen TV. I'm missing the season premiere of *The Bachelor.*"

Thumping footsteps, hard and heavy. Two sets. Her taunts had worked!

Heart thudding against her ribs, she hurried to the cot to—nope. Dismantled leg, remember? Right. She sat in the corner instead and leaned against the wall, as if she hadn't a care. Perfect timing. Both Xerxes and Thane returned, stopping in front of her cell.

They said nothing. But then, words weren't needed. They radiated extreme hatred and rage.

As she watched, their images dulled, becoming as insubstantial as smoke. Side by side, they slipped inside the cell.

I nailed it! No door. Even better, the plan was working! Excitement spread through her, and she battled to maintain a neutral expression while whisking her gaze over the males, searching for a weapon...finding none.

"You hope Bjorn dies, hmm?" Thane leaned down to clasp her upper arms in a vise-grip and yanked her to her feet. "How about we make *you* wish to die instead?"

"There's only one way to do that. You're going to have to make a pass at me." Instinct demanded she fight, and fight hard. Punch the cot's screw into his throat. Knee his balls into his abdomen. Something! But she suppressed her temper, only struggling against his hold half-heartedly.

"I am devoted to my wife. She is a woman of worth," Thane snapped. "I have no need for another, much less someone like you." His lips peeled back, revealing straight pearly whites. "Perhaps I should summon my Elin to make introductions. As a phoenix shapeshifter, fire is her specialty. She can burn you alive while I watch and cheer."

Oh…shit. Fox combatted a shudder. She'd warred with phoenix shifters before, but only because she'd been backed into a corner. They were a bloodthirsty lot, with a higher pain threshold than any other species. When you killed them, they came back to life ten-times stronger. But the real reason Fox avoided them whenever possible stemmed from her one and only fear. Burning alive…again.

Her mother had died at the stake, and Fox had tried to save her, bravely throwing herself into the flames. The pain… The only reason she hadn't scarred was because she'd carried a vial of her mother's blood. Drinking it had hurt almost as much as the burns. The last remnants of her mother's life just…gone.

There was no stopping a shudder now. The fact that Thane considered Fox unworthy didn't bother her in the slightest. Nope. Not even a little. He meant nothing to her. His opinion meant less than nothing.

"Elin can have her," Xerxes announced, "*after* I've had a turn."

Thane canted his head, studying Fox more intently. "Are you ready to tell us what you did to Bjorn?"

They still believed her responsible for their friend's abysmal condition. Batting her lashes, she told him, "Nah. But I *am* ready for you to try and beat the truth out of me."

"Let's get started, then. I'd hate to keep a female waiting." He tightened his hold on Fox's arm and nodded at his friend.

The other male moved behind her. If not for Thane, she would have spun to keep him within sight. All she could do? Stand there, grinding her molars.

From the shadow he cast, she thought Xerxes produced two items from thin air. What were those? Boomerangs? Whatever they were, they had a half-moon shape. Worry scraped her nerves raw. What did he think to do with those?

A second later, something cold and heavy settled around her neck. A clicking sound assaulted her ears—a type of death knell.

A grinning Thane released her and stepped back, a handheld mirror appearing in his hand. She caught a glimpse of her reflection and swallowed a horrified gasp. Not a boomerang. A metal collar, with a small hook in the center. A thin chain hung from the hook.

He thinks to lead me around like an animal? Red dotted her vision.

Suppressing her temper ceased being a possibility. She readjusted the screw she'd positioned between two fingers and punched, slicing into his throat. At the same time, she kicked him. He failed to block the first strike, but successfully blocked the second, clasping the chain and yanking. The collar constricted her airway, and she wheezed for breath she couldn't catch. Then he ripped the bloody screw from her grip.

He hauled her forward. Just before he reached the bars, he became mist. He didn't reach back to touch her, but the next thing she knew, she turned to mist, too. A cold, weightless sensation washed over her a split second before her senses flatlined. For a moment, she felt and smelled nothing. So weird!

One after the other, they exited the cell. Xerxes kept pace at the rear.

Being re-embodied was just as weird, her senses coming back to life with a rush of heat.

A soft, soft whisper wafted across the back of her mind. *You cannot beat these men. Why try? You are too weak.*

Was she too weak? She—

Argh! Stupid demon. Guess he'd gotten over his fear of Bjorn. *I will succeed, whatever the cost!* She just had to wait for the right moment...

They passed other cells. Some contained prisoners, some didn't. Those prisoners recoiled the moment they spotted Thane, but whimpered when they caught sight of Xerxes.

When Thane turned a corner, Fox spotted a staircase at the end of the new hallway.

Now!

Fox launched into motion, latching on to the chain and yanking, just as he'd done to her. She stepped to the side as Thane stumbled backward; unfortunately, he didn't drop his end of the chain. Very well. She would use it against him.

As soon as he passed her, she jumped up, stepped on his thigh and wrapped a leg around his shoulders. At the same time, she wound the excess chain around his neck and jerked, cutting off *his* airway.

When Xerxes attempted to grab her ankle and rip her off his friend, she kicked him in the face. The heel of her foot met the bridge of his nose, and cartilage snapped. He roared with agony and fury, blood running down his mouth and chin.

With a hiss, Thane threw a fist up and back. Wham. Wham. Wham. That fist slammed into Fox's cheek, eye socket, and mouth. A bomb of pain exploded inside her head. One of her eyes swelled, blurring her vision. Her cheek stung, and her lower lip split. But the one thing she didn't do? Budge. She punched him right back, doing her best to blind him in the process, and shoved the heels of her feet into his gut. At the same time, she continued to hold Xerxes at bay.

"Pass out already!" she growled.

Thane stopped fighting, surprising her. He clasped her legs, keeping her perched atop his shoulders and fell backward. Shit, shit, shit. *Should have expected this.* They crashed into the floor. Her skull hit first, then the rest of her, with Thane's weight smashing into her.

Her lungs emptied in a single heave. As she struggled to breathe, a feather made its way into her mouth, and she coughed. Through it all, she retained her hold on the chain. She even gave a hard yank to shorten the slack and choke him out faster.

Suddenly, fingers combed through her hair and closed into a fist, pulling the strands. Xerxes! The bastard yanked her out from under Thane. *Now,* she lost her grip on the chain. Before she had a chance to fight back, Xerxes slung an arm around her neck, catching *her* in a chokehold.

Thane clambered to his feet, glared at her while flicking his tongue over an incisor, then turned on his heel to resume his journey. Once again, Xerxes followed. He kept her tucked against him, never loosening that chokehold.

Her lungs burned, and her head swam. They entered a bar-free cell bigger than her own, with tables piled high with instruments of torture. Knives, saws, tools, and other goodies often used in a violent and bloody interrogation. Sweat beaded on her nape, a droplet trickling down her spine. Though she fought, her captors successfully anchored her to a tall wooden beam, her arms secured overhead.

A whipping post? She faced the beam, keeping her back exposed.

Thane sauntered to the table and traced a fingertip over several blades. Ultimately, he selected a whip, just as she'd suspected. "Bjorn is one of the best males I've ever known. He has survived horrors and tortures you cannot even imagine, yet you hope to cause him more?" With every word, malice deepened his voice a little more. He moved behind her, joining Xerxes. "For this, Executioner, you will pay."

"Sure," she said, hating these men. Hating *herself.* Once again, she'd failed a mission objective. "Should I write you a check? Someone fetch my purse. Oh, wait. I left it in my other cell."

"You joke now, but soon...soon, you will beg." He stroked the base of the whip. "Did I forget to mention the whip is laced with *infirmədē* to ensure you cannot heal?"

Infirmədē. A nightmarish demon venom. It prevented even the smallest wounds from healing without some kind of antidote.

"One," Thane said and cracked the whip.

Searing agony sent a scream barreling out of her mouth. Nausea churned in her stomach, and her eyes blurred again.

"Two." He lashed her again. And again. Until he reached ten. Then he passed the whip to Xerxes, who whipped her ten more times.

By the time they finished, her T-shirt was shredded, and so was her back. Her knees gave out. All she could do was hang against the post, her shoulders nearly sliding out of their sockets.

Her voice was broken from her continuous screams, but at least she hadn't begged.

Xerxes moved in front of her, pinched her chin and forced her gaze to lift. Those neon red eyes projected undiluted rage. "What did you do to Bjorn?"

"I gave him...a massive...hard-on," she said between panting breaths. "My bad."

He jostled her, pulling the wounds on her back. "What did you do to Bjorn?"

Tears scalded her cheeks. The pain...almost as bad as the burns she'd once sustained. But she pressed her lips together, choosing silence. She couldn't say she wasn't the one who'd hurt Bjorn, because at some point, she *had* hurt him, so Xerxes would taste the lie. Her best bet now? Her *only* bet? Keep taunting the two and pray they left her tied to the beam, thinking her too weak to mount an escape.

"Be honest," she croaked. Deep breath in, out. Her panting slowed, but not by much. "You're going to jerk off to images of my torture, aren't you?"

He hissed in her face before stalking behind her and starting the whipping all over again...

Chapter Seven

Bjorn awoke gradually. First, the lights came on in his mind. Then, all the shops began to open, vendors selling their wares—memories, awareness, and rage. He sensed Thane and Xerxes nearby and suspected they paced around his bed. Whispers reached his ears.

He caught the snippets "whipping," "took it too far," and "furious." Had Alana whipped him after she'd drained him? Maybe, but he felt no pain.

As he blinked open his eyes, Bjorn did his best to focus on his surroundings. A room. A bedroom. Perfunctory furnishings: a bed, a wardrobe filled with weapons, a dresser and a nightstand. No knickknacks, decorations or photos. *His* bedroom.

He maintained no friendships outside of his boys, no permanent or temporary lovers, so he had no need for photos. He pursued no hobbies, either. If he wasn't hunting and slaying demons, he was running the club. If he wasn't running the club, he was dealing with Alana. Nothing more, nothing less.

In the whole of his life, he'd loved only one woman. Leema the Loyal, who'd earned her moniker when she'd braved a hail of gunfire to save her family. A fellow Sent One with wings of solid white. A Messenger who traveled between the heavens and the mortal realms.

They'd met on assignment. The second-in-command before Clerici—Germanus—had ordered him to guard a human traveling overseas. Ten hours into the trip, Leema had shown up with new instructions from his boss. Leema's beauty instantly captivated Bjorn, but her warmth and kindness sealed the deal.

They fell for each other fast and even moved in together. He'd been happy. Content. Then, the demon-torture happened.

Bjorn fisted the sheets and peeked into the darkest part of his past...

The demons had clawed at his robe, stripping him before they chained him inside a cell with Thane and Xerxes, who'd also been naked and chained. Every day, two of them were forced to watch as the third was beaten and worse. Bjorn, though...the demons were particularly obsessed with him. The things they did to his body...

Skin peeled off, inch by inch...

Organs cut out of my abdomen and eaten in front of me...

Eyes removed and hung from necklaces.

Limbs amputated, regrown, then amputated again...

Constant pain and degradation quickly dehumanized him. To survive mentally and emotionally, he'd had to build a stone wall around his heart.

Leema had been ill-prepared to meet the new Bjorn. A man unhappy, malcontent, intense, combative, explosive, violent, and utterly dependent on Thane and Xerxes. They understood his anguish in ways others could not. More than that, she'd fallen in love with another Messenger during Bjorn's absence. But fearing the loss of her *loyal* designation, she'd stayed with Bjorn and continued to see her lover in secret.

Her reputation had mattered more than the male she'd professed to love and adore.

He bit his tongue until he tasted blood. Six months passed before he caught the two together—in *his* bed, with portraits of him and Leema hanging all around. To this day, Bjorn cringed when he recalled how he'd beaten the male so severely, he'd required Water of Life to survive.

Healers claimed his organs would have fared better in a blender.

As for Leema, Bjorn had tossed her out, destroyed her possessions and their cloud, then worked to change her designation to "the Disloyal."

Kick me while I'm down, and I'll retaliate on my way back up.

Since then, he'd avoided any kind of emotional tie with anyone but his boys. But the occasional one-night stand—before Alana's arrival—had never satisfied him. Nothing had. He hadn't experienced genuine satisfaction or desire since...

"Fox," he croaked. Her name echoed inside his head, waking up other parts of him. Nerve endings tingled to life. Muscles tensed, and blood heated. *Beautiful warrior.* She'd faced her crimes without flinching, blatantly admitting to the truth. Such strength. Such wit. When they'd

fought, she'd cared more about Galen's and Legion's safety than her own.
So different from Leema and Alana.

Bjorn wished he'd had another memory of her childhood.
Something. Anything!

His friends rushed to his side and helped him ease into an upright
position.

"She remains in the dungeon," Thane told him.

Good, that was good. So why did the male look away rather than
meet his gaze?

"Galen the Treacherous has been blowing up your cell phone with
calls and texts," Xerxes said. "He says you are his new pet project, and
whatever you do to harm Fox, he will revisit upon you a thousandfold."

So protective. Had Bjorn been mistaken before? Were the two
lovers?

He wished he knew more about the woman. The memory he'd
dreamed about her childhood—he stiffened. The memory. *Her* memory.
His chest did that clenching thing, the ensuing pangs nearly splitting him
in two. Why had he glimpsed into her past? *How* had he glimpsed into
her past?

Bjorn drew in a deep breath to clear his mind. Instead, he became
more aware of his body's needs. "I'll deal with Galen later. Bathroom
now."

His friends had assisted him every time he'd returned from Alana's
and now knew the drill. Each male latched on to one of his arms and
helped him stand. Then, they acted as crutches as he hobbled to his
private en suite, his knees too weak to hold his weight.

Voice diamond-hard, Thane said, "You will be avenged."

"Your tormentor has suffered and will continue to suffer. No
mercy," Xerxes grated. "I want her to hurt."

"Drink, my friend." Thane handed Bjorn a small vial.

Only a few precious drops remained inside. The Water of Life came
from the heavens. A single drop could drive a demon from a body,
depending on the person and situation. Also, depending on the person
and situation, it could cure any disease and heal any injury. The Water
could even revive the dead.

Once Bjorn ran out...

Don't think about that. He unplugged the vial and tipped a single drop
onto his tongue.

Moments after swallowing, a cool, effervescent sensation invaded his veins and traveled through every inch of him. Suddenly, he felt cleansed from the inside out. His mouth tasted minty fresh. His every blood cell sparkled—surely—as if they'd received a vigorous polish. Strength seeped into his muscles.

After re-corking the vial and hanging it from his neck, he stripped and showered on his own, scrubbing the queen's soot and scent from his skin. Xerxes and Thane stayed close, just in case.

When one of the three had a need, the other two gave without hesitation.

No man had better friends. Bjorn loved them both dearly. They kept him sane, giving him a reason to look ahead rather than continually glancing back at the horrors of his past.

He dried off and donned a clean robe, then returned to the bed on his own, easing onto the edge of the mattress. Time for the Q and A portion of his recovery. "How long have I been out this time?"

"Three days," Xerxes said.

Blink, blink. Three days. An eternity. "Tell me you cared for Fox while I was out. Tell me you fed her." In the memory, she'd been starved. The thought of her going hungry again...

The two shared a glance loaded with tension.

"What did she do to you, exactly?" Thane asked at a lower than usual volume. "Not even Alana has harmed you to such a degree."

"Not Fox. Alana. She flew into a rage when I ignored her summons, choosing to stay close to Fox." New memories flooded in, and his hands fisted. How Alana had stepped inside his body to possess him. How she'd roughly syphoned his energy. How blood had rushed from his extremities in seconds, pooling in his abdomen to protect his vital organs. How he'd continually vomited and blacked out. How he'd cried like an infant, a sense of violation unwavering.

How much abuse could one being take before he stopped recovering?

Razor-sharp guilt pulsed from the warriors, rousing dread in Bjorn. Something had happened while he slept. Something terrible. "Tell me," he demanded.

Massaging the back of his neck, Thane said, "We assumed Fox was responsible. We...punished her for it, Bjorn. Severely."

He went still, not even daring to breathe. "What did you do?" But he divined the answer before he finished the sentence. *Whipping. Too far. Furious.*

"The day you collapsed, we whipped her," Xerxes said, confirming his suspicions. "Forty lashes from a whip laced with *infirmədē*."

Denial screamed inside Bjorn's head. Proud Fox, whipped and unable to heal... Red dotted his vision.

He should revel. *Exactly what she deserved.* But dark fury sparked. She'd been whipped for a crime she hadn't committed, not the one she had.

"We also denied her food and water," Thane added.

The fury intensified, devouring his calm façade. "I did not want her harmed." He leaped to his feet, demanding, "Where is she, exactly?"

Thane bowed his head. "The cell we use for torture. She told us she hoped you died and we...reacted. After the whipping, we left her hanging on the whipping post."

"Of course, she wants me to die," Bjorn snarled, surprising both men. "I plan to kill her."

Forty lashes. Three days of starvation. The fury slashed at his insides. Guilt joined the party, pouring salt on the wounds. Usually, only demons were left on the post, and only to increase the amount of pain they experienced before their execution.

Fox murdered ten Sent Ones in cold blood. She deserves this. So why did his guilt continue to grow?

Bjorn scoured a hand over his face. "I need to see her. Alone." No telling how she'd react to the sight of Thane and Xerxes. "I will be sharing the Water of Life with her."

His friends reacted as if he'd issued a bomb threat.

Thane gave his head a brutal shake, saying, "We have so little, and she is so...unworthy."

Xerxes ran his tongue over his teeth. "The demon-possessed cannot drink the Water without suffering debilitating pain."

"Better pain than death," Bjorn ground out.

Thane spread his arms wide. "Why save someone you plan to kill?"

Excellent question. Bjorn didn't know the answer. He only knew he couldn't *not* heal her. To allow her to suffer for a crime she had not committed... *I'd be as bad as a demon.*

"Acquiring more Water is nearly impossible these days," Xerxes said. "If we run out before your next visit with Alana, how will you recover?"

"I'll find a way," he replied, standing and nodding. Eager to aid Fox, he strode to the door.

"The Elite have a mandatory meeting this evening," Thane called, stopping him in his tracks. "Axel's cloud, seven sharp."

Axel. An irreverent Sent One as misunderstood as Bjorn, Thane and Xerxes. The guy took nothing seriously, slept with anyone breathing, and pissed off anyone forced to partner with him. But he never judged the people around him, and it hadn't taken long for Bjorn to fall in like with him.

"I'll be there." Finally, he strode from the bedroom.

Halfway there, his limbs began to shake, his knees threatening to buckle. These days, a drop of Water no longer revived him fully. He'd built up a tolerance and required more. A drop merely strengthened him, speeding up the healing process. So, as he made the trek to the dungeon, he fought to remain upright.

Priceless antique furnishings and luxurious surroundings soon gave way to disrepair and crumbling stone walls littered with claw marks. Marks made by demons as they were dragged to their cells. Bjorn crinkled his nose, the air saturated with a mix of filth, body odor, and death.

Someone had died. Someone like Fox?

He snaked around a corner, finally reaching the torture chamber.

His stomach twisted into a thousand knots. There she was. Fox the Executioner. She'd fought her way free of the post, but she hadn't made it far. She lay on her stomach, a metal collar secured to her neck. Though she slept, pain contorted her features.

Three days had passed, yet her back…

A growl of rage rumbled deep in Bjorn's chest. Her back was mutilated. What remained of her skin and muscle resembled raw hamburger meat. In a few places, a bone protruded. She'd bitten off her nails, mangled her ankles, and broken her thumbs.

No doubt she'd broken her thumbs in order to slide her hands out of her bonds. Then she must have clawed her ankles free.

As he removed the collar and picked her up as gently as possible, careful not to brush against any open wounds, she flinched, and the twisting of his stomach worsened. A bloody outline of her body remained in the dirt. A body at least ten pounds lighter than he'd last seen it. Crimson streaked her skin in multiple places. Her dark locks were tangled and caked with mud. A metallic scent wafted from her.

He wished he could give her the Water here. Anything to ease the anguish she'd been forced to endure. But the Water would pain her more than the whipping. At first. If she thrashed, he'd have an easier time controlling her movements in his private bathroom.

Somehow, Bjorn found the strength to carry her there. Yes, he stumbled along the way, but he never dropped her. To his relief, Thane and Xerxes were gone.

He didn't blame them for what they'd done. Had the situation been reversed, he would have whipped anyone who'd harmed either of them. *Hurt my boys, suffer the consequences.* But. He wasn't happy with them.

Perhaps the whipping could be Fox's punishment for slaying the ten? That, and oh, ten years behind bars? He just…he didn't want to kill her.

There. He'd admitted it. What good would killing her do, anyway? Why rid the world of her strength and cunning?

He stripped Fox out of her only remaining garment: the thong. Trembling now, he eased her onto the lid of the toilet, letting her cheek rest against his shoulder. With one hand, he cupped her nape to lean her backward. With the other hand, he uncorked the vial and poured a drop onto her tongue. Then a second. Then a third.

Several minutes passed. An eternity. He remained tense. What if too much time had passed, and she was too far gone to be saved? He—

She threw back her head, her spine bowing, and unleashed an ear-shattering scream. Those screams only intensified as muscle and flesh wove together. A process more agonizing than the initial injury—a process far worse for someone like Fox. The Water healed her, yes, but also attacked the demon. Distrust's pain was her pain.

When no more gashes remained, she sagged against Bjorn, her features relaxing at last. Relieved to have the worst part over with, he fiddled with knobs, starting the shower. Then, he picked her up and carried her into the stall. Hot water rained over them both, soaking his robe and washing the blood and dirt from her skin.

He expected her to wake as he washed and conditioned her hair, but she never even cracked open her eyes. He expected her to wake when he scrubbed every inch of her body…nope. When he stripped out of his robe and dried her off…again, nothing.

Still not looking at her naked form. Not even a swift peek.

Maybe a peek.

No, no! Resist!

One of his hands brushed the side of her breast, and he fought to silence a groan.

Moving on. Still expecting her to wake, he gently eased her atop the bed…brushed her hair…and dressed her in a large T-shirt. The material bagged on her small frame, but he liked it. A lot. *Adorable female.* Or maybe he enjoyed seeing her dressed in his clothing?

With a sigh, Bjorn tucked the covers around her. Midway through, he caught himself smiling. In slumber, she lost her murderous edge. She looked young and innocent.

Fool! There was a chance she would awaken, attack him, and run. He should cuff her to the bed, he knew it. But...

I don't want to restrain her. Which meant "fool" was too kind a designation for him.

In the end, he slid in beside her. A mistake! Moaning, she rolled to her side and cuddled into his. Her curves... *Soft, where I'm hard.* Heat radiated from Fox, enveloping him. *Searing* him. He sucked in a breath, her sweet scent filling his nose and fogging his head.

Bjorn hadn't held a sleeping woman in centuries. Not since Leema. With everyone else, he'd bailed as soon as he'd come.

Sighing, Fox snuggled more comfortably against him.

Bail. Yes. Bail now!

Too late. His cells caught fire, lust burning through him. Need clawed at him, and sweat beaded on his brow.

Not because of Fox. He hadn't self-pleasured lately, that was all. Pressure had been building for months. He would have reacted this way to anyone.

Ignore the near-euphoric sensations. He gritted his teeth and fit a wing underneath her, then turned, becoming the big spoon. He draped an arm from one of her shoulders to the other, thereby pinning her in place. If she moved, he would feel it and awaken. *If* he fell asleep.

Oh, he would most definitely fall asleep.

He might have slept the past three days, but he hadn't rested. He'd merely rebuilt his energy—energy he'd used up taking care of Fox. Already, his eyelids were too heavy to hold up. Strain seeped from his bones, his muscles.

Bjorn didn't resist. He let himself drift off as he wondered: *How can Fox the Executioner fit against me so perfectly?*

Chapter Eight

Fox moaned with surprised pleasure. Since the whipping, she'd existed rather than lived, agony her constant companion. Every time she'd breathed or moved, she'd cried like a stupid baby, her pain worsening. The slightest breeze had made her pray for death. Meaning, she'd prayed for death every moment of every day. Now, she felt amazing! Better than. She was brand-new, cleansed from the inside out.

Distrust hadn't gone silent, but he'd stopped speaking in favor of groaning. As if *he* suffered, too. Perhaps he'd gotten injured while Fox slept? Was that possible? And if so, how?

Wonderfully groggy and sublimely full, she stretched. Oh, the bliss! Not a single twinge of discomfort.

Someone must have carried her to a bed because oh, baby, she lay on the warmest, softest sheet of all time. *Probably a silk-cloud blend.* Mmm, and they smelled incredible. Like sandalwood and…Bjorn?

Heart rate picking up speed, she fluttered open her eyelids. Ugh. Blurry vision. Where was she? And where was Bjorn? He hadn't visited in days.

Movement at her right. She tensed and lifted her head, blinking rapidly. Her vision cleared at last. Bjorn! He *was* here, stretched out beside her, one of his soft, downy wings cushioning her from neck to ankle.

I'm in bed with Bjorn.

I'm in bed with Bjorn, and we're cuddling. Naked?

Heart racing faster, she lifted the covers. She wore a T-shirt but no panties. He wore—air hitched in her lungs. He wore nothing but his tattoos, and they looked good on him. Really, really good. A wealth of symbols and old language letters decorated his powerful lower body.

An-n-nd her heart picked up speed yet again, knocking against her ribs. Had she ever seen a more beautiful male? Sunlight bathed him, his bronzed skin glistening with a slight mother-of-pearl sheen she'd never before noticed. *Mesmerizing.* In certain light, the color appeared as dark as ebony. In others, as pale as snow. And his long, thick black lashes must be the envy of every false-lash aficionado, and his lips…plump, pink and kissable.

Arousal stirred, hot and liquid, threatening to melt her bones. Different parts of her ached in the best way. All of her *needed.*

When she could breathe again, she inhaled his erotic scent deeper into her lungs. Mmm. A sensual fog formed around her mind. Wait. She sniff-sniffed. The guy did not have morning breath. He had cotton candy breath.

Did she? She covered her mouth, breathed out and sniffed. She did! As if she'd gargled with sunshine and rainbows. But how? Why?

Mumbling something unintelligible, Bjorn drew her closer. His eyes remained closed, even as he glided a hand up the ridges of her spine to cup her nape. She luxuriated in each caress.

Kill him and leave. Now! Before he kills you.

Now she tensed, preparing to leap out of the bed. Then realization hit, and she relaxed. Stupid demon! Obviously, Distrust hoped to feed, so he could strengthen and heal from that mysterious injury he may or may not have. Either way…

I shouldn't give him what he wants. Last time I listened to him, I murdered the ten.

Fox's inhalations turned shallow. Just to be contrary, she softened against Bjorn even more. Not for any other reason. Nope. Not a single one. But, oh, this felt incredible.

"Do you have any weaknesses?" she whispered, tracing her fingertips along his jaw. Dark stubble tickled her, and she shivered. Miracle of miracles, her blood turned into wine. No, champagne. For the first time in her life, she felt drunk. No wonder humans loved alcohol. So, she did it again, tracing his jaw, applying more pressure and covering more ground.

He had the softest skin, but his lips…his lips were even softer.

As she shivered, his eyelids popped open, those rainbow irises glittering as if dusted with diamond powder. She gasped and yanked her hand back to her side. But he moved quickly, too quickly for her to track, and latched on to her wrist to forcibly flatten her palm on his chest, just above his heart.

"Why did you stop?" he rasped.

Their gazes met and locked, and the heat of a thousand suns seared her. Her skin flushed and sensitized, everything else fading from her awareness. Her world revolved around Bjorn.

"I…you…" Inner shake. Where had her wits gone? *Easy. My panties.* Except, she wasn't wearing any.

They stayed in that sexually suggestive position for endless minutes, neither moving, neither speaking again. The urge to kiss him sparked, shocking her. Kiss her captor? No, thanks. And yet, the desire refused to ebb.

He must have felt it, too. He eased his legs apart and tugged her closer until she was all but draped over him. His eyes! Her jaw dropped. Blue had consumed one eye, and green had consumed the other. Both contained a wicked, sinful gleam. *Irresistible.*

"Why do your eyes change color?" she asked, breathless.

"I am a Dread. Half Dread, anyway, half Sent One."

An actual Dread? Wow! She'd had no idea the 'Dread' in Bjorn's designation referenced a race of warriors known for being the originators of nightmares. Unfeeling monsters so cruel the gods had kicked them out of Mt. Olympus. In other words: her role-models! Every time she buried her emotions, she used their technique.

Fox had liked Bjorn's transformation before. Now? *Love!* His ferocity and intensity made more sense and—

Her palm. Her palm on his chest. His heart raced against it, drumming just as swiftly as hers. She sucked in a breath. She'd excited a Dread, and she loved that, too, her determination to resist him crumbling in an instant. Sexual desire eclipsed even the demon's desires, his whispered commands no longer computing.

An all-you-can-eat buffet of masculine delights stretched out beneath her. *I'm starved.*

Abstain? Impossible. Already, frustration mounted.

With a ragged moan, she swooped in, pressing her mouth against his. She expected protests from him. A shove. Something! Instead, the hand on her nape inched up to fist her hair and hold her in place. Then…oh, then he opened up and thrust his tongue against hers.

They kissed slowly, languidly, an exploration unlike any she'd experienced before—*better* than anything she'd experienced before.

He is taking the time to learn what I like? But, but...why? Unless he planned to use her body, then kill her while she recovered from an orgasm?

Such a suspicion should have sent her fleeing. But just as quickly as the doubt formed, it dissipated. Bjorn wasn't like most men. He couldn't lie, and he was too strong to resort to subterfuge, especially with a woman he'd been ordered to slay. *I think he might, maybe, possibly, truly desire me.*

This suspicion caused her arousal to spike.

Want more. Need it! He didn't just kiss, he conquered, making mincemeat of her lingering reservations. Seriously, did Sent Ones have some kind of aphrodisiac in their saliva? Her breasts ached, and her nipples tightened into hard little points. Her belly quivered. Her control? Completely obliterated.

Their tongues tangled together. He tasted as good as he smelled and...and...still she needed more. All. Everything. Her entire body quaked with need. He'd made her ache, and she wasn't mad about it.

Fox combed her fingers through his hair, rested a leg between his— and gasped. He wasn't just shirtless, her man was one hundred percent naked, his erection a white-hot battering ram, ready to storm the gates of her castle.

She stiffened. *Her* man?

Need for release overwhelmed her, blanking her mind. All she could do? Writhe against him. Every time her feminine core ground against his thigh, another moan left her. The pleasure...so much. Too much. Not nearly enough.

The aches expanded as he kneaded her breasts and pinched her nipples, lightly at first. Then hard. Harder. Tremors skated through her. When she flattened a palm on his chest, he captured her wrist just as before. This time, he urged her arm lower.

When she reached his shaft, she curled her fingers around the base. *Well, hello!* The man was big. Bigger than she'd realized. Huge! Her inner walls clenched, desperate to be filled.

As she stroked him, a bead of moisture wet the tip. She licked her lips, imagining licking him like a lollipop.

With a groan, Bjorn rolled her to her back and wedged his hips between her legs. His weight settled over her, pinning her down. Yes, yes! He snapped his wings open. Those gold feathers blocked out the rest of the room. The Sent One was all she could see, all she wanted to see.

"Want me...to stop?" he asked between rough breaths.

"Never!"

After a beat of hesitation, his gaze searching hers, he slanted his head for another kiss and nipped at her tongue. After another beat, he kneaded her breasts once again and rubbed against her with increasing force. The friction... She rocked in time to his thrusts, seeking deeper contact.

Why had he paused, though? Only two answers made sense. Either he fought to stop this with all his might, or he wanted to do so many things to her body, he wasn't sure where to begin. Even the thought of the latter unleashed an onslaught of pleasure, scrambling her brain.

He hooked an arm beneath both of her knees to force her thighs farther apart, creating a deeper cradle for his erection. As he kissed along her jaw, ran her earlobe between his teeth, and continued playing with her breasts, she thrashed beneath him, clawed at his back and tugged at his hair.

Who could have known a Sent One could be so wonderfully aggressive in bed? Or that she'd like it—Bjorn—so much?

In the past, Fox had gravitated to more submissive males. As much as she loved money, she loved control more—money was simply a tool to *gain* control of her life. But this...Bjorn...

He'd shredded her control and exerted his own. He decided the tone and speed of the kiss. The angle of her body. The placement of her hands. All she had to do? Relax and enjoy. *Really* enjoy. *Never knew I'd prefer to* relinquish *control.*

Bjorn went still. She moaned a protest, and he lifted his head to peer down at her. His panting breaths matched hers. He studied her face, and she studied his. Sweat glistened on his brow and trickled down his temples. Lines of tension bracketed his eyes and mouth. His lips were red, puffy, and damp.

He looked like the incarnation of sex.

"Why did you stop?" she croaked.

"We shouldn't...we..." With another groan, he dove back down.

Their mouths met once again. This time, they ate at each other, *devoured* each other. This...he... She shivered wildly. *More.*

As if he'd heard her internal cry, he maneuvered a hand under her, cupped her ass and urged her into a faster rhythm. At the same time, he rocked his hips forward and back, forward and back, his erection brushing against her clitoris again and again.

Oh...oh! Pleasure fragmented her thoughts until only one thought remained in her head. *So good, so good, so good.*

Then he readjusted her, draping her legs around him, freeing his hands. As he continued to rock against her core, he caressed her...everywhere. Inside her, pressure built, every point of contact leaving her shaky and breathless. *So amazing, so amazing, so amazing.*

No. *Amazing* wasn't a strong enough word, either. Magnificent? Hmm, yes.

Wet and achy, she ran his bottom lip between her teeth and pinched *his* nipples, one after the other. He tightened his hold on her ass, his grip bruising. Tomorrow, she would feel him and remember this one, blissful moment each time she took a step.

Must have this man. "Bjorn," she rasped against his lips. "I want more...want everything. You are—" *Married.* The word crashed into her mind, her body going cold.

That's right. Bjorn had a wife.

Horror punched Fox dead center in the chest. *He has a wife, and I kissed him.* A wife he'd visited before returning to the dungeon injured. Now, she wondered. Had he gotten injured defending the woman he'd loved enough to wed? Had he visited the wife while Fox recovered from the whipping? Perhaps he'd been too sated to check on the prisoner his friends nearly killed. Either way...

Her hands curled into fists. How could Fox have forgotten his mated state, even for a moment? "We're stopping. You're married." *And I'm an idiot.* How could she have forgotten his wife, even for a moment? "Unless you're in the process of divorce?" Ugh. Had that hopeful tone truly come from Fox?

* * * *

Control, soon to shatter...

Bjorn went still as Fox's words echoed in his head. *I want more...you're married...we're stopping.*

More. Married. Stopping.

All night, he'd held Fox in the shelter of his arms, unable to sleep. He'd wallowed in guilt and shame because of what he'd allowed to happen to her. At first, he'd cared only about her recovery. But as her breathing evened out and color returned to her flawless skin, his thoughts became more and more sexual. When she'd healed completely, his true torment had begun. The feel of her body against his…

Her softness to his hardness. Heat against heat, with her silken hair spread over his chest, and their legs intertwined. Climbing into bed with her had been the best decision and worst mistake he'd ever made.

Finally, though, he'd drifted off…only to awaken when she caressed his jaw. When their gazes had met, desire had flared to life all over again, only stronger than ever before. In that moment, resisting his body's need for her had been futile.

Celibate? No longer.

Now, with the sweetness of her taste branded into his memory and filling his mouth…with her soft curves pressed against his hardness…with her feminine heat wetting his shaft, he didn't know if he'd *ever* be able to resist her again.

Anytime he remembered this moment, he knew he would crave her again. And again. But the worst part? He suspected no other female would do. A ridiculous thought! *Anyone* else would be better suited for him. The *nightstand* would be better suited for him.

"Bjorn," she repeated with a groan. "Any answers or comments? Questions? Thoughts?"

Arousal softened her features and flushed her skin. Those hazel eyes projected earth-shattering need, rousing his most primitive instincts. Lips swollen from his kisses remained parted as she panted.

No longer were her features simply arresting. They were *exquisite*. A layer of anger had been stripped away, revealing a startling vulnerability and a hint of…adoration? For him?

No, no. No way she adored him. "I despise Alana and the marriage she forced upon me." But even still, he needed to resist Fox. Yes? At the moment, he couldn't recall a single reason to combat the hot tide of desire raging through him. He couldn't think straight. *Need to think.* "She is Queen of Shadows. A parasite. As soon as I can reach her without a summons, I will kill her." Of course, he would have to find a way to sever their bond first, or he would die with her.

"She forced the marriage? Then you are *not* married. You're single, baby, and ready to mingle." Fox nibbled on her bottom lip and traced circles over his pec. "If you'd like to make your single-hood official, I can portal you to your wife—" She pursed her lips. "I can portal you to *the queen*. Without a summons. Vow to set me free, and I will. I'll even throw in a sweetener and help you kill her."

If not for the bond, he might have taken Fox up on her offer. Even still, the temptation proved overwhelming. "She isn't just a Shadow; she is a *queen* of Shadows. She can possess your body and drain your soul before you comprehend what's happening. And, to set you free is to risk my place in the heavens. To what end? So I can die when you kill Alana? So you can be hunted again? Another Sent One *will* be sent to slay you." He stiffened, already furious with this nameless, faceless Sent One.

"Yeah. So?"

"So, I would never forgive myself if they harmed—if *you* harmed them." Could he forgive himself for sinking so low and kissing Fox, the murderess? Not just kissing her, but liking—*loving*—it. Time to make the madness stop. He disengaged from her, untangling their bodies. "If you're hungry, there's a feast over there." He stood and pointed to a small bistro-style table piled high with platters of food. "Please, eat."

"Why? Is the food poisoned?"

She thinks I will heal and kiss her the same day I plan to kill her?

Will I?

The answer hit him, and hit hard. No. He wouldn't. He would not be harming a hair on her head today. Perhaps not tomorrow, either.

Chest clenching with relief, Bjorn stalked to the closet, his hard-on bobbing with every step, all but pointing at her. He ground his teeth, irritated beyond measure, and donned a robe. He wouldn't be kissing her again, either.

"My friends whipped you, and I'm sorry for all you suffered, Fox. That wasn't supposed to happen."

"Oh. I see." Frowning, she sat up and lowered her head. Dark hair fell forward, shielding her face from view. "So, the feast is a make-up gift?"

A muscle ticked beneath his eye. He continued without addressing her question. "The kiss should not have happened, either. I choose to be celibate."

"What?!" She glanced up for a moment, only a moment, her eyes wide. "Did you just say you're celibate?"

"For roughly a year, yes."

"I've gone five…hundred years, eight months, and six days, but who's counting?"

Now, *his* eyes widened. "Fox the Executioner hasn't had sex in over five *hundred* years?"

"Well, I had trust issues long before Distrust," she said, defensive.

Reeling. "You chose to break your sexual fast with me, the male tasked with your murder? Why?" *Are we more alike than I realized?*

And what is it I think I'm doing? Playing with temptation is never wise. Stop!

"No, don't tell me," he said next. "I can't change what happened in our pasts, but I can change what happens in our futures. We will *not* kiss again."

Her head wrenched up. Humiliation and dejection burned pretty pink circles in her cheeks.

His chest clenched with more force. So much, he swore several ribs cracked. The rejection had cut her as much as the whipping. He nearly dropped to his knees to apologize.

Fool! This is a trick, only a trick. He balled his hands into fists. She would have to care about his opinion to give a damn about his rejection. She didn't. She couldn't.

But what if she did? What if her feelings for him were just as complicated as his feelings for her?

Hope blossomed, only to wither. Rejection hurt, period. Even when someone you hated rejected you, it stung.

"You don't want to kiss me again? Fine," she snapped. "Don't kiss me again. Good call, by the way. I'd bite off your tongue. Now. I'm done playing the role of prisoner. Either you fight me, or you watch me walk away."

"I will do neither. I will put you in your cell, and that's that."

"Why? Are you hoping I'll forget your vile behavior and sign on to be your temporary dick handler?"

Dick handler? *Now I want to laugh.*

Get your head in the game. Bjorn extended his arm and curved his hand, a sword hilt appearing there. As he closed his fingers around it, fire spread over the blade. With his free hand, he motioned to the door. "Exit the bedroom, Fox."

Fox raised her chin, and it was clear the humiliation and dejection had morphed into fury. Another trait to admire. Anyone else would have sobbed or begged for mercy. This woman would fight until she took her last breath.

She smiled slowly, coldly, and said, "Make me."

Chapter Nine

Bjorn remained immobile. He watched, fascinated, as another startling change transformed the enigmatic Fox. First, she'd been soft, warm and needy, not just receptive to his kiss but an active participant, writhing against him. Then she projected hurt, dejection and embarrassment. One hundred percent his fault. Now? She looked hardened, cold and emotionless.

What she didn't do? Panic.

No longer did she resemble a sleepy, just-kissed lover hungry for more. No, she appeared every inch a killer...yet he still craved her. No, he craved her even *more*.

Bjorn found the different aspects of her personality intriguing, and wondered if he wielded enough sensual prowess to make her go soft again. *Without* going soft himself.

His mind a minefield of desire, regret, and fury, Bjorn struggled to focus, to think straight, answers beyond his skill set at the moment. Questions were a different story entirely. Why did he heal and kiss an enemy at all? Why did he enjoy the kiss more than any other he'd ever experienced?

When could he do it again?

No, no. *Lock her back in the dungeon, as decided. Clear your head. Finally think straight and figure out a new plan of action.* Maybe he'd have a fresh memory of her?

He tensed. He needed to tell her about the first one. How would she react?

As graceful as a ballerina, she stood and smoothed the wrinkles from her oversized tee, treating the garment like a formal gown. "Be honest. You're afraid your crush on me will turn *Fatal Attraction*-ish if you dress me in something other than a crappy T-shirt, right?"

Her confident teasing threw kindling on the flames of his desire. "I do *not* have a crush—" The remainder of the sentence disintegrated, leaving a foul taste on his tongue. He pressed his lips together. Apparently, he *did* have a crush on Fox. As a Sent One, he could speak no lies. In the end, all he could tell her? "Someone thinks highly of herself."

"What, I wasn't supposed to notice the robe-tent you're currently sporting?" she sneered, poking at his inner bear. "Sorry, but it looks like you're smuggling a Shake Weight under there."

Shake Weight? "It is a bodily reaction," he grated.

"Let's be real. You don't want to lock me away for my crimes. You want to lock me away because you blame me for your desire. You're lashing out, because I dared to turn you on, as if females aren't blamed for a male's actions and reactions all the time. Tell me, Bjorn. Which of these scenarios works best for you? I pretend not to notice your arousal...and you consider me prudish. I point out that you obviously like the look of me...but I'm conceited. How about I explain to you how you can't possibly want me...so you can ding me for being insecure? If ever you compliment me, should I accept it and come across as needy, or reject it like a baby-back-bitch? There's just no winning with you or anyone, so, I'll stick with the truth. You want me because I look like a tasty snack, and we both know it."

She...wasn't wrong. The wisdom of her words knocked him breathless. Sent Ones worshipped truth, and she'd just given him a healthy dose of it. "I...apologize," he said, and he meant it. He scoured his free hand over his face—tired, so tired. So much to do. So much he didn't *want* to do.

She blinked, shook her head, rubbed her ears. "Am I in the middle of a delusion?" Rolling her hips provocatively, she crossed the room, closing in on him, daring him to strike at her. "It sounded like you—a stubborn, self-righteous tosser—just apologized to your number one target."

The fact that she stood within striking distance, unafraid, all challenge and sensuality while he held a fiery sword... Did she hope to disarm him? Or did she hope to pick up where they'd left off?

His shaft throbbed harder than ever.

If ever he received an opportunity to select a woman from a catalogue, he'd pick someone like Fox, right here, right now. Dark hair mussed. Strong but vulnerable. Lithe body draped in his T-shirt, and only his T-shirt. Lips that were red and puffy from his kisses. How had he never noticed the little freckles that dotted her nose? *Adorable.*

His chest clenched. *Adorable? No! She is lethal seduction, and I must remain on guard. Always.* "You are not deluded. You are a beautiful woman, and your confidence is commendable. I never should have implied otherwise."

More blinking. Head canted to the side, she said, "Why didn't you kill me in my sleep? I would think *you* would think it'd be kinder than healing me, locking me up, keeping me stressed about D day—death day—until you finally got the balls to do your duty. Or maybe you were too busy snuggling with me?"

"My reasons are my own," he said, shoving the words past his gritted teeth. The hardness of his tone should have told her more than his words: *Ask another question at your peril.* "Do *you* not think dying in your sleep would be better?"

"Hell, no. When I go, it will be in battle. I will face death straight-on."

Such bravery. Such courage. Such strength. His admiration for her multiplied.

"How am I healed?" she asked, forging ahead. "Your buddies whipped me with *infirmədē.* I should have suffered until my death. Did you do something to aid me?"

Maddening female. "I will not reveal the reason." While the Water of Life wasn't a secret, exactly, Sent Ones rarely confirmed or denied its existence. Already, immortals attempted to storm the heavens on a daily basis to hunt and find the river where the Water flowed.

"In other words," she said, smug now, "yes, you did do something to aid me. I'm gonna guess…Water of Life? Yeah, I know about it. I do my homework. Anyway. I'm confused about your reasons. Why save me from pain rather than completing your mission?"

Maddening, *perceptive* female. His actions confused him, too. "Kissing you must have addled my brain," he grumbled. If only he'd resisted the all-consuming urge. He wouldn't know the sweetness of her taste, the softness of her body when it pressed against the hardness of his, the intoxicating scent of her arousal—a heady perfume—or the drugging warmth of her silken skin.

Now I must give her up?

In her arms, he'd forgotten his troubles. For a few minutes, the stress he'd carried for so long had ebbed. But, as soon as the kiss ended, those troubles and stresses rushed back.

"I didn't ask you about the kiss," she snipped at him. "But. Since you brought it up, let's do it. Let's go there. I'll break this down for you, and you'll listen like a good boy, m'kay?"

Though he knew he should protest, he nodded, eager to hear what her keen mind observed. "Go on. I'm listening."

Go on she did. "You want me, you just don't *want* to want me. You can't resist this"—she waved to indicate the length of her body— "and *that* is why you want to keep me around a little longer."

He clenched his jaw, the muscles taut. Maddening, perceptive, *smart* female. "You are cold, calculating and conniving, and I cannot be sure of your motivations. You care for nothing—"

"Wrong! If you're going to malign my character, at least do so accurately. I care for Galen and Legion, control, money, success, gold, jewels, money, victory, weapons, money, and killing the deserving." Her shoulders sagged the slightest bit, and he didn't have to wonder why. She'd remembered the ten. They had not been deserving.

A second later, she squared those shoulders. Had he not been observing her every move, he would have missed the entire byplay.

Realization: *She* isn't *cold. She does feel. She just fights her emotions.*

He reeled, his chest clenching again. This time, the clenching didn't let up. As long as he'd lived, he'd observed many people who'd fought their emotions. They'd all had one thing in common—they felt too much. Usually, due to some sort of trauma in their past.

What did he know about Fox's past? Only what he'd seen in his dream. How long had she wandered the streets of Ancient Greece, starving, dirty and vulnerable? Had other soldiers harmed her? What other horrors had she endured?

Bjorn squeezed the sword hilt tighter. He knew Galen the Treacherous had found and protected the girl at some point. *I am to be the villain, the one who locks her away, while a male known as* the Treacherous *is the hero?*

Bjorn opened his sword hand and lowered his arm, the fiery weapon vanishing. Annoyed by the situation, by Fox, by *himself*, he sighed, weary, and said, "I do not wish to fight you, Fox."

"So? If you try to lock me up, a fight is *going* to happen. You have the Fox gold-star guarantee on that."

"What if I pay you to walk yourself to the dungeon?"

Intrigue glittered in her lovely hazel eyes. "I hear the disapproval in your tone, baby boy. You consider me materialistic."

"I do." No reason to deny it.

"Maybe I like material gain because it allows me to save the people I love. Ever think of that? With an overflow of cash, I can buy weapons, mystical artifacts, homes, food, computers and vehicles—all necessities for surviving an immortal war. Wait. I can already hear your response." Mimicking and mocking him, she wagged her finger in his direction and said, "Now, Foxy, my sweet. You should have a lady boner for helping everyone, not just your loved ones."

Lady boner? The things this beauty said had a way of stabbing his high horse to death, leaving him reeling, without a solid foundation to stand upon. *Worth it.* Fox made life more exciting. She even made arguments fun.

Tension ebbed from his muscles. He canted his head to the side and told her, "You make a valid point. But I think you have forgotten a basic rule of humanity. Everyone you hate and consider worthy of elimination is *someone else's* loved one."

Her breath hitched. She opened and closed her mouth without making a sound. Finally, she settled on, "You make a valid point, too. Damn you!"

He took a step closer. *Why are you doing this? Stop!*

Can't stop. Can't stay away.

Drawn to her, he took another step closer, and another, until only a whisper of air separated their bodies. She stilled and stiffened, as if uncertain about his intentions. But, as he did nothing more than inhale her innate fragrance, awareness crackled in the air between them, little lightning strikes against his skin. They both began to pant.

"Back off, Bjorn," she croaked.

"Why?" he asked, mimicking her. "Because you lack the strength to back away from *me*?" *Is she as weak for me as I am for her?* Even the notion thrilled him.

"Because you plan to kill me one day, and I can't trust you."

"You can trust me today, for I vow I will not harm you. Unless you attack me, and I must defend myself." Always best to add a qualifier. "But back off? No. I'm a little too busy mentally stripping you out of that shirt." Only minutes ago, he'd held her breasts in his hands. Those plump beauties were more than a handful, firm yet soft, and absolutely, utterly perfect.

She snorted. "Please. You aren't just stripping me. You're also imagining parking your boner in my garage."

He fought a smile. Damn her!

As much as he disliked this woman—no, that wasn't true. He didn't dislike her. He disliked what she'd done. The real problem? He liked her more than he should.

I'm not going to kill her—ever. He would have to find another path.

There has *to be another way.* He wanted to help this woman, not harm her.

The truth drifted through his mind, found a spot to camp, and erected a tent. He'd had a hard-on for her ever since he'd spied her flying out of that shower stall, wet and naked. Every interaction since had only increased his desire for her.

She was just so different from Alana, who lied to anyone and everyone to get what she wanted, no matter who she hurt in the process. Fox told the truth, no matter how upsetting, and dealt with the consequences, hurting only herself. Alana expected to dominate her lovers. Despite her own strength, Fox had willingly surrendered to Bjorn, allowing him to set the pace. Alana often played victim, blaming others for her problems, all *so unfair this* and *so unfair that.* When she messed up, Fox admitted it, even to her own detriment, and he *admired* her for it. Bjorn would rather save a loyal villain than a disloyal hero. He would rather work with a truthful enemy than a deceptive ally.

He had no doubt the ferocious beauty would go to the mat for her man, putting her life in jeopardy to protect the one she loved, remaining loyal until the end. Alana only cared about herself.

Bjorn stiffened. *Do I want to be Fox's man...long-term?*

"What thoughts tumble through your mind, hmm?" she asked, yanking him back to the present.

Only that you are everything I never knew I needed. Maybe, with Fox, he would experience true satisfaction.

She smiled slowly, the corners of her mouth curling up. Not with amusement, but wicked delight. "Look at you fighting *yourself.*"

He balled his hands into fists. Had he mentioned her perceptiveness?

"You won't hurt me today if I refrain from attacking," she continued. "I won't go back to the dungeon willingly. So, how do we proceed from here? You gonna try to A, force me back in the dungeon, B, make out with me, or C, let me go? Make a decision. Just know that option A will get you battered, because I won't go down without a fight...and I'll probably behead you during my escape. I'll give you three seconds to decide, then I make the decision myself. Three...two..."

Chapter Ten

"You chose option A? Seriously?" Fox shouted as Bjorn walked away from her cell. Somehow, the bastard managed to carry her to the dungeon *without* harming her.

"I have a meeting with the Sent Ones," he called, never looking back. "I'll return shortly, and we'll finish what we started."

"At least put a TV in here. And buy me an access pass to my favorite reality TV shows!"

Silence. She launched into a swift pace. Wearing a T-shirt, and only a T-shirt, she felt shockingly vulnerable. No, Bjorn and his mind-bending hotness made her shockingly vulnerable.

She should have killed him during their first meet-cute, but nooo, she let herself get captured, imprisoned, and whipped instead. Then she kissed him. Like a fool! *Then*, like a greater fool, she offered him three options to decide her fate, willingly ceding control to him.

Like the greatest fool of all, she'd pulled her punches during the ensuing grapple. Now, she occupied the same cell as before—with a few changes to the decor—Bjorn long gone. On his way out, he grumbled about needing to meet with the Sent Ones before he and Fox could finish what they'd started.

With a sigh, she settled atop the mattress. Yep, a mattress rather than a cot. He'd exchanged a dirty sheet for plush bedding. He'd also provided a small, round table piled high with an all-you-can-eat buffet of snacks and beverages. Chips, cookies, a carafe of wine, a block of cheese, fruit juice, candy bars, and bread.

Why be nice to her at all? And why the hell had she pulled her punches? At no point in the past had she ever hesitated to make a kill in order to self-preserve. Actually, she'd killed anyone who'd ever even uttered a threat. So why hesitate here and now, with him, with her appointed executioner? What made him so special?

Her hormones screamed, *Hell-loo! He apologized for the whipping with words* and *action, and he isn't even the one responsible. He's a good guy, and one with a working moral compass.* That *is why he's special.* The fact that she'd never apologized for what she'd done to the ten…

I suck. And what had Bjorn meant, finish what they'd started? The fight about what to do with her, or the make-out session?

Shivers tumbled down her spine. *I know which option has my vote. Focus up.* How should she proceed from here?

She still didn't want to harm Bjorn. But she *did* want…need another kiss. Bjorn had revved her engine, then left her aching. She yearned to have his big, strong hands back on her breasts, kneading. Longed for him to pinch her nipples. Craved his mouth on her—every inch. Would he take her hard and fast or tender and slow? What did he like in bed?

The demon stretched inside her mind, getting comfortable. *What if this was his plan all along? Rev you up and leave you desperate for more, giving you false hope about a possible relationship. Just another form of punishment.*

A lump grew in her throat. What if Distrust was…right?

Now, her stomach flip-flopped, suddenly queasy. She had a weapon available in her arsenal, something she hadn't utilized yet. Not fully, anyway. That weapon? Bjorn's attraction to her.

Whatever Bjorn's intentions with the kiss and vow to leave her unharmed today, he wanted her. What if she made him fall in love with her? Anticipation sparked. Excitement, too. If she somehow won him over, he would prevent other Sent Ones from coming after her. Since they were the only species able to negate her portal-opening ability, stopping their attacks would be big. Huge!

How did they negate her portal-opening ability?

Distrust laughed, gleeful. *You are so good at sex, you can make a two-pump chump fall in love with you?* More laughter. *Good luck with that. Guaranteed, he likes to ditch a bitch as soon as he nuts. And if you think you'll get any pleasure out of the deal, you're even stupider than I thought.*

Unleashing our inner frat boy, demon? Go flame yourself.

If the fiend had called anyone but Bjorn a two-pump chump unconcerned about a "bitch's" pleasure or emotional wellbeing, she would have agreed. But she wouldn't, couldn't believe such a thing of Bjorn.

The male had too much honor…unlike the douchebags on her favorite reality shows.

The baby-fine hairs on the back of her neck stood up, and she frowned. Next, the temperature dropped a couple thousand degrees, dark shadows spilling down the walls like ink on paper. Growing, spreading, covering more ground, getting closer and closer to Fox's cell.

Her muscles went taut as realization struck. Alana had returned. Great! Just great. This should be fun.

A gust of smoke blew through the dungeon, only to part, revealing Alana. She strolled toward Fox, glaring. She wore another dress made of sheer scarves, displaying more skin than it concealed. She'd plaited her hair, then wound the multitude of braids into a crown. Rage iced her irises.

The woman had come for a reckoning, hadn't she?

Fox comprehended there were two ways to play this. Prove Alana could not intimidate her, or pretend to be afraid, putting Alana at ease, thereby making her cocky enough to relax her guard.

"Who are you? What is your name?" the spouse demanded.

Afraid, Fox decided then. With the right incentive, she might be able to convince Alana to set her free…

Here goes nothing. Fox wrapped her arms around her middle and stepped back, as if she feared what Alana might do. "I—I'm Fox. No one."

Alana must have craved a high, because she basically snorted Fox's *fear* like a drug. "I felt Bjorn's arousal and thought I'd do my wifely duty and put him out of his misery. I just left his bedroom. He wasn't there. Want to guess what was? Your scent in his bed. If you'd like to live, you will tell me why."

Fox balled her hands, fury rampaging through her. Put him out of his misery? Hardly. The bitch had planned to force Bjorn to sleep with her, no doubt about it.

Be scared, remember? Right. Schooling her features, she croaked, "I had been whipped…was dying. He put me in the bed to help me heal. I woke up and…I…I kissed him, but he pushed me away." Truth. Would it push her over the edge?

Rage flared in Alana's abyss-like eyes. "You dared to kiss my man? Bjorn the One True Dread is mine, and I do not share."

If only Fox could cry on command. "It was a mistake. L-let me out of this cell, and he'll never see me again. I promise!"

"I have a better idea." A tendril of black smoke wafted from Alana's nostrils. "I *kill* you, and he never sees you again."

Fox recalled Bjorn's warning about Alana. The woman could possess a body and drain it of energy.

Unable to open portals, Fox would be at a disadvantage once again. Plus, she'd never actually fought a Shadow, had only ever heard rumors about them. They were broken into two factions. The Lux—light—and the Sine Lumine—without light. The latter exhibited the worst traits of her three most-hated species: vampires, demons, and phantoms. Living dead who hungered for life? Check. Hive-minded and parasitic? Check. Able to become intangible and tangible, walking with spirits *and* the embodied? Checkmate. And Alana was their sovereign.

Fox shuddered. *Doesn't matter. I'm armed with my wits. I've got this.* Sticking with her pretense, she rasped, "P-please, don't hurt me. I don't...I can't..." Ugh. *Am I overselling?*

With a smug grin, Alana extended her arms at her sides. Dark shadows seeped from her pores, swiftly engulfing her in a cloud, attempting to bypass the cell's bars, only to bounce back.

Alana cursed and tried to slip through the bars again. An-n-nd she failed again.

So. Only Sent Ones could enter the cells? *Must, must, must find out how they negate our abilities.*

On Alana's third attempt, she ricocheted backward with more force, crying out in pain.

Do not smile. The corners of her mouth twitched. *Seriously! Don't you dare.*

Ultimately, Alana gave up and stomped her foot like a child. "This isn't over," she grated.

"Please, don't hurt me," Fox repeated. "I'm just a poor nobody with—"

The woman vanished as quickly as she'd appeared, no sign of her remaining.

"—a lady boner for your demise," she finished with a harder tone. No wonder Bjorn hated the woman. A one-minute conversation revealed a trash bag hidden beneath skin and smoke. Spoiled, selfish, without shame or guilt.

Killing Alana would be a privilege and a favor to Bjorn. Although, why hadn't *he* killed Alana?

Whatever the reason, a four-part plan took shape in Fox's head. *Act charming to seduce Bjorn. Make him fall in love with me. Kill his wife. Get pardoned by the Sent Ones.*

Despite the obstacles littering her path, Fox caught herself smiling with excitement. No part would be simple, or easy, but damn if they weren't going to be fun.

* * * *

The door to Axel's cloud was open.

Bjorn did his best to push Fox from his mind as he entered, Thane at his right side, Xerxes at his left. Like them, Axel was a former Warrior who'd received a promotion soon after a demon-possessed male set off a magical bomb in the heavens, killing most of the original seven as well as hundreds of others.

Axel reminded Bjorn of, well, him and his boys. Utterly untamed.

If you are so untamed, why are you playing it safe with Fox?

Not thinking of her. Not now.

He focused more surely on Axel. The male had black hair, electric-blue eyes, and a powerful build. He loved practical and impractical jokes with equal intensity, never took anything seriously, and enjoyed a new lover—or two—every night.

Unlike the other Elite, Axel wasn't a full-blooded Sent One. No, not true. He might be. No one knew his parents. As a child, he had been found wandering around the heavens with a mind as blank as an unpainted canvas. He'd grown up to resemble another warrior Bjorn knew. William the Ever Randy, a powerful enforcer of mysterious origins, who was just as likely to stab a friend as an enemy.

No one knew William's origins, either. Long ago, Hades had adopted him, making him a prince of darkness. One of only a dozen. There was no worse enemy to have.

If—when—Bjorn killed Fox, he would be declaring war with William, who allied with all Lords of the Underworld, including Galen, who allied with Fox. The Ever Randy had a No Harm, No Exceptions policy for his allies. A strike against any member of William's crew equaled a strike against William himself, something Bjorn greatly admired. If anyone were to harm Thane and Xerxes, Bjorn would retaliate. No mercy.

Bjorn was only surprised William and Galen hadn't teamed up to work together. Galen wanted *his* Fox back, and texted a new threat to

Bjorn every day, claiming he would sneak into the Downfall and murder Bjorn in his sleep.

He balled his hands into hard fists. *Not his Fox. Mine!*

Why can't I get her out of my head? No doubt the newly mated supervillain would try to make good on his threats soon. And if not Galen, any of the Lords and Ladies of the Underworld.

So why do I still crave Fox?

Tone low and quiet, Thane said, "I see no sign of the others."

"Nor do I." Since Bjorn had never been here before, he cast his gaze throughout the ten- thousand-square-foot structure. Luxury at its finest, with ornate furnishings. All gloriously preserved antiques. Countless crystal vases filled with roses. Portraits framed with solid gold. Plush rugs.

This did not fit the irreverent Axel in the slightest. Where was the stuffed roadkill wearing baby clothes? The posters of half-naked women? The blow-up dolls, or *conversation starters*?

The money-loving Fox would probably adore this place. No doubt Bjorn's minimalistic approach to decorating struck her as sad. He popped his jaw. *Not going to think about her anymore.* Or their kiss. Or the long, long list of things he yearned to do to her exquisite body as her moans of rapture filled his ears, her sweet scent teased his nose, and her amazing taste tantalized his tongue.

Damn this! He wanted to think about her, so, he would think about her. The cherries on top of her attributes? Her intelligence and her dry sense of humor. The woman had a talent for reading each person and situation she encountered, and she possessed a merriment Bjorn did not recall experiencing himself in…ever.

He'd always been the serious one, even before his imprisonment and torture. But every time Fox spoke, he fought a smile. Boner garage. Seriously? Not to mention her love of reality TV. Even thinking about those things intensified his hunger for her, desire rolling through him like an avalanche, growing in strength and speed. His blood heated, and his muscles bulged with tension.

His friends must have taken his body language as a sign of distress, because Thane and Xerxes placed a hand on Bjorn's shoulders. A gesture of comfort. Of reassurance. They could face anything, as long as they remained together.

Some of the tension seeped out of him.

Axel materialized in the living room, frowning when he spotted them. "There you are. Come." He waved them over before vanishing.

Confused but unconcerned, Bjorn and his boys crossed the distance…

As soon as they passed an invisible threshold, the living room faded from sight. Instead, a dome with walls of energy surrounded them, the other Elites already there, standing in a circle. Every member of the Elite 7 owned wings of the purest gold. They wore white robes trimmed with topaz, a color representative of the Most High. But that was where their similarities ended. Together, they were an assortment of hair, eye and skin colors, sizes and heights, from all over the universe.

There was the uber-stubborn Zacharel…brilliant Calypso, known as Caly…and hot-tempered Ravensara. Also present, by-the-book Lysander, who used to be an Elite. Now, he was something more. He would be overseeing their meetings until he believed everyone understood their new position and the responsibilities that came with it.

Axel stepped into the center, saying, "I called this meeting because we have been tasked with a mission. Each of us is to recruit an army of one hundred Warriors and move to the Underworld, where we will team up with the Lords of the Underworld to slay Lucifer and his demons. Lucifer is the ultimate blame for the bombing that killed our friends. He has been building *his* army, and the number of soldiers grows daily—his demons, other immortals, allies, and even spirits of the dead."

Move to the Underworld, the asshole of the immortal world? Icy fingers of dread crept up Bjorn's spine, while white-hot fingers of fury slid down his sternum. "When is this move to take place?" One way or another, the Fox situation had to be dealt with beforehand. One way or another. He couldn't, shouldn't, *wouldn't* cart her to Hell, where she would grow in power, thanks to Distrust. Where other Sent Ones might not resist the urge to tear her to shreds.

Unless taking her to Hell was the way to save her life?

An idea formed, not yet complete but worth mulling over.

"Ten days," Zacharel replied, and Bjorn reeled.

Ten days to perfect his idea and save Fox. Ten days to do everything he longed to do to her body. Only ten. *Not nearly enough.*

As if he'd read Bjorn's mind, Lysander said, "I'm assuming Fox the Executioner is dead, as ordered." His tone was as dry as the desert.

While the strict male had lightened up since his marriage to a beautiful Harpy, one of the bloodthirstiest species in *mythology*, he still erupted over any hint of disobedience.

"She is imprisoned," he admitted, earning a chorus of disappointed rumblings from everyone but Thane and Xerxes. "She is a resource. A rare Gatekeeper," he added, unable to stop the words from leaving his tongue. Though the idea wasn't fully fleshed out, he had to run with it. What other options did he have? "We can use her to get our armies in and out of Hell in seconds." Most Sent Ones could not flash. Usually forced to fly, they wasted precious time in do-or-die situations. "We can even portal in and out of Lucifer's home. Gatekeepers do not need to see a location before they can portal there. They only need coordinates. What's more, we can portal our wounded to safety during battle." *If* he could gain Fox's cooperation. Could he? And could he trust her to follow through with any kind of bargain?

The chorus went quiet at least, everyone mulling over his words.

"I will speak with Clerici," Zacharel finally said. "Do not slay Fox until you've heard from me."

Relief stormed through him. Knowing the emotion would seep into his voice, he opted to nod, remaining silent. All the while, his thoughts whirled.

Ten days to raise an army.

Ten days to move to Hell.

Ten days to save Fox.

Ten days to learn every detail about her past and every facet of her personality.

Ten days to kiss and touch her.

With a deadline now set, a sense of urgency overtook him. *Get to Fox. Now!* What he'd do when he got there, he didn't know. Yet.

Chapter Eleven

"What are you doing?"

Bjorn's deep, husky voice shattered the quiet, and Fox jumped up with a curse. *Caught red-handed.* She'd been digging in the far corner of the cell, where the shadows were thickest. Her plan? Secretly create a tunnel beneath the cells until she reached the doorless whipping room. From there, she'd have a straight shot to the club and then the exit.

She'd been listening for footsteps, and also sniffing for any hint of Bjorn's incredible scent, but she'd gotten nothing. Now, he was here. The guy she shipped. The cream-filling in her life Twinkie. And what the hell had she inhaled with all that sniffing because, duuude. Life Twinkie?

As she'd dug, she'd smelled a metallic odor of blood and a hint of cotton candy. Blood and candy, the same mix she'd tasted when she'd woken up in bed with Bjorn three days after her whipping. Why?

Figure it out later. Heart thudding, she pivoted on her heel…and gasped. Bjorn stood a few feet away. Meaning, he stood *inside* the cell. Excitement buzzed along her nerve endings. In an instant, her skin flushed, her nipples puckered, and her belly quivered.

She gulped. Maybe he wouldn't notice.

Oh, he noticed, all right. His eyelids hooded. His lips parted and softened, as if preparing for a kiss. Tension pulled his skin taut and bulged his muscles.

He looked good. Better than good. His dark hair stuck out in wild spikes. His rainbow eyes glittered brighter than ever before. A dusting of stubble shadowed his strong jaw, and a flush gifted his bronzed skin with a coppery sheen.

Wait. He'd asked a question, and she had yet to answer. "Obviously, I'm giving myself a dirt mani-pedi. All the rage...cool kids...you get it." Earlier, she'd decided to seduce him to make him fall in love with her. *No better time to start.* Stepping closer and waggling her fingers near his face, she said, "Do you like the end result?"

He snapped his teeth in the direction of her fingers, half-playful, half-serious, before saying, "Slipping through the bars has a higher likelihood of success than digging under the walls. There are myriad traps set throughout the foundation to ensure diggers lose their hands and perhaps a bit of brain matter."

He sounded so matter-of-fact, as if the escape attempt hadn't surprised or angered him in the least. Another shock.

Sent Ones cannot lie, but they can mislead, Distrust whispered. *You've been digging for hours, and nothing has happened. Stop now, and he will laugh about your gullibility with his friends.*

She swallowed a groan. Distrust had healed from his injuries and now hoped to feed. Too bad, so sad. In this, she wouldn't entertain a single doubt. While she and Bjorn hadn't known each other long, she had already learned a ton about him. He wasn't the type to misdirect. Or laugh.

"Thanks for the heads-up," she grumbled. Wait. There was something different about him. Several somethings, in fact. A stronger, sharper intensity...a primitive wildness...a panty-melting ferocity... Warm shivers spilled over her. Who or what caused these changes? Because she needed to send a Thank You basket.

"Come," he said, holding out his hand.

Her frown deepened as she wrenched backward. "Why? You've claimed you won't harm me today or kiss me again, so, what are you hoping to do with me?"

A muscle ticked beneath his eye. "I will escort you to my bathroom, where you will shower and change into clean clothes."

Seriously? *Do not reveal your excitement.* "Fine. Whatever. I'll shower and change because you insist. See what a good little prisoner I am?" *He's all but begging to be seduced.* She hurried over to accept his hand, only to draw back just before contact. "But again, I have to ask...why?" What was his endgame?

"Your execution has been temporarily postponed," he admitted. "I will not discuss the reasons until—"

"Why was it postponed?" she interjected. Deep inside, hope went to war with suspicion.

"—we are out of the dungeon." He sighed and intertwined their fingers. His calluses produced the most delectable friction, sending a lance of heat up her arm, down her torso, and to her core.

Remaining silent, he turned them both to mist, the sensation just as eerie as before. As soon as they cleared the bars, she expected to be released. Instead, he tightened his hold.

As they trekked upstairs, she attempted to open a portal with her free hand. A test, just in case. Once again, she failed. Gah! How did he negate her ability so easily and so consistently?

Allowing him to lead her through the house, she traced her gaze over every inch of him, searching for any hint of a weapon to steal. Again, just in case. Alas, if he'd strapped a dagger anywhere, the robe hid it well. But then, he might not have need of daggers. The guy forged a sword of fire from thin air.

He led the way, his steps clipped and hurried as he all but dragged her behind him, her shorter legs unable to keep up. "If you attempt to escape while you're out of your cell…". His voice trailed off.

"Let me guess," she said with a wry tone, "I'll suffer in ways I've never imagined possible."

He didn't deny it, which made her think he maybe, might, probably decided not to harm her…at all? The hope returned, stronger than ever. Probably too strong. *Getting ahead of yourself.*

"If you succeed," he said, "I'll turn my sights to Galen."

Oh, that burned. Rather than yelling at him, accomplishing nothing, she changed the subject. "How'd your meeting go?" she asked, not really expecting a response. Information was power, after all, and there was always a chance something she learned could aid her escape.

"As well as expected," he said, surprising her. "Each member of the Elite must recruit an army of a hundred Warriors. We must then move to Hell, where we will aid the Kings of the Underworld, as well as their allies, the Lords of the Underworld. Both factions currently war with Lucifer."

First, why would Bjorn share so much information with her unless he planned to use her in some way?

Second, Galen loved the Lords and their assortment of Ladies. Actually, Galen *was* a Lord. Technically, Fox was a Lady. Knowing her friend would have fierce Sent Ones at his back amid every battle pleased her greatly.

Unless the Sent Ones plan to take out the Lords, too.

The demon's dig hit its mark, tanking her enjoyment. Sent Ones despised demons—pure evil—and rightfully so, but they also tended to dislike the demon-possessed. Galen needed Fox. "You should take me with you," she told Bjorn, doing her best to erase the eagerness from her tone. "I'm a nifty tool to have during times of war." She would personally guard Galen and Legion, just as they would defend her. Things would go back to normal. They'd be a family again.

Longing nearly rent her chest in two. Family. A foundation on which to stand. A support system in times of trouble. Built-in cheerleaders. Therapists who offered free sessions, listening to her problems and offering advice. People obligated to love her no matter what.

"The war is what I wished to discuss with you outside of the dungeon." He gave her fingers a comforting squeeze. "My leader is deciding whether or not to use your portal-opening skills during battle. There are problems, of course. We do not know if we can trust you not to portal us into a trap or harm us in some way. And what if the demon influences you again?"

Hope rose and crashed again and again like a freaking carnival ride. Nothing she said would convince Bjorn to trust her, so she didn't even try. "I guess you guys will just have to decide if the risk is worth the reward, because I'm a hundred percent in."

He flicked a glance over his shoulder, his brow furrowed with confusion, as if her easy acceptance baffled him.

"What? I like the idea of helping you," she admitted. "I'll be helping Galen and Legion, too." And talk about a choice notation for her resume! Killer of Lucifer the Destroyer, Prince of Darkness and King of Deception. Plus, she relished the chance to cheer for Bjorn during battle. Would he be cold and methodical, or fiery and unpredictable?

When they reached the upper suites, she caught sight of Thane and Xerxes. The two were talking and laughing in a communal sitting room. The waystation between three different hallways. Thane sat upon a couch, a gorgeous brunette perched on his lap. She must be the cherished Elin.

Envy poked at Fox. He had his strong arms wrapped around his wife. A protective, possessive, adoring hold. The kind of embrace Fox had never experienced for herself.

Xerxes sat across from the couple. Spotting her and Bjorn, the threesome went quiet. As soon as they noticed the position of her hand, tension electrified the air.

Fox pasted on a sunny smile and waved. "Hey, guys. I'm so glad we ran into you. Isn't it time for my weekly whipping?"

Thane scowled. Xerxes ran his tongue over his teeth.

Voice coated in frost, Elin said, "You're the one who killed those Sent Ones."

Never going to live that down. "So, you're not going to sign the roster to become my new best friend?" Fox hiked her shoulders in a *whatever* shrug. "I'll try to get over my disappointment."

A corner of Bjorn's mouth twitched, surprising her.

Xerxes arched one white brow, asking Bjorn, "We reward prisoners for escape attempts now?"

How did he know she'd tried to escape? Unless...

They'd put cameras in the dungeon, hadn't they? She bit her tongue, tasting blood.

"Of course, she attempted an escape," Bjorn said, and still, he sounded anything but upset. "Just as we tried to do when we were prisoners of the demons." He offered no more, just led a flabbergasted Fox to a bedroom in the second hallway.

He'd defended her. To his friends. Bjorn, her executioner, had actually defended her to his friends. She couldn't...she hadn't... Shock propelled Fox into a wild state of suspended animation.

They entered his bedroom, the same room as before except—wow. He had all new furnishings and tons of knickknacks. *Bejeweled* knickknacks. Pure luxury. On the bed were soft sheets and a plush comforter. The softest rug in the history of ever made her feel as though she walked on pillows. Oh, oh, oh! He now had a ginormous TV!

"What's with the overhaul?" she asked, quashing the urge to jump up and down, clapping with excitement. "And did you get those all-access passes I mentioned?"

"I wanted a change. And, yes, I did." He said no more, just hauled her into the bathroom.

Reaching over her head, he pushed the door shut behind her. His chest brushed against hers, a stream of pleasure flowing straight to her core. Mmm. More. She wanted more.

Be leery, Distrust whispered. *Why would he help you? Must be trickery of some sort.*

Yes. Trickery. Disappointment set in. Did Bjorn hope to torment her with what she couldn't have? He—*what are you doing?* Listening to the demon always ended with blood and pain.

Needing a distraction, she cast her gaze up at Bjorn. Whoa, whoa, whoa. The glint of arousal flared to life in his eyes, promising a whole lot more. More shivers. Another stream of pleasure. Goose bumps broke out.

She must be mistaken, right? "Are you hoping to watch me shower…or join me?"

He crossed his arms over his muscular chest, highlighting the broadness of his shoulders. "Which would you prefer?"

What!? Her heart kicked into warp speed, fluttering as surely as her stomach. He'd just implied he wanted to have sex with her. Had he…accepted his desire for her?

Gulping, Fox shifted from one bare foot to the other. Did she want to sleep with him? Yes. Could she trust him? No, not really. Did she appreciate his unwitting willingness to help her seduce him? Absolutely. But, damn it, what had brought about the change? She needed to know!

"Are you horny and looking to bang and bail?" she asked.

"Yes?" he said, a question rather than a statement. A moment later, he smacked his lips as if he tasted something foul.

Interesting. He'd given himself permission to score…and then what? "Before I decide what to do about your, uh, offer, I should make a confession. Two, actually." Voice ragged, she said, "One. I—I'm sorry for what I did to the ten. If I could go back, I would send Galen to the temple and stay home."

Admiration lit his eyes, surprising her. "And the second thing?"

"Alana came to see me today."

His muscles seemed to petrify right before her eyes. "Tell me."

Nope. No one had seen her. Otherwise, Bjorn would have come running. "She sensed your sexual arousal and came for a visit, hoping to get busy with you. Then she scented me on your sheets and returned to the dungeon. She tried to get past the bars but couldn't. She wanted to kill me."

The muscle began jumping under his eye again, only faster.

But Fox wasn't done. "If you leave me defenseless, and she returns…"

He narrowed his eyes. "I suppose I'll just have to keep you by my side. Now. About that shower…" He took a step toward her, though it seemed like so much more. The space between them shrank considerably.

New shivers plagued her. "Let's say I invite you to join me. What happens next?"

Another step. "I will be on you...and I will be *in* you."

Stronger shivers. *He* wants *to be seduced.*

Trembling with excitement, Fox gripped the hem of her T-shirt and yanked the material overhead. Cool air caressed her warm flesh. Naked, she lifted her chin and squared her shoulders, letting him look his fill. And look he did. He sucked in a breath when his gaze found her breasts. Her nipples hardened. He looked lower...

Heat pooled between the apex of her thighs.

"Never have I seen a body as fine as yours," he rasped. "Your curves...your tattoos..."

Jungle scenes covered prime real estate on her torso and back, a butterfly in the center of it all. The mark of Distrust. "If you look close enough, you'll see little foxes hidden throughout the foliage. 'Fox' is the nickname my mother gave me as a little girl." A woman she'd loved with every fiber of her being. "After she died, I hoped to feel close to her again, so I dropped my given name."

His stance softened. "And what is your given name?"

"No way I'll—"

"Tell me, and I'll let you watch reality TV all night."

"With popcorn?"

"Multiple bags of popcorn."

"Desdemona," she rushed out, her cheeks already burning. "My given name is—was—Desdemona."

He blinked, shook his head. Then, a full-blown smile broke out, lighting his entire face, and he laughed. A laughing Bjorn...

Eyes wide, jaw dropped, she stared at him, unable to look away. He. Was. Gorgeous. Incomparable. Perfection. She found herself blurting, "My middle name is Anastasia."

"Desdemona Anastasia." Now he threw back his head, his laughter booming.

The door burst open, shoving Fox forward. Bjorn caught her, stiffened, and shoved her behind his back, acting as her shield.

"Out," he ordered.

"I thought she'd harmed you," Thane said, and he sounded shaken. "But you were laughing."

"Laughing," Xerxes echoed.

Ugh. They'd both come running. But why were they so surprised about his merriment, anyway? Were they unable to amuse him or something? Uh...it just happened to be the easiest job ever.

Ignoring both males, she cupped Bjorn's ass.

He released a soft puff of air, almost a moan.

High on feminine power, she rose on her tiptoes to peek over his shoulder and make a kissy face at his friends.

They narrowed their eyes.

Grinning now, she pressed her breasts against his back and ran his earlobe between her teeth. "Get rid of them," she whispered. "I made my decision. I want you in the shower with me."

"Out," he repeated, the word like a detonated bomb. "Out now!"

Though the pair hesitated, they did leave in the end. Footsteps sounded. Hinges squeaked. A soft snick rang out.

Bjorn spun around, facing her. He looked predatory and aggressive, and her body loved it, aching for his.

"You want me?" he demanded.

"I want you," she confirmed. "And I'm going to have you."

Chapter Twelve

Desire *seethed* inside Bjorn. Earlier, he'd wondered if he'd been playing it safe with Fox. At this moment, he could play *nothing* safe. Fox…naked… She stole his breath. Though slim, she possessed the sweetest feminine curves and the most sublime muscle definition. A magnificent combination. Dusky nipples crested pert breasts. Passion-flushed skin highlighted the freckles on her nose. Between her legs, there was a small triangle of dark curls.

Her body is a treasure map; triangle marks the spot.

Though, to be honest, a battle seemed most likely. He wondered if she had a plan: feign arousal and knock him out as soon as he got her into bed. Perhaps not. Either way… He fought the urge to sink his fingers into her core. Would he find her wet?

Never wanted anything so badly… Would risk everything for this woman.

Bjorn removed his robe, baring his entire body to Fox. She watched as he stripped, her sizzling gaze as arousing as a caress. Did she like what—?

"Look at you," she said, breathless. "A walking aphrodisiac."

Oh, yes. She liked.

She flattened her hands on his pectorals, her fingertips resting atop his nipples. Her flesh burned as hot as her gaze, her palms callused from handling weapons. Every point of contact maddened him, sharpening his lust.

A groan slipped from him.

"So many muscles," she continued. "No lasting scars because of your immortality, but oh, oh, oh, what do we have here?" She waggled her brows and waved a finger to indicate his lower body. "From the waist down, you are covered in tattoos, and I need study time. Extra credit. Maybe answers, too." Excitement laced her tone. "No images, only symbols and text. Why? Are they names?"

A clipped nod. "I'll tell you about the names later. My reason for branding myself will ruin the mood."

"Counterpoint. Nothing can ruin the mood."

Oh, really? "They are the names of the brothers and sisters I've lost in battle. Including the ten. I hoped to honor their sacrifice for our people."

"Okay. The mood is ruined." She lowered her head and raised her hands, resting her face against her palms. Then she pressed her forehead against his chest.

He clasped her wrist, then hooked two fingers under her chin, forcing her gaze to lift. "Let's see if we can un-ruin it, yes?"

She nibbled on her bottom lip but nodded.

"Did I mention that you…Desdemona Anastasia,"—he motioned to the amazingly detailed jungle scene etched into her flesh— "are the sexiest piece I've ever beheld?"

Those long-lashed hazel eyes widened with surprised euphoria. "You did, but I'm expecting you to tell me at least five times a day from now on."

How long was "from now on?"

"Want to hear something funny? Well, boo-hoo funny," she corrected. "You are the first person to compliment me in years."

Truly? "The males in your life are fools."

Preening, she told him, "I guess sleeping with you was inevitable. Because *you* are the sexiest piece *I've* ever beheld. When you broke into my bathroom, I considered jumping your bones."

He detected no lie. Fox had wanted him from the start? His head spun.

Inner shake. Concentrate! Before they could be together, he had to explain the rules—to them both. Voice firm, he said, "We've called a temporary truce, though you still wish to escape. I still can't let you. Therefore, the times you aren't under my direct supervision, you'll be returned to the dungeon. If my leaders refuse to pardon you, allowing you to work with us…" *What will I do then?* "We'll have to come to some other arrangement. Are these terms acceptable?" *Please, be acceptable.*

"Let's see if I can read between the lines," she said. "We're sleeping together to preempt regret, not for any other reason, and I shouldn't get my hopes up that you'll ever develop feelings for me?"

Perceptive Fox strikes again. "Exact—" He pressed his lips together, going silent as a foul taste coated his tongue. Apparently, he *wasn't* sleeping with her simply to prevent regret.

A pause laden with tension stretched into what felt like days, weeks. Peering at him through the thick shield of her lashes, she quietly asked, "Did you redecorate your bedroom to impress me?"

Yes, but also to make her more comfortable. However, admitting the truth would be foolish. Remaining silent, he entered the shower stall and turned a knob, water gushing from the showerhead. Steam billowed, reminding him of early morning fog.

Fox followed him in, but stopped on the other side of the waterfall. At first, they remained immobile, staring at each other. Then, she made a move, reaching through the water to run her hands over his wings, ruffling the feathers.

Another groan slipped from him, his mind momentarily engulfed by bliss.

"Rumor claims a Sent One's wings are an erogenous zone," she said, sounding enchanted.

"You heard correctly." The fact that she didn't know for sure… "You've never been with anyone like me before?"

"Nope. You're my first."

And your last. The possessive thought rooted him in place. Possessive, yes, but also dark. If his leaders voted to end her rather than save her, he would be her last everything.

His chest did that awful clenching thing.

"By the way," she said with a teasing smile, scrambling his thoughts. "Don't think I'll be easy to please just because I've gone five hundred years without sex." As she stepped under the water, soaking her hair, the dirt washed from her skin. "I'm *really* good at pleasuring myself."

That visual… He sucked in a mouthful of air. Fox, naked and in bed, working her clitoris and thrusting her fingers as deep as possible.

The visual would be forever branded into his mind. "I will watch you do this. Later."

"Oh, you will, will you?" she purred.

"I will." Nothing would stop him. "And you'll love every second of it."

"How about you make me love every second of this shower? Let's stop eye-banging and start banging-banging."

Yes! Satisfaction poured through him, eroding any lingering resistance. Gripping her by the hips, he spun her around and tugged her backward, pressing her spine against his chest. He'd been celibate for a year, every new touch was overwhelming. *Too much, but also somehow not enough.*

With his lips hovering directly over her ear, he whispered, "My bold little vixen loves her pleasures."

"She does, she really does," she replied, with a throaty voice. He snickered, then he got to work, shampooing and conditioning her hair. Next, he sudsed his hands with soap to wash the rest of her. She was so soft yet strong. So perfect. Every point of contact magnified his lust until need utterly consumed him. A bead of precum glistened on the head of his shaft.

"Unfortunately," he said, "I bathed before I came to you. We'll have to shower again, so you can wash me."

"Deal." She leaned into his every touch, her eyelids heavy and hooded, her lips parted. Lips he wanted wrapped around his erection... Soon, she began to pant.

For too many years, Bjorn had despised being touched by anyone other than Thane and Xerxes. The only people in existence who understood his inner torment, because they'd lived through the nightmare, too. Once he'd begun to crave human contact again, he'd wanted to inflict pain, not pleasure, and the guilt had eaten him alive. Here, now, with Fox, the woman he should enjoy harming, he only wanted to pleasure. *I am some kind of messed up.*

Perhaps parts of him had finally healed?

Reeling again. If she agreed to be with him merely to manipulate his emotions... He stiffened. *I'll bear those wounds all over again.* "Before, I told you not to tell me why you decided to break your sexual fast with me. Now, I have to know."

"Because I like you, okay? You're the most amazing man I've ever met."

Again, he detected no lie. He marveled, his shaft pulsing with so much force, he feared he might come. For the most amazing woman to consider him the most amazing man—was there any finer compliment?

"You are already clean," she said, anticipation crackling in her tone, "so how about we get you dirty?" She spun and wound her arms around his neck. Enlarged pupils. A reaction she couldn't fake. "I want my hands all over you."

Control fraying… Waterdrops clung to her lashes. Rapture flushed her cheeks. Not kicking her legs apart and plunging inside her, required every ounce of his might. How tight would she be? How wet? "Touch me anywhere you desire." He rubbed the pad of his thumb along the seam between her lips. "With us, nothing is taboo."

"Good to know." She melted into him, a wanton smile nearly unmanning him. "I think I'll start with your lips."

As she rose to her tiptoes, he bent his head. Their mouths met, and he opened up, greeting the thrust of her tongue with one of his own. They kissed and kissed and kissed, all thoughts drowning as wave after wave of heat and yearning flooded him.

Bjorn walked her backward and pressed her against the wall, or rather, the wing he wrapped around her, ensuring she didn't get cold. He fisted a lock of her hair and tilted her head farther back, deepening the kiss. With his free hand, he cupped the underside of her knee and lifted her leg. He placed her foot on the bench beside them and spread her legs, leaving her open to him.

Shivers rocked her. A frenzy overtook him, spurring him on. *Need more. Now!* He kissed her harder, faster. From a slow, drugging exploration to a wild, wicked devouring. When she scoured her nails down his spine and gripped his ass to yank him ever closer, the pace of the kiss accelerated yet again.

When he shifted, the tip of his shaft brushed against her core. She released a plaintive moan, and he hissed, his blood running hot. Boiling. Sweat beaded on his brow. He needed this woman in ways he'd never dreamed possible. Growls percolated in his chest. Had he ever enjoyed a female's reactions more?

"You are"—*everything*—"exquisite." He ground his aching length between her legs. At the same time, he cupped her breasts. Kneading the giving flesh, pinching her nipples, he licked and sucked his way down her neck, where he flicked his tongue over her racing pulse.

Her breaths turned shallow. She rolled her hips, seeking—chasing—a more intimate contact. "Bjorn. Mmmm. It's been…too long…I want…need…more!"

More. Yes. Could he truly handle more after going so long without a hint of pleasure?

He must. He couldn't get enough of this woman. Dazed, he sank to his knees, laving and sucking her nipples on his way down. The dusky pearls teased and tantalized him. Then he kissed a fiery path down the center of her stomach, licked a circle around her navel, and nibbled lower...lower still. When he hit his knees at last, he paused to look up, wanting to take in all of her, rather than his new portal to paradise.

Soaked strands of jet-black hair clung to her. Water droplets sluiced down her heaving chest, catching on puffy nipples several shades darker than before. Her spine was arched, her head back. Her belly quivered. With her foot still resting on the bench, he had a clear view of paradise— her swollen, needy little clit, and those pouty pink folds that glistened with feminine honey.

Ravenous, he licked his lips. Then he licked her. A grunt escaped, his eyes closing in surrender. Never, in all his days, had he tasted anything so sweet. Maddened, already desperate for another sampling, he set in with more vigor, licking, sucking, nibbling. Mimicking sex.

Soft cries left her in a rush as his tongue penetrated her core. He wished to penetrate her with something else, too. Something bigger. Harder. He craved the sense of communion experienced only between two lovers. But again, he wasn't sure he could handle the emotional fallout—yet. *Will take this a step at a time.*

She arched her spine more pronouncedly, thrusting her breasts up, giving him better access. He skimmed her inner thighs, then palmed the curve of her ass. A perfect handful.

Goose bumps spread over her, fueling a return of his satisfaction. *My beauty craves more, too.* He traced a fiery path to her core...and thrust a finger into her heat. *Wet* heat.

"Yes!" When he withdrew the digit, she shouted, "No!" She shifted her hips, blindly hunting for his hand.

Such exuberance! So demanding! Loving her reactions, he thrust his finger inside her once again, adding a second this time, stretching her. *So tight. So hot. So wet—dripping.* Her inner walls clenched around the digits, another cry bursting from her, this one higher, longer, almost a scream.

The urge to come intensified, pressure building. No, no, no. *Fox first. Then me.* As he worked her over, he sucked on her clit hard. Between panting breaths, he told her, "Never tasted anything so sweet."

She gasped, then cried out once again. He sucked harder.

"Bjorn!" Fox came on his tongue.

Chapter Thirteen

An orgasm tore through Fox. *So good, so good, so good.* Muscles contracted. Blood heated as it rushed through her veins. Her mind soared through the clouds, forming a complete thought suddenly beyond her skill set.

The demon went quiet, and she didn't know if he orgasmed too and *couldn't* speak, or if her satisfaction drowned him out.

Before she could come down from the high, a new tide of lust crashed into her, rendering her satisfaction nothing but a fond memory. She felt as though she hadn't come in…ever. Tremors vibrated in her bones, stronger aches plaguing her.

Need to be filled. By Bjorn, only Bjorn. A powerful Sent One who listened when she spoke and never went to war with wisdom, simply because it came from a woman. Who treated his enemy—a target for elimination no less—with respect. He never lied, and he always remained loyal to his friends. Not once had he complained about her habit of detaching from emotion. He controlled his temper, exhibiting a perma-calm veneer. Basically, he was a walking, talking grenade to her life plans, with the pin already pulled. But…

She wasn't sure he was ready for sex. She wasn't sure *she* was ready for sex. Bjorn would be her first lover in centuries. Good or bad, she would feel bonded to him afterwards. Already, oral sex had made her feel tender toward him. And ultra-clingy. *Never want to leave his side.*

Steam billowed around him, creating a dream-like haze as he straightened. Dewdrops glistened on his skin. Tension tightened his features, his inhalations ragged. His gorgeous golden wings arched over his broad shoulders, the edges rimmed by a bony substance that glittered in the water.

Intrigued, she reached out to trace the ridge with her fingertips. At first contact, he hissed in a breath. She moaned. *Hard as steel and white-hot.*

When she pulled back, aggression pulsed from him. His eyes... Fox shivered. Those rainbow eyes, so lovely and unique, blazed with sexual hunger.

As she watched, he dragged his tongue over his bottom lip to taste her again.

Hot. As. Hell. In a bold one-two move, Fox cupped his nape and spun him around and to the side. The underside of his knees hit the edge of the bench, and he plopped onto the seat. Wasting no time, she dropped to her knees, positioning herself between his powerful thighs.

Shock and excitement emanated from him. He wore them both well. Very, very well.

For a long while, she debated. Climb into his lap and impale herself on his ginormous shaft, or suck him down. In the end, she unveiled a slow, wicked smile and purred, "Time for *your* tongue-lashing, baby."

His air of excitement intensified. She thought she also detected a note of relief and disappointment. Like her, he must want sex but fear his reaction to it.

We are definitely more alike than I ever realized.

Trembling, she leaned closer and flicked her tongue over a nipple, then the other. He combed his fingers through her hair and fisted the strands. What he didn't do—apply pressure, forcing her head to lower. No, oh no, he merely clung to her, as if he couldn't bear to let her go.

Her traitorous heart skipped a beat. *He's starting to care for me, isn't he?*

She was delighted. No, horrified. No, delighted. Argh! She was delightfully horrified. He deserved better than Fox, the woman planning to win and shred his heart just to escape imprisonment and death. Bjorn would save himself a world of grief if he exiled her from the heavens *Survivor*-style. Or refused to give her a rose à la *The Bachelor.* Better yet, evict her from the house like a competitor on *Big Brother.* Seriously, by the time they parted, Bjorn would have brand-spanking-new trust issues.

Guilt iced her...until the heat of her desires melted it. Mouth watering for him, Fox opened wide and sucked him down.

Roaring, he bucked his hips, sending his length deeper into her throat. "Sorry, sorry," he croaked, easing up.

"Don't be sorry for enjoying my kiss." Down she went. Up. Down again. He was so big, he stretched her jaw. So hot, he scorched her tongue. So sweet he reminded her of morning sunshine. And, yes, okay, morning sunshine had no taste, but no other words properly described the compilation of heat, light, and…perfection. At the moment, her world revolved around him.

When she picked up the pace, he unleashed a series of curses. "Don't stop. Please, vixen, do not stop."

Never! But she did pause. "Would you rather be inside me?"

"Yes. No." He scrubbed a hand down his face. "Yes?"

Definitely not ready. "Soon," she vowed. And had he just referred to her as a vixen, another word for female fox? Love!

At first, she used one hand on his shaft, following the motion of her mouth, while the other hand played with his testicles. But, the more she sucked on him, the stronger her own arousal became. Finally, she released his testicles to slide her hand down her body…and sink two fingers into her soaked channel.

Having those fingers inside her only ratcheted up her need for more, more, more, satisfaction dancing just out of reach.

Bjorn tightened his grip on her hair, lifting her head. "You are so hungry for your man, you can't even wait for a second orgasm?"

The awe he evinced had her groaning as she sucked him down again. Sucked him…fingered herself…any second she would blow, the need to climax already clawing and gnawing at her.

"If you do not finish me with your hand, vixen, I will jet down your throat."

The endearment pushed her over the edge. Pleasured crashed over her, and she screamed around his shaft.

"Fox!" he shouted, her climax spurring his. "I'm coming. I'm coming!" As promised, he poured his satisfaction down her throat.

She swallowed—no, *savored* every drop. She'd earned it.

When she came down from her second high, panting and trembling, a sense of vulnerability hacked at her emotional lock-box. Suddenly, she felt like an exposed nerve, stripped bare, with no internal armor. Or a Twinkie with an ooey-gooey cream filling. Yet, she couldn't regret what they'd done. Or even what they hadn't done.

This wasn't a one and done deal. They'd be together again; she knew it. This kind of wanting demanded a response.

Needing a moment to compose herself, Fox crawled into his lap and buried her face in the hollow of his neck. Wait. Did *he* regret what they'd done? Would he blame her for his inability to resist her charms? No doubt he considered his desire for her a weakness. But, as one minute bled into another, he remained relaxed, holding her close with one arm, petting her hair with the other.

Eventually, he stood, still cradling her in his arms. He carried her out of the stall, cool air kissing her damp skin, raising goose bumps. She shivered as he set her on unsteady legs. Holding her up, he dried her off, then himself.

Her mind whirled. "Are you taking me back to the dungeon?"

He opened his mouth. Closed it. Opened. Closed. No sound emerged.

Hadn't decided yet, huh? She switched gears—for now. "I need clothes," she told him, struggling to project an easy, carefree vibe. "Good ones."

"To aid your escape, yes?" Once again, he didn't sound upset by the idea, just matter-of-fact. "Don't deny it. I was a prisoner once, too, only my captors were demons."

"Captivity is captivity, no matter the host." Though she did not like the thought of him suffering at the hands of demons. Or anyone! The horrors he must have endured...

"You are not wrong."

Gah! Did he have to be so reasonable? "But I'm sorry for what you must have suffered. No doubt you fought to escape every minute of every day."

"I did."

"So why are you chastising me for doing the same?"

His brow furrowed. "I cast no blame. I understand why you do what you do."

Great! Wonderful! More reasonableness. And she liked it—she liked *him* more by the second. *At this rate, I'll be in love by tomorrow night.* "I have no problem escaping naked, baby." Truth. "You've seen me, right? I'd be doing any witnesses a favor."

The corner of his mouth twitched. "I cannot argue your point."

Smart man. "So, if you want to head off any escape plans, you'll have to meet my demands."

He stiffened but said, "And what are those demands, hmm?"

"For starters, I require a cell phone. Galen and Legion must be worried out of their minds."

An-n-nd he got stiffer. "I will contact Galen on your behalf."

"Not good enough."

"And yet it's as good as it's going to get." Bjorn took her hand, something he'd done before. This time, he linked their fingers, as if they were partners working together, versus a captor leading his captive.

Her heart nearly burst from her chest.

He escorted her to the closet, where he donned a robe and gifted her with a clean white T-shirt and—surprise, surprise—a thong, the butt floss of underwear.

Normally, she would rather go panty-less than don a stupid thong. But. She remembered his reaction to the last pair, and couldn't resist taunting and tempting Bjorn with another.

Wait. A thought hit, and she shuddered. "Where did you get the thong? Because, if you gave me someone else's undergarments and I come down with panty crickets, I will choke you with your own intestines!"

He snorted. "I sent a Downfall employee out to shop for you. Every article of clothing is new."

That snort…utterly adorable. But, gah! She must be making serious moon eyes at him right now. How embarrassing for her.

What if he took a scheme from your playbook and now hopes to make you fall in love with him, so you'll do whatever he asks?

Ugh. She could always count on Distrust to ruin her day. *Ignore the fiend, and enjoy Bjorn while you can.* "What'd you put on that shopping list, exactly?"

One corner of his mouth twitched again, making her heart skip a beat. "The list had one notation—undergarments, with two sub-notations."

"Let me guess. Sexy and sheer?"

"And make you feel like an object? Hardly. I asked for as little material as possible. You know, for your comfort. And airy, so you wouldn't get overheated."

A laugh bubbled up. She'd never seen this playful, teasing side of him. *I am living for it!*

Just like that, he went still, not even seeming to breathe. He stared at her with…awe? Whatever it was, it caused the air to crackle with awareness. She labored for every breath.

Distrust hissed. *Such a fool! You long to bed him now so he can kill you later? Run! Or suffer the—*

Shut up! If she fled in fear, she would never know what could have been.

Oh…crap. *What could have been.* She'd never planned to escape him, had she? Not really. She'd merely needed an excuse to try and build something with him. She *was* a fool.

Like they would ever be able to make a relationship work. Deep down, whether he admitted it or even realized it, a part of him would forever resent her for the harm she'd caused his people. And she would never be happy with a man who resented her as much as he wanted her. Not long-term. So, she'd have to enjoy him while she could, and do a better job of guarding her heart. No more softening! And maybe no sex, period. But orgasms were fine. Better than fine.

Anyway. Unless and until he agreed not to imprison her, she would willingly stay with him. After all, she owed the Sent Ones a debt. If given half a chance, she would help during their war.

Decision made, she shimmied into the thong, pulling the material up her legs. Bjorn's pupils expanded, a puff of air parting his lips. Well, well. From now on, consider her the #1 fan of thongs.

"Be honest," she said, looping the hem of her shirt through the collar, creating a half-shirt. Then she turned to display her spectacular ass. "Do these panties make my butt look amazing...or magnificent?"

Voice like smoke and gravel, he offered, "Amazingly magnificent. If I didn't have one hundred Warriors to recruit—something you made me forget—I would toss you onto the bed and go for round two."

Don't ask to go with him. Don't you dare. Instead, she opened her mouth to graciously accept his compliment. "Why don't I accompany you?" Argh!

"You may," he offered while strapping a pair of sandals to his feet. The fact that the affirmation wasn't accompanied by a caveat or thirty... "But I'm not going out today. Just pouring through a bunch of books with names."

Fox got stuck on his first two words, reeling after a punch of shock, a kick of awe, and a double jab-jab of excitement. "I want to be sure I understand this correctly. Tomorrow you plan on taking me out in public, where I will socialize with Sent Ones at your side. You're trusting me not to portal away for good?" Would she regain her ability once she left this stronghold? "You're trusting me not to portal you and your chosen ones to dangerous terrain and leave you? And since we're on the subject of portals, why can't I open one here?"

"I'm not trusting you, no. I'm testing you. There's a difference." He pinched a lock of her hair, rubbing it between his fingers. "Flunk my test, and suffer the consequences. Get an A and earn my trust."

So…a game. Fun! "Oh! I should warn you. While you're testing me, I'll be *charging* you. I expect a daily wage for staying by your side, and a bonus for every portal I open. My friends and family discount is ten thousand dollars per eight-hour shift. Therefore, you'll owe me *twenty* thousand a shift. I expect tips."

The mouth twitching started up again, and damn, it was a gorgeous sight. "I do not receive a lover's discount?"

"Maybe if you put out more."

Twitch, twitch.

"Also," she continued, "I'll be testing you, too." She stepped into his personal space to pat his cheek. "Don't give me a reason to ditch you and—spoiler alert—I won't ditch you. Give me a reason, and *you'll* suffer the consequences. Meaning, no access to my goods."

"Is that so?" He clasped her wrist, yanked her against the hard line of his body, and forced her arm behind her back. Her spine arched, thrusting her breasts against his chest. "Shall we play a game, then? You will tempt me sexually, and I will tempt you. The first one to cave—without self-pleasuring—loses. Winner receives a boon of his—"

"Her," she interjected.

"—*his* choice. Deal?"

Bjorn, doing his best to seduce her…

Fox, doing her best to seduce him…

She'd get to put her hands all over him and say the most suggestive things, all in the name of a game… *Yes, please. Sign me up.* "Before I agree to your game, you must agree to my payment plan."

He arched a brow. "You are *that* in love with money and control?"

"Don't be ridiculous. I'm more in love with money and control than anything ever." Why deny it?

To her bafflement, his expression softened. He tenderly smoothed a lock of hair behind her ear. "Very well. I agree to your payment plan. But you must help me study tonight."

Her chest clenched. Why had he softened? Why hadn't he tried to negotiate the extreme prize? Whatever the reason, it only made her like him more. Wait. A thought occurred to her. "You put on your shoes to study?"

"I did. You'll be showering soon, and you never know when an enemy will kick down a door to fight you."

She snorted. Then she held out of her hand and said, "We've got ourselves a deal."

Chapter Fourteen

Bjorn spent the entire night with Fox. First they'd studied at his desk, then they'd climbed into bed, laying side-by-side. He maintained his distance, certain he would be the one to cave—again—if they touched even the slightest bit. A truly torturous experience for him. The best and worst night of his life.

He tossed and turned, tormented by arousal and the sounds she made while she slumbered. Breathy moans, soft purrs, and raspy gasps. A few times, she even talked in her sleep. Silly things he would love to hear again in context. Like: *Go ahead. I'm into it.* And: *I don't have a dollar. I don't even have a penny.*

He'd chuckled then, and he chuckled now. He'd grown to appreciate her love of money; it was her way of showing people how much she cared, especially when she locked down her emotions. She let her actions speak for her. He admired her survivor-by-proxy mentality, the preservation of her friends more important to her than the preservation of self. What Bjorn did not like about that fact? The one she adored above all others. Galen. The male continued to blow up Bjorn's cell with death threats.

According to Thane, Galen had shown up at the Downfall last night. If Bjorn had been present, they would have come to blows. And he knew beyond a doubt Fox would have sided with the winged blond. Bjorn bit the inside of his cheek, tasting blood.

He peered at her sleeping form, and his mental chaos died down. How? How did she affect him so strongly? He craved Fox, and Fox alone. No other would do. No one else tasted as sweet, or fit him so perfectly, as if she'd been created just for him. The missing puzzle piece his life so desperately needed to be complete. But that couldn't be right. The two of them could never make something work long-term.

The bed shook as Fox began to stretch. Arms overhead, back arching. Was she soon to awaken? He tensed with excitement.

That excitement blossomed as she fluttered open her eyes, then jolted upright. Not clasping her by the waist and yanking her against him required every ounce of his strength. Rumpled dark hair framed an exquisite face he would forever see in his dreams.

"Good morning," he said. He was propped up against the headboard, the sheet bunched at his waist. He wore no robe, no shirt, his chest on display…and he caught himself flexing for her. Anything to tempt his vixen to make the first move, so he could win their bet.

He knew the moment she recalled their bargain. Heat flushed her cheeks, and her eyes narrowed. She traced a fingertip between her breasts and said, "Good morning, baby. See anything you want? I'm running a buy one climax, get one free special."

He shot harder than steel. "What a coincidence. I'm running the same special."

She laughed, the sound raspy from slumber. Why had he made a bet that involved keeping his hands to himself, anyway? No longer celibate, he longed to do anything and everything with Fox, his chosen partner. Craved contact and communion. Meaning, yes, he should have sunk inside her while he'd had the chance.

Need *to get inside her.*

She rubbed at her eyes, cast him a glare, as if every problem in every part of the world stemmed from him, then stumbled out of bed. "What's on the agenda today?" she grumbled.

Not a morning person? Or just as needy as he was and trying to hide it? He worked to subdue a smile, then had to work to hold back a frown. Why did he find every aspect of her personality so charming?

"I must meet with the Sent Ones I hope to recruit for my army of one hundred."

Worry flitted over her expression. "Right."

That worry… She expected him to put her back in the dungeon. He should. He knew he should. Yet, he'd rather have her where she belonged—at his side.

My side? Mine? The thought should have panicked him, blown his mind, something! Instead, he nodded as if it were the most natural thought in the world.

As they readied for the day, brushing their teeth side by side, showering together, changing clothes, they barely spoke and hardly touched. But. Words and touches weren't necessary for seduction. The heated way she looked at him…the heated way he must be looking at her. His heart raced, the rest of him overheating.

Temptation almost proved too, well, tempting.

Naked, she rooted through the clothing he'd fetched for her. She bent over. Arched her back. Made her breasts bounce. All the while, he sweated as if he'd entered a sauna while wearing sweatpants and a coat. Ultimately, she selected a black tank and matching leathers.

Gothic chic was a good look for her. Very good.

Who was he kidding? *Everything* looked good on her.

When she plaited her hair, gothic morphed into mythological warrior goddess, and he seethed with arousal. Had anyone ever appeared so tough yet delicate? So arresting? So enchanting?

He cursed. As he'd waxed poetic about her appearance, he'd missed which undergarments she'd selected. Another thong, just to push him over the edge?

A moan escaped him. If he kept up this line of thought, he'd have to deal with a robe tent situation. He just…craved her more with every second that passed. He *needed* contact with her.

Resisted all facets of intimacy for a year. Now I can't go a day without my captive?

Do not touch her. Do not kiss her. Remember the bet. She would make the first move, damn it. She would!

Maybe, if he reminded her of what they'd done, she would beg for more? "What we did in the shower…" he began.

"No!" She rushed over to flatten her hand over his mouth. Contact! Finally. "We're not going to talk about that until after a winner is declared."

Fair enough. What wasn't fair? That body of hers. If she'd dressed to scramble his mind—mission accomplished.

If only it were mission*ary* accomplished. *One can hope.*

He negated the bloodline around the bedroom, secretly disturbing the line of blood and Water he'd drawn around the bedroom's perimeter. Now, Fox could open a portal, no problem.

Was he making a mistake, trusting her to keep her word? Time would tell.

He clasped her wrist, kissed and nipped her palm, then lowered her arm, freeing his mouth. "I have a gift for you," he said, withdrawing a velvet bag from the nightstand. *Try to resist me now, vixen.*

She accepted the bag, leery, only to evince excitement as she withdrew and donned the contents—an assortment of weapons he'd selected from the club's treasure room. He'd personally selected a necklace with a small, bejeweled dagger hanging from the center, a pair of spiked armbands, and an electrified ruby torque. A split second of contact would fry someone's insides.

"Aren't you afraid I'll attack you?" she asked, brows furrowed with confusion.

"A test isn't a true test if the variables are inaccurate." He tilted his head and leveled his gaze on her. "Will you attack me?"

"No!"

"Will you attack other Sent Ones?"

"No," she said, her teeth gritted.

Just to be contrary, he told her, "Be a good little vixen, then, and open a portal to these exact coordinates." He rattled off the latitude and longitude of a sub-realm in the heavens. A good place to meet with certain Warriors, because it led nowhere. If ever Fox returned, no big deal.

Her eyes widened with surprised excitement. But she used a grumpy tone when next she spoke. "FYI, this vixen will pee on your rug and shred your robes if you condescend to her again."

He grinned, loving her reaction. The woman took no shit from anyone.

She flipped him off, and his grin only widened. "You are so irritating when you refuse to get irritated," she mumbled, rolling her neck and shaking her arms. She tapped her fingers together, sparks flying from the ends. A toothy grin spread as the sparks burned a hole in the air. A hole that grew and grew until a doorway to the other location opened up.

He marveled at her ability and the undiluted power—magic—she wielded. Sent Ones had a hate-hate relationship with all things magic, a poison to their bodies.

As they walked through the magical doorway, a thousand needles seemed to prick his skin. The effects of the magic. He and Fox entered a too hot and too cold cloud-land with puffy white hills in every direction. Yes, the air was both hot and cold. It was an impossible phenomenon but true all the same. Bjorn, Thane and Xerxes often trained here. The more awful the conditions during your training, the better you fought afterward.

With Fox at his side, Bjorn trekked forward. He expected an escape attempt, but Fox never struck at him, or darted off. Of course, the woman never did *anything* he expected.

At his left, a demon shot from the cloud. A scaled beast with a forked tongue, two claws sprouting from each fingertip, and pus dripping from multiple gashes on his face. Probably one who'd hidden here, hoping to torment a Warrior. Or maybe one intended for use during training.

Either way, demons had the ability to solidify outside of Hell; this one made full use of his tangibility, swiping those double claws at Bjorn's jugular.

He swished his wing to blow the bastard backward before contact. Too late. Those claws continued to descend, ready to rip into flesh.

Fox spun into the demon's line of attack, shielding Bjorn while slicing a dagger through the bastard's throat. Bjorn did not sustain a single injury. Nor did Fox.

As the demon fell, gasping for breath he couldn't catch, black blood spurted out. Bjorn yanked Fox to the side, avoiding contact with the substance far more corrosive than acid. Then, he palmed the sword of fire to finish the creature off.

That done, he turned to Fox, baffled. "You saved me from injury."

"I know. That'll cost you another ten thousand dollars." Smiling sweetly, she cleaned the bloody dagger on his robe.

He could almost see the dollar signs in her eyes and fought another smile of his own. "So, you are a bodyguard as well as a badass. Good to know."

What was he going to do with this woman?

* * * *

Bjorn recruited fifty soldiers, while Fox stood at his side, unmoving and quiet. The Warriors glared at her with hatred and menace, and his mood continued to darken.

Why didn't she ask questions, or share her thoughts about each individual?

That night, he slept on one side of the bed, and she slept on the other. They did not speak, touch, or try to tempt each other sexually. His emotions were too rough and raw, and they did not improve with the rise of the sun.

And yet, when he climbed out of bed, he felt as if he'd shed a hundred pounds of baggage. He'd slept with a beautiful woman he admired. Someone he hungered to possess, who made him smile with her quick wit and guarded his back as well as Thane and Xerxes. Fox might be pardoned today. What did he have to complain about?

Bright sunlight filtered through the bedroom window, bathing Fox, who still lay on her side, eyes closed. His shaft ached to fill her.

Trembling like a lad, he reached out to trace his fingertips along the rise of her cheeks, only to snatch his hand back before contact. Would his willpower splinter with the first touch?

The mattress suddenly bounced as Fox jolted upright. "What? What's wrong?" she demanded, reaching under her pillow. Where she usually kept a dagger? "Did Alana summon you?"

Took him a moment to realize she directed the question at him. That she hadn't glanced in his direction but remained aware of him...the *sweetest* progress.

"There's been no summons." Alana always waited two or three weeks between summons to ensure he'd regained his strength, just so she could drain him again.

Although, Alana must have sensed his arousal last night. Must sense his arousal even now. Perhaps she would believe he'd self-pleasured. If ever she learned the truth...

A ragged growl brewed in his chest. If Alana harmed Fox, Bjorn would...he would...

He balled his fists. Nothing seemed dark enough.

He forced his thoughts to the matter at hand. "We have more meetings today."

She groaned. "Can I call in sick? Yesterday, I stood at your side and stayed quiet. Don't think I didn't realize everyone glared daggers at me, hoping you'd slay me while they watched. And I'm not complaining. I deserve it. I did them bad, and I need to make amends."

This was the first time she'd spoken about making any kind of amends, and damn if he didn't shed another hundred pounds of baggage.

"At least your presence mutes Distrust some," she grumbled, then blew a lock of hair from her eyes.

A tendril of satisfaction wafted through him. So, he aided her with Distrust just as she aided him with his past. "Have you ever been in love?" The sudden change of subject proved jarring, but he didn't snatch back the words.

"Nope," she answered, not missing a beat. "You?"

"Once. Her name was Leema, and she left me for another male."

"Then she's an idiot." Fox reached over to pat his shoulder. As he'd feared, contact nearly obliterated his resolve. How would he ever win their bet? *Control slipping...* "You're the best person I know."

Awe punched him so hard, he lost his breath. Ten words, yet they profoundly impacted his life. Fox found genuine worth in him. Him.

If he didn't get out of this bed right now, he wouldn't be getting out at all. He would strip her, pin her beneath him, spread her legs, and finally, blessedly surge inside her.

She must *make the first move.* He would receive a boon of his choice, and he wanted, *needed* to request a second chance for his friends. They were a part of his life...but so was Fox. The three had to make peace.

He had to get this woman to break. Soon!

* * * *

Seven more days passed, yet Fox never broke.

The frustration Bjorn had expected to feel on day two? It plagued him relentlessly now, and he wondered what boon she hoped to ask of him. Freedom?

Pang. He'd gone eight days without sleep. Eight days without a kiss, a caress, or a climax. He missed the giving and receiving of pleasure as much as a limb.

Shockingly enough, he'd begun to trust her. She'd made zero attempts to flee, and she hadn't attacked him once. Instead, she'd protected him as if she actually...liked him.

Did she?

Doesn't matter. Focus. He had a job to do. And he'd already rewarded her for her actions, allowing her to text Galen about her well-being.

This is focusing? Mind on the matter at hand. Right. So far, Bjorn had recruited ninety-seven Warriors. Three more, and he would complete his Underworld-bound army.

A group of twelve stood before him now, listening to his spiel. *I will be fair but demanding...betrayal of any kind would not be tolerated...opportunity for advancement...*

Leema occupied a spot in the audience. When Bjorn was promoted to Elite, she had been promoted to Warrior. He'd invited others, and one of them issued the invite to her.

Twice she'd attempted to pull him aside for a chat. The first time, he'd kindly let her down. The second, he'd been blunter. Rumor suggested she and her partner split not too long ago. He wondered if she hoped to rekindle their romance.

How should I feel about that? He didn't know.

What he did know? No matter how many times his gaze returned to her, his body remained unaffected. Which surprised him. She hadn't changed in the least. Same fall of pale hair, same golden skin. Same sparkling blue eyes and plump, pink lips. Same short but curvy figure with large breasts and wide hips. Once, he'd considered her the most beautiful female in all the worlds. Now? She did not compare to Fox, who radiated strength, admiration, and calm.

He towered upon the dais usually reserved for the band, Fox at his side as usual. Thane and Xerxes had finished selecting their Warriors early this morning, and they flanked Fox. They watched her intently, but not with their usual malevolence. He—

Hardened like steel when he finished his speech, and Fox rose on her tiptoes to whisper into his ear, "Why is the blonde undressing you with her gaze?"

He pinched the bridge of his nose, as if praying for patience before whispering back, "I used to date her."

"What!?" she blurted out. "Seriously?"

A nod, then he resumed his speech. Half of the males and all of the females cast Fox glance after glance. Some crackled with hostility, others smoldered with curiosity. Some burned with lust. The first sparks of fury scalded his chest.

Finally, Bjorn snaked an arm around her waist and tugged her in front of him, staking a visual claim. She leaned back, a little smug and a lot sexy, and got comfortable.

Now everyone's eyes widened, the crowd agape. Pointing to the males with lust in their eyes, he said, "You, you, you and you may go. I suggest you hurry."

The four males remained in place, frowning and glancing around, obviously confused.

"You do not look at my wo—prisoner in such a way and receive a reward," he grated. Had he almost referred to Fox as his woman amid a crowd of Sent Ones? Did it matter? Since he spent every waking second thinking about getting her naked, she kind of *was* his woman.

"Does he need to repeat himself, or do I need to start beheading?" Thane asked with a casual tone.

He and Xerxes stepped out of the shadows, two menacing towers of strength. The foursome jumped to their feet and raced from the nightclub.

"You, you and you can go, too," Fox said, then turned her attention to Bjorn. "I could have snuck up on them at least a dozen times and slit their throats. They are too easily distracted, and they'll cost you in battle."

Excellent point. When the four looked to him, as if waiting for him to admonish Fox, he didn't hesitate to send the threesome out the door, as well.

Leema leaped up, her chair skidding behind her. "Is she the kind of person you spend time with now? Why are you associating with her, Bjorn? You're better than this. You know that she murdered ten of our people, yes?" Fury crackled in her voice. "She's vile, disgusting trash and she deserves—"

"Enough!" he roared.

Fox tensed, only to relax a second later. He knew what that meant, and it pushed him over the edge. She'd just gone cold, probably in hopes of avoiding a well of hurt.

"She did murder the ten," he snarled for one and all to hear. "Something she regrets with every fiber of her being. Something I understand. I, too, have killed indiscriminately in the past, and not just during battle. Many, many species would relish my capture and punishment. How can I despise her for something I have done, as well?" Today, he'd come prepared for questions like Leema's. He dug into his pocket and withdrew ten small pebbles. Using a play in the Sent Ones' handbook, he tossed those pebbles at the crowd. "For those of you who have made no mistakes in your life, please, be the first to stone Fox the Executioner."

Silence. Not a single stone was hurled in her direction.

Bjorn raised his chin. "Now, ask me if she cheated on the male she's supposed to love."

Embarrassment burned two red spots in Leema's cheeks. "I...you..."

"I want you out." He didn't hate Leema, but he harbored no love for her, either. Not anymore. She'd done him dirty, cheating on him when cutting him loose would have been far more merciful, but he'd since moved on. However, she'd just hurt Fox and, for some reason, that particular detail pulled the pin on his temper, setting off the bomb. "You may leave. Now."

Jaw dropped, she gaped at him. "But. But—"

Ignoring her, Bjorn pointed to the soldiers he thought would work best in his budding army, thereby completing his task. The unchosen hurried out of the club—everyone but Leema—the others remaining behind. "Go home and pack," he told them. "Tomorrow, we move to Hell."

The chosen hurried off next, but still Leema remained behind with Bjorn, Fox, his friends, and club's employees.

"I think Leema hopes to watch us make out before she leaves?" Fox turned, resting her head on Bjorn's shoulder. With one hand, she combed his hair. With the other, she traced the rim of his wings.

He swallowed a groan, the sensations maddening. His resistance began to crumble. Would making the first move truly be such a bad thing? So he would lose their bet. So what? If she requested freedom, he could secretly tag her with a GPS chip in the back of her neck. A douche move, but at least he would always know where she was.

No, no. Fight this. Make her crave you so desperately, she cannot think past it.

Lowering his grip to cup her ass, he bent his head and quietly told her, "I want inside you."

Her breath hitched, and she jolted. Her hands stilled, her nails digging into his scalp and his feathers. Goose bumps spread over her arms, the rest of her going liquid as she melted into him. The pulse at the base of her neck raced, a mini-heartbeat.

Seeing her reaction to his words—to him—threw kindling on the fires of his desire.

An impatient huff brought him back to the present. They still had an audience. Right. His ex had made a derogatory statement before deciding to disobey him and remain in place.

He glared at Leema until she got the message, lifting her chin, stomping her way out of the building. Her departure gave him no satisfaction. But he felt no guilt, either. Fact was, he couldn't *not* touch Fox. If others couldn't bear to watch, they could leave.

Moving before him, standing on her tiptoes, and pouring her words into his ear, Fox whispered, "You've got a hard-on pressed against me. I'm pretty sure that makes me your meat shield."

His mouth curled into a half-smile. The things she said never ceased to entertain. "My apologies. I—"

"No, you misunderstand. I like it." She leaned into him. "I'm into it."

The same words she'd used during her dream. Had she, perhaps, dreamed about Bjorn?

Even the idea excited him.

"Besides," she added, waggling her brows, "the time has come for a showdown. We've got to stop playing it safe and start playing for the win, you know?"

He chuckled, the sound rusty. Well, not as rusty as it'd been before Fox entered his life. During the past week, she'd wrenched more smiles and laughs from him than...anyone. Ever. Now, however, the amusement was overshadowed by lust, his body on fire for her.

"Agreed," he croaked. Whisper-quiet, he added, "Do you surrender, then, and admit you're ready to get rid of our guests and race to our bedroom?"

Their bedroom? The wordage gave him pause. When had *his* room become *their* room?

She licked her lips and said, "Do *you* surrender?"

He...did. Bjorn couldn't survive another day without staking a claim to Fox the Executioner. *Mine! I will have what's mine. Finally.*

Yes, yes. Soon, he would be gloved by her hot, wet core. He would know true satisfaction at long last. *Need this. Need her.* No one else would do. Not now. Not...ever?

He traced his fingertips along Fox's hip bone, saying to his boys, "Isn't there something you wish to discuss with Fox?"

"There is." Thane raised his chin and stepped forward. "We apologize for whipping you. What you are doing for Bjorn...we cannot thank you enough."

Xerxes nodded in agreement. "We've never seen him so light or free. For that, you will forever have our support."

Fox shivered against him, then stilled. He suspected she had just buried her emotions—again—to avoid softening toward the males who'd harmed her, in case they ever voided said support. It was a defense mechanism, and it made his heart hurt.

"She will consider forgiving you," he said with a wink at her, "for one hundred thousand dollars. From each of you."

She gasped and jolted, zooming her gaze to him. His defense of her in front of hundreds of Sent Ones hadn't elicited such a delighted response, and he didn't have to wonder why. She liked that he supported her interests, liked being defended when she preferred to take care of herself. "That is, hands down, the sweetest thing anyone has ever said to me." As her eyes watered and widened, she pressed a fist above her heart. Was she too overcome with awe and admiration to continue burying her emotions?

"I, like, need your autograph," one of the waitresses called. Bellorie, one of his favorites, as well as Elin's best friend. All the waitresses were her best friends, which meant Thane, and thereby Bjorn and Xerxes, guarded the females with their lives.

"Guess what? You're my new best friend," another waitress said. Savy.

The third, Octavia, grabbed a bottle of whiskey to pour shots for everyone—wrong, only for herself; she hadn't used a shot glass, had just drunk straight from the bottle.

Part of Bjorn wanted to linger, to give Fox a chance to befriend his friends and employees. People he greatly respected. He also hoped to give everyone a chance to get to know Fox better. They'd love her. They must. But, he'd been a live-wire of lust for eight days, and the thought of making small talk...*I'd rather cut out my tongue.* But he needed his tongue to win Fox. Today. Now.

Don't fail. Turn up the heat. "Now that apologies are done, there's something I must discuss with Fox. If you'll excuse us…"

Catcalls rang out as he led Fox away, everyone shouting different *encouragements.*

"Yeah, baby. I'm sure you give good discussion."

"Will this chit-chat involve a flesh-colored bullhorn with a slit in the tip?"

"If the room is rockin', it ain't boots they're knockin'."

Laughter joined the catcalls, but Bjorn hardly noticed. Anticipation consumed him.

Chapter Fifteen

Smoldering with sexual prowess, Bjorn opened the bedroom door and motioned Fox inside. She stood rooted in place, uncertain. One of them was about to lose the bet. As horny as she'd been, as horny as she was, she had a sinking suspicion the loss would go to…drum roll please…her. Fox the Executioner.

Eight days. Eight days she had ached for this man—his dirty kisses, and his every touch—with increasing intensity. She'd dreamed of him each night while breathing in his masculine fragrance. Watched his rainbow eyes glitter with every smile. Fantasized about all the things they could do to each other. What she hadn't done? Broken the rules. No getting herself off. The near-constant pressure had honed her body into a conduit of sensation. Aching nipples. Fluttery belly. Weak knees. Raw, primitive desire coursed through her veins, demanding a climax.

Did she affect him as strongly?

Does it matter? You are a passing fancy to him. A new conquest, easily had, easily forgotten. A joke. A source of amusement for years to come. Go ahead. Have sex with him. Fall in love. You deserve all the heartache headed your way.

Ouch. Distrust went for the jugular. Fox wrapped her arms around her middle, but the action failed to help. Never had she felt so exposed, so vulnerable.

At last, she swept past Bjorn, trembling all the while. Along the way, she brushed her hand against his robe. Or, more specifically, against the erection underneath the robe. He sucked in a breath; she swallowed a laugh, her nerves appeased. She did, in fact, affect him as strongly. *Take that, Distrust. It matters!*

Tonight, Fox and Bjorn would be together, ending the week-long torment…after one of them broke, of course.

She came to a halt at the foot of the bed, then spun to face him.

Where to begin? How to make him break? So far, she'd done little to try. Because, if she won, she'd have only one real boon to request—*let me go*—and she hadn't been ready to leave him. *Foolish girl.*

With his gaze glued to hers, he shut and locked the door, then prowled closer. An-n-nd her nerves jacked up once again. A predatory ember crackled in those eyes, and determination stamped on every deliciously hard inch of his body.

"Take off your clothes," he rasped, his low, husky words infiltrating her ears, amplifying the sensations plaguing her.

See Bjorn make Fox break first. No, no. He wielded incredible sex appeal...but so did she. Toying with the collar of her shirt, she purred, "I'm happy to take off my clothes. As soon as you admit defeat."

"Keep your clothes, then. Keep mine, too." He tore off the robe, putting his bronzed skin and bulging strength on spectacular display, then tossed the garment her way. "You have only to speak two words—*I surrender.* Then, all of this is yours." He waved to indicate every inch of his incredible form.

I want it. Give it to me!

Look away, look away! Anywhere but my own personal Temptation Island.

Pride demanded she fight her attraction until the bitter end. Somehow, Fox found the willpower to say, "Counteroffer. *You* say those two little words, and all of *this* is yours." Yanking her tank and bra overhead, she kicked off her boots. She shimmied out of her leathers and panties.

Suddenly, they were both naked, standing only a few feet apart. His breath caught while hers disintegrated, the sight of him blowing every circuit in her mind. *Beyond beautiful. At this rate, I'm going to lose in a matter of minutes.*

"I think we should change the rules," she blurted out. "We agree to make a move at the same time. Then, the one who climaxes first is the loser." *And, simultaneously, the winner.*

"Agreed," he rushed out, as if he feared she would change her mind at any moment.

They wasted no more time. As she pressed a kiss at the corner of his mouth, he gripped her hips. A split second later, she soared through the air and landed atop the bed. Fox laughed as she bounced, that laughter genuine and as intoxicating as champagne. Face it, Bjorn's desire made her giddy.

He pounced, shooting onto the bed to pin her down. Dark but

playful, wicked but sweet, he stared down at her. Her laughter died in an instant, and she gulped. Never had he looked so fierce.

Not just beautiful. Mesmerizing. He *owned* this moment.

Continue on this path, and he'll own you, too.

Stupid Distrust! He will not ruin this for me.

Fox had never willingly ceded control to anyone, for any reason. Now, she wondered if Bjorn hadn't, either. She'd seen his dealings with Alana, and he'd mentioned being captured. He might *need* control.

But. *There's always a* but *with me.* She sighed. Their relationship had begun on uneven footing. He'd burst into her life, determined to slay her. He'd negated her ability, imprisoned her, and set her up for a whipping. What had she done to him? Besides murder ten of his people, of course.

Winning the bet might put them on equal footing at last.

One minute ticked into another, neither of them looking away. Neither of them making a move, either. The way he looked at her...

*As if I'm the most beautiful woman in the worlds. As if I'm...*special. Her stupid heart filled with something akin to rainbows, nearly bursting. She wasn't sure she'd ever been special to anyone...ever.

The more time that passed, the more his eyelids hooded with desire, and the more her awareness of him intensified. The dark stubble on his jaw beckoned her hands. *One touch...maybe two.* His muscled chest beckoned her mouth. *One taste...to start.* His erection beckoned her hands *and* her mouth.

The man beguiles me.

Lust heated her inside and out. Her blood began to boil, steam wafting. That steam caused pressure to build inside her, stealing her breath. Meanwhile, Bjorn low-key panted.

A realization jolted her: *He's mine, and for the rest of time, I will not share.*

Oh, she'd known he belonged to her. At least in part. She just hadn't known she'd planned on keeping him forever.

She wouldn't win his heart just to escape, and she refused to settle for a temporary arrangement. Not with him. She wanted to win his heart because...because... *Do it. Say it.* Because *she* was falling into major like with *him.* There. She'd done it, said it, breathed life into the thought, giving it an opportunity to wipe out her doubts.

I am. I'm falling. I'm falling into like with him hard. She wanted him today, tomorrow, and every day after that. Long-term, baby! Excitement bubbled over, spilling through her.

You saw the way other Sent Ones view you. They'll never approve of you. Being with you will get Bjorn exiled. He'll grow to hate you, and rightfully so.

What sucked the most? The bastard wasn't wrong. She ground her teeth.

Expression softening unexpectedly, Bjorn glided the pad of his thumb along her bottom lip. "Distrust is doing his best to make you walk away from me, yes?"

"Yes," she croaked. The fact that he'd sensed her change in mood only made her lo—like him more. *Not yet ready for the L word.*

Yet! Yet? I will not fall in love—ever. I won't! Like was acceptable. Love? No. Even the thought of it made her panic. Love invited pain and disappointment, giving the other person power over you. She'd much rather return to her emotionless state.

A lock of hair tumbled over his forehead, the dark strands a startling contrast to his bronzed flesh. As she grappled with a desire to smooth the lock away, he said, "Let's teach the demon a lesson. Every time he strikes at you, we'll strike back with pleasure, something he surely despises."

Snort. Tricky Sent One, trying to work the situation to his favor. "Excellent plan. Gentlemen first," she teased, rubbing her knee along the side of his body.

Just like that. Their good humor took a nosedive, their bodies too achy to be ignored any longer.

"You are the most exquisite creature in all of creation," he rasped. "Outwardly delicate but inwardly tough, a contradictory and intriguing combination. You madden me."

Her breaths accelerated. On fire for him, she said, "All week, I've imagined you perched above me like this. You play with my breasts, pinch my nipples, and slide your fingers deep inside me, preparing me for something much, much bigger…"

With a moan, he lowered his head. With a groan, she raised hers. Their lips met in the middle, their tongues thrusting together. There was nothing gentle or tentative about the kiss. No exploring. Only fierce, unstoppable need. They devoured each other. She breathed for him, and he breathed for her.

A passion-flush spread lightning-fast, heating her cells. How had she gone so long without this? Unable to remain still, she rubbed her sex against his shaft. Oh, the bliss! Every point of contact sent a new shockwave through her. Soon, her every thought revolved around the next hit.

Addicted. Want this three times a day—at least!

He laved the pulse at her neck, pressure mounting, the need for release all-consuming. Still, she tried so hard to be gentle with him. No clawing. No biting. If she caused him pain, guilt would destroy her. After everything he'd suffered with Alana and his captivity, he deserved only pleasure. But...

She muttered a curse. Carnality just took the wheel, driving her every thought to one of three conclusions. "Yes. Please. More."

"More. All. Everything." He lifted his head to kiss her lips. Their tongues twined together again and again.

No clawing? No biting? No way. She raked her nails along his scalp, then down the center of his wings, finally sinking the sharp tips into his ass to yank him closer. Yes, yes! No! His erection hit the center of her desire, nearly wrenching a climax from her. *Must hold out. Must!*

He hissed in a breath.

"Sorry," she croaked, plucking her nails free. She fisted the sheets. "Didn't mean to hurt you."

"Not hurt." A ragged growl rumbled from him as he wrenched his face from hers, drowning out a stream of protests from Distrust. "Put them back."

Them? Her nails? "No. Must resist." Gah! Sounded like she was speaking her thoughts...while her mind was blank. But, oh! None of the guys she'd been with in the past were as strong or intense as Bjorn. Having tasted the perfection of his passions, she doubted any other male would do. "I *could* hurt you," she tried to explain between panting breaths.

"I love your reactions to me. Love *earning* them. Do not deprive me of such bliss."

Darling man. "You know what this means, yes? I'm next level girlfriending, and you owe me." Once again, Fox sank her nails into his ass. She wrapped her legs around his waist, locking her ankles. She drew his earlobe between her teeth and whispered, "I won't fight my reactions to you anymore. I'll surrender. *If* you'll do something for me."

"Anything," he said. "I will be the one to surrender."

She almost smiled. Almost. "Fuck me, Bjorn. Please."

* * * *

Sweat beaded on Bjorn's brow, Fox's words echoing inside his mind.

His muscles knotted with strain, and his heart pounded against his ribs. Beneath him lay the sexiest female in the history of ever. Tangled dark hair framed her delicate features. One lock even curled around her nipple, playing peek-a-boo with his gaze.

She is the incarnation of desire...

He kissed and licked a fiery path to her breasts, nudged the lock of hair out of the way, and sucked that nipple hard. Her back bowed, a cry of bliss filling the air. He sucked harder. Only when she thrashed and mumbled incoherently did he switch to the other, sucking it just as hard.

Can't think, can't think. The bet had ceased to matter. Never had he wanted something as desperately as this.

With a flare and flap of his wings, he lifted Fox off the mattress. After flipping them both, he rested atop a mound of pillows while she rested atop *him*. Breasts bouncing, she straddled his hips and nestled her hot, drenched sex against his erection.

She stared down at him, her expression tender, indulgent, her excitement and anticipation palpable.

When she rolled her hips, grinding on him, pleasure and pain collided, whipping him into a frenzy. *Waited so long for this—for* her.

He hissed another breath and went still. He *had* waited for her. Deep down, he'd known—hoped—someone exceptional would come along, the bright future she offered eclipsing the past. On paper, Fox should not be that someone. As different as they were, they should drive each other nuts. Instead, she made him better, complementing every aspect of his life.

"Bjorn," she said softly, only to go quiet. Whatever emotion she noted in his expression—burning lust? frenzied need?—intensified both the excitement and the anticipation.

"Yes, vixen. Yes." He curled his wings around her, the ends caressing her back.

Shivering, moaning, she traced a fingertip around both of his nipples. "How badly does my baby crave a climax? Will you go off as soon as I slide down your length?"

Yes! No. Maybe? He would fight with every ounce of his might. "Let's find out." But first, he had to prepare her.

He urged her to her knees. The moment he spied a visible gap between their bodies, he reached down to plunge a finger deep into her core. With a ragged cry, she dropped her head back and bowed her spine. The ends of her hair tickled his thighs.

As he moved the digit in and out, in and out, her inner walls squeezed him. On the next inward plunge, he added a second. She gasped—a gasp that tapered into a moan. He scissored the two together, stretching her. In, out. In, out. Every time he withdrew them, she writhed, chasing them, eager for more.

When she began to pant his name again and again, he wedged in a third. She gasped with more force, her hips jerking. All he could do? Pray for strength. *Too good. Too much. Not enough.* In, out. White-hot. Wet. Soaking. In, out. Feminine honey drenched his hand.

The way his vixen responded to him...

Will never *get enough.*

She slapped one hand against his chest then the other. Then she raked her nails down his abdomen, leaving eight perfect trails he would admire for hours to come.

He hadn't lied to Fox. He loved the sting. Loved knowing he'd pushed her past thought and reason, making her a slave to sensation. Loved knowing she'd left her marks on him. Her brand.

The woman held nothing back, and he realized this wicked, wild, uninhibited desire was everything his life had been missing. Everything he'd hoped to gain when he'd bedded those soft, gentle women he'd thought he preferred.

Trembling, panting faster, he lifted his head. Fox's nipples were damp, red and puffy—ready. Her passion-flush had deepened, and her pupils were blown. All signs she'd reached the point of no return.

Need her. Now. "Ready for me, vixen?" *Please, be ready for me.*

Voice ragged, she said, "Please! I—I'll be the first to come. I will. Just make me come!"

The provocation to sate her proved more overwhelming than the urge to tease her. Control in shambles, he shifted her to her knees a second time. Her pupils expanded, covering more of that glittering hazel as he positioned his shaft at her entrance, breaching the inner ring by an inch.

His eyes nearly rolled into his head. The pleasure! And he had only inserted the tip. What would happen when he thrust hilt-deep?

Not yet, not yet. As she watched, he licked her essence from his fingers. Again, his eyes nearly rolled into his head. So sweet!

She got wetter. Hotter. Because of his size, she did not slide down his length. He was too big, and she was too tight. Incredibly tight. He gritted his teeth, the urge to come all but strangling him.

He skimmed his fingers along her inner thighs, drawing goose bumps to the surface of her skin. "You ready for more?"

"Mmm." Chewing on her bottom lip, she gave her hips an experimental roll. A gasp. A groan. "Yes, please. More! Now, now, now."

Clasping her by the waist, Bjorn planted his feet on the mattress, bent his knees, and lifted his hips. Slowly, he forced his length deeper, impaling her. Deeper. Deeper still. Not slamming all the way to the hilt required more strength than he possessed, but somehow, he managed it.

Once she'd accepted every inch, he stilled, letting her get used to his invasion. Tension thrummed inside him. Sweat trickled down his temples and his back. He shook.

"Tell me when…you're ready," he gritted out.

Experimenting, she rose up slightly, then sank down gingerly. Again. Then again. It was pure, unequivocal torture for him, yet he loved every second of it. Finally, she rushed out, "I'm ready!"

Wait, wait, wait. This felt good. Too good. Better than ever before. Why?

Realization stabbed him, and he flinched. "Need to pull out. Not wearing a condom. Shouldn't risk pregnancy." *Could* he pull out? His every cell shouted a protest.

"No! Stay! Just got you here. Not ready for you to leave, even for a moment." She locked her legs around him. Only took a heartbeat to realize what she'd done. She unlocked and whispered, "You can't get me pregnant like this. Will explain later. Please, Bjorn."

Hearing her plead for his possession…

With a grunt, Bjorn utterly unleashed. He thrust up, and she slammed herself down. For a moment, he saw stars, but he did not go still. No, he hammered inside her, the headboard slapping against the wall. In and out. Faster. Harder. In, out. In, out. Her inner walls clasped him tight, surrounding his shaft with heat and arousal. In-out, in-out. Faster still.

He'd been posed at the razor's edge of desire for far too long. Now, passion ruled him. He reached between them to circle his thumb around her clitoris while working her little bud between two fingers.

Then. That moment. Fox threw back her head and screamed, her inner walls clenching around his length.

The next moment, Bjorn roared to the ceiling, pouring jet after white-hot jet of satisfaction into his woman.

Chapter Sixteen

Hours passed before Fox's heart calmed and her breathing slowed. She'd never been a snuggler, but she spent every minute tucked against Bjorn's side, her nails buried in his chest. Like a predator intent on keeping her prey. He combed his fingers through her hair. A suspended moment of communion and connection more satisfying than the sex. Well, just as satisfying.

Almost as satisfying.

A real close second.

As silence continued to reign, worry plagued Fox. Last time she and Bjorn had gotten busy, the Queen of Shadows sensed his arousal and came gunning for him. Would Alana sense his arousal today, too?

If the bitch returned, Fox could kill her *without* opening a portal. The perfect silver lining. Oh! Oh! Maybe Fox and Bjorn could work together to end Alana. *After all, couples who slay together, stay together.*

I want to stay with Bjorn.

What they'd just done…Earth-shattering, world-changing. The man had *worshipped* her body. Nothing had mattered but his next touch. Never had she felt closer to another living being. Now, she wasn't sure she could live without the sensation.

Fool! I told you before, but I'll tell you again, because your puny brain is not computing the truth. His leaders will never pardon a sinner like you. When the time comes, Bjorn will strike at you.

The demon whispered his poison, and her stomach filled with acid. Perhaps she should put a little distance between herself and Bjorn, just in case. "I guess we can't declare a winner of the bet. We came in a photo finish."

"I suppose we must have sex again to break the tie," he teased.

Teasing. Now. Her heart squeezed.

He frowned and rubbed the center of his chest, as if his heart squeezed, as well. "I'm being summoned by Alana."

All thoughts of maintaining distance vanished. *Knew the bitch would try something like this.* Stomach now roiling, stirring the acid as if it were a simmering stew, Fox said, "Give me her coordinates. We can kill her together. Today! Please, Bjorn." She flattened her palms, one against the other, creating a steeple. "Please, please, please."

He opened and closed his mouth once. Twice. Thrice. Finally, he settled on, "During one of our first conversations, Alana told me she used to live in Hell, as a concubine of Lucifer's."

What!? "Are we talking Lucifer, Prince of Darkness, adopted son of Hades, brother to William the Ever Randy? Or some poor bastard who got stuck with the worst name of all time?"

"Prince of Darkness." Bjorn pinched and lifted a lock of Fox's hair, tracing the end against his cheek. "Took her centuries, but she ultimately escaped him. She claims she will never return to Hell, not for any reason."

Fox knew girl-code, which meant she knew the translations for Alana's vow. *This bitch gonna be coming for her hubby in Hell.* Jaw clenched, she said, "Do you believe everything she says, Ofalana?"

He frowned. "Ofalana? What does that mean?"

Rather than explaining the intricacies of sexual subjugation in *The Handmaid's Tale*, she said, "I've never asked you for anything, Bjorn. Not anything important, anyway."

"I know. You do not ask. You issue demands."

"Are you complaining?" she asked, one brow arched. "No, seriously. Are you? Maybe give me a list with my worst traits, and I'll work on—"

"You misunderstand." Bjorn rolled her over, his heavy weight settling atop her, stopping her flow of verbal diarrhea. "I'm thanking you. Social cues are not my talent, and your forthrightness puts me at ease."

She fluffed her hair, feigning nonchalance. Meanwhile, she squealed like a fangirl inside her head. Too many people overlooked the value of comfort, calling it "boring." Not Fox. When you'd been uncomfortable for the bulk of your life, you clung to whatever security, reassurance, or encouragement you could find.

"I think someone has a serious case of Foxitis, and I'm here for it."

Trying for flirtatious—probably achieving creepy—she batted her lashes at him. "You trusted me with your army. Trust me with Alana's coordinates, and I'll make you glad you did."

Bjorn drew in a deep breath, then held it for an endless eternity. After exhaling slowly, he told her, "I'm not just married to Alana." Shame coated his voice. "I'm bonded to her; my life-force is tied to hers."

The admission lashed like a whip—and Fox should know! "So, Alana isn't just a bitch. She's a straight-up POS." No doubt the queen had forced that bond to prevent Bjorn's friends from avenging his mistreatment. Whatever injuries one spouse received, the other endured as well. "I'm a Gatekeeper, Bjorn. Do you know what that means?"

"Only that you can open portals to any location."

There was so much more to it than that. Toying with the ends of his hair, she said, "I've visited more worlds, realms and dimensions than anyone else on the planet. One of those worlds is Phantasia. The citizens are phantom-like. They can reach inside your body to unwind, detach and remove any mystical bonds, then patch up the damage left behind."

His eyes widened. "Like surgery on your spirit."

"Exactly." There were dangers, of course, but the rewards far outweighed the risks. "Problem is, time passes differently on Phantasia. Spending one day there would cost us a decade here."

Disappointment etched every line of his face. "Unless I'm willing to fall, I cannot spare a decade until the war in the Underworld ends."

Bjorn, a Fallen One...nope. No way. A life devoid of his brothers by circumstance, immortality, wings and mission to kill as many demons as possible would only lead to unfulfillment and regret. "Then we take out Alana today, and you immediately bond to me." Her cheeks burned with heat. "Or anyone! Whomever you prefer. Someone who will agree." Ugh. Did she *want* a permanent bond with Bjorn? Maybe. Maybe not. The new one would infuse him with new strength. In theory. "That option is a lot more dangerous, though. The longer a marital bond is in place, the stronger it becomes. There's no way the new one will be as potent as the old. Still, you're stubborn and mighty, and the odds are in your favor." Again, in theory.

Expression alternating from hopeful to hopeless, he shifted to the side. His shaft rubbed between her legs, sending a spear of pleasure to her belly, her breasts, and her mind. In that order. Mmm. *Focus!*

"Why aid me in such a way?" he asked, his brow furrowed.

Holding his gaze, refusing to look away, she admitted, "I like you. I like being with you, and I want to keep being with you. Plus, I plan to do anything and everything to make up for my actions. This is a good place to start."

His features softened. His *body* softened. Well, everywhere but his fun zone. "You are forgiven, vixen. What I failed to remember the day we met? Everyone makes mistakes. And just because you welcomed the demon doesn't mean you are happy about the choice you made. You hate him. You fight him daily. You learn from your mistakes and work to do better. To be better. Something only a rare few do. You are one of the rare few, and that should be praised, not punished."

Her eyes burned as if she—no. No way. No way she teared up like a pansy. "What will happen if you're told to kill me?"

He stiffened but said, "Your execution will be stayed. I know it."

"But what if it's not?" Sent Ones were stubborn. "I need a plan B, C and D." Also, a plan E, F, G, H, I, J, K, L, M, N, O, P, Q, R, S, T, U, V, W, X, and Y wouldn't hurt, either. A girl couldn't be too careful. And, yes, she'd purposely left off Z. As a letter, Z sucked. *End my alphabet? Go screw yourself.*

A muscle jumped in Bjorn's jaw. "Did you sleep with me merely to ensure I would keep you safe?"

Ugh. One day. One day soon, hopefully, he would think the best of her rather than the worst. "Would I sleep with you to survive? Yes." Moving quickly, she grabbed a pillow and bashed his face. "But I didn't. I wanted you more than anyone ever. I know you don't believe me—yet—but I'm not deceiving you, and I'm not going to betray you."

The jumping muscle gradually slowed, and he expelled a heavy breath. "I'm trusting you, Fox. Not just with my life, but with the lives of my cherished friends. Heed your own words, and do *not* betray me." His tone hardened at the end.

"I'm not going to betray you," she repeated, and she meant it. "After last night, you earned a spot on my coveted Never Harm list."

He grinned, the sight nearly her undoing, and kissed her temple. "You may change your mind. I should have told you sooner. Should have apologized. But, the day Alana visited, I saw a memory from your past. I'm not sure how, or why."

Knew it. A lump grew in her throat. "What did you see?"

"You were a little girl, starved and dirty, wandering the streets. A soldier dragged you to a dark alley and ripped your clothes." He pressed his lips into a thin line as black spread through his irises, turning the rainbow into an endless abyss.

The change proved astonishing and wild, nothing "True Dread" about it. It spoke of primitive desires and raw need, his every emotion clearly heightened.

"Did you see what happened after?" she asked.

He gave a terse shake of his head.

"I killed him before he could do what he wanted. Even as a child, I could open portals. I wasn't very good at it, wasn't very powerful, but I could do it unless stressed. I was stressed that day, obviously, but I managed to open and close a small one around his ankle, amputating his entire foot. While he screamed with pain, I took his sword and beheaded him. He was my first kill."

"Good girl." Bjorn bent his head to kiss her brow. "So, how did I see the memory?"

"I fed you my blood." When he jolted, she rushed to add, "You had just returned from your meeting with Alana, and you were in incredible pain. My blood is supercharged and helped you heal at a faster rate for roughly twenty-four hours. The memory was a side-effect."

As she spoke, he stared at her mouth, his irises sizzling hotter and hotter. Voice low and throaty, he said, "So I will see more of your memories if I consume more of your blood?"

"Correct." Wait. "Do you *want* to see more of my memories?"

"I do." He nodded for emphasis. "You remain a mystery to me, and I will enjoy learning all your secrets."

Bjorn, intrigued by her. Her! She shivered. "I'm like a candy store. Open for a select clientele, sometimes sweet, sometimes tart—just depends on what you're in the mood for—and always the leading cause of heart disease among immortals." She gently pinched the lobe of his ear. "You can ask me anything."

He smiled with ease, no more twitching. "Before we had sex, you told me you couldn't get pregnant. How is that possible?"

Had sex on the brain, did he? Oh, yeah. He did. Her body cradled his, and she felt his every reaction. He hardened; she shivered again.

"Gatekeepers are only fertile once a year," she said, "and only for four weeks at a time. Which could be the reason we're near extinction. Any other questions?"

"Not at the moment. I have…other things on my mind."

"Like?" she prompted.

"Like our upcoming move to Hell."

She waited for him to continue. He didn't. At first, she pouted. Then she wiggled beneath him. *There we go.* He sucked in a breath.

"That's it?" she asked, all teasing and temptation. "Nothing else consumes your thoughts?"

His eyelids turned heavy, sinking low over his eyes. "Perhaps I...the feel of your body gloving mine..."

"Shhh. Too much talking." Fighting a smile, she combed her fingers through his hair. "I've got a better use for our mouths."

* * * *

The next day

A bead of sweat trickled down Fox's spine. "So, this is Hell," she muttered. Or rather, one of ten territories in Hell.

Earlier today, Bjorn had asked her to open a portal to this very spot. One by one, his soldiers had rushed through. Then Thane's. Then Xerxes'. She'd had to keep the portal open for hours, a first for her.

Bjorn had remained next to her. Toward the end, she'd been so drained, he'd had to hold her up. Finally, he'd ordered her to close the portal. She'd protested. The last section of Warriors hadn't made it through, but he'd insisted.

Then, the argument ended...because she'd passed out, exhausted...only to awaken inside a completed cabin, alone, next to a note.

Because of your portal, we were the first to arrive in Hell. We had our pick of territories, and I owe you thanks. Which I will give as soon as I return...and you're naked. If you're reading this, I'm somewhere outside helping my soldiers get settled. For safety reasons, I ask that you stay put. Please? Yours, Bjorn. P.S. I've taken your weapons.

She heaved a sigh, her shoulders rolling in. He didn't trust her, and she understood, but it still hurt like a punch to the gut. Would he *ever* trust her? Was he ashamed of their budding relationship? Or maybe just Fox herself? Maybe he didn't want his peers to know he cared about her?

That hurt, too. Actually, that hurt worse.

She stepped outside, the breeze sweltering and scented with sulfur, and studied her surroundings. This territory happened to be owned by Hades, one of the nine Kings of the Underworld. His son, William of the

Dark—aka the Ever Randy, the Panty Melter, and a prince of darkness—often stayed here, in a massive fortress made from brimstone and gold. *The home of my dreams.* In the backyard, there was a boarded-up stable also made of brimstone and gold.

As hundreds of Sent Ones erected cabins all around the stable, whispers abounded. Ultimately, she concluded William kept a young woman locked in the stable. Some claimed she possessed a beauty beyond imagining. Others called her plain. Some said she had blue hair. Others said pink or white. Some said she had brown eyes. Others said green or blue. Everyone agreed she had to be something special to obsess the Ever Randy, who liked to select a new lover every night.

Uh, maybe he had multiple women in there? One way or another, Fox would find out. For the right price, she would free the woman/women...and, depending on her/their attitude, either sell her/them back to William or escort her/them to—

No, no, no. Stop! Fox had traveled here for Bjorn, not a job. Besides, she owed him. Big time. By fighting to save her life, he'd put his reputation on the line. From now on, her actions would be a reflection upon him. She had to behave.

Determination rooted in her heart as she studied the remaining terrain. Smoke and soot covered the ground. A ground that spontaneously spit streams of fire into the air, turning the area into an oven. There wasn't a single plant or weed in the vicinity. No signs of life, period. Unless she counted the demons hiding around the property, spying on the Sent Ones.

Suddenly, the fine hairs on the back of her neck stood at attention, and she frowned. Feeling as if she were being watched, Fox scanned the area—there. Him. Those little hairs practically vibrated. With white-gold braids and skin to match, he had a distinct appearance she would have remembered if ever they'd met. Which meant, they hadn't met. However, he'd clearly heard of her. He stood a hundred yards away, glaring as if she'd murdered his cat.

Note to self: I should get a cat. Though she wanted one, badly, she refused to repeat her mistake with Tawny, living in fear that an enemy would strike at the animal just to hurt her. But, now that she and Bjorn were together, her pet could have Sent One protection twenty-four-seven.

Wait. *Was* she together with Bjorn?

They'd never had a talk about their relationship. She knew he desired her sexually, knew he had fun with her. Did he think about her when they were apart, the way she thought about him? He must.

Had he truly forgiven her for her past actions? Surely. Otherwise, he wouldn't have slept with her. Right? Right. On the other hand, he'd left her defenseless, so, how much did he really care for her?

Would he get in trouble with his bosses for dating a war-criminal? Probably. Had he fallen for her even a little? Please, please, please.

Where was he now, exactly? *I miss him.*

Ugh. What kind of romantic loser had she become?

Pounding footsteps yanked her from the mental Q and A. And subsequent pity party. The male who'd glared at her stomped across the sea of Warriors, supplies, and cabins, radiating menace. The tips of his white-gold wings dragged the ground, collecting soot.

Part of her longed to face off with him. But…what if he was related to one of the ten? He deserved a chance to spew his fury, and she deserved the rancor. The other part of her demanded she honor Bjorn's wishes and go inside to avoid making a scene. If the man threw a punch at her, she'd have to block…and fight back. He could get hurt, and she'd have an eleventh casualty to add to her tally of wrongdoings.

Sighing, she backed up, one, two, three steps. After passing the open door, she kicked it shut. Now what?

The cabin had three rooms—a living room, a kitchenette, a bathroom, and a bedroom with a second, private bathroom—but few furnishings. Only two love seats for gamers, a TV with multiple streaming services already programmed in, and a bed.

Her heart raced. Had he gotten the chairs and TV for her?

No way he's ashamed of me. Fox grinned from ear to ear. Perhaps she'd re-watch an old season of *Big Brother*, then do a little internet trolling. Could you get wi-fi in Hell?

If not, she could open a quick portal to her home, where she kept an antenna she'd built with magical wire able to power anything, anywhere, at any time. Why not fetch the antenna, anyway? It'd come in handy in other ways.

Problem: she tried to open a portal and failed.

Fox ran her tongue over her teeth. Once again, Bjorn had done something to negate her ability, which meant he trusted her less than she'd thought. Another gut punch. But again, she understood. She really did. And she would fight, fight so hard to win him over. Giving up wasn't an option. She—

The door swung open, the white-gold-haired man stomping inside.

Great! Thanks to Bjorn, she had no weapons, and no way to open a portal. *Isn't life grand?*

Without looking away from Fox, he kicked the door shut, shaking the entire cabin. He held a dagger in each hand, the metal glinting in the light.

Her heartbeat sped up, sending a prickle of unease down her spine. She raised her chin and squared her shoulders, going cold. The best—only—way to battle.

Must kill him before he kills you, Distrust whispered.

She ground her teeth. Exactly what the demon said when she'd faced the ten.

Ignore him! Easier said than done. Flippant, she asked, "Did you hear about my sale and come running? Well, you should have brought a friend. For a limited time, I'm giving two spankings away for the price of one!"

Rage mottled his face. *Guess I'll call him Mr. Rage.*

He pointed a dagger tip at her. "I do not know how you convinced a male as honorable as Bjorn to spare your life, and it doesn't matter. I will stop you, and one day, he will thank me."

Mr. Rage lunged for her, swiping the daggers in her direction.

Fox jumped backward, avoiding a strike. But, unused to the home's layout, she slammed the backs of her knees into a recliner, and fell. Damn it! Before she could jump up, Mr. Rage flared his wings and spun.

Contact. A sharp sting erupted in her cheek, and blood dripped down her chin. Realization: There were hard, razor-sharp hooks hidden beneath his feathers, and she'd just gotten a taste of their capabilities.

He spun again, no doubt intending to run a hook across her vulnerable throat. Reflexes on point, she pulled the lever on the chair, whooshing back. The hooks missed her face by half an inch. At the same time, she grabbed a fistful of feathers and yanked.

He howled. She grinned.

She kicked out her legs, nailing his man-junk. Air left his lungs in a mighty heave as he hunched over. She kneed his chin. He bellowed in pain and stumbled backward. As she stood, he planted his sandaled feet against the wood floor and hurled a dagger at her.

A pained gasp parted her lips, the blade embedding in her collarbone. Trembling, queasy, she yanked it free. Ow, ow, ow. Despite a surge of adrenaline, the pain proved agonizing. Black dots wove through her vision. A river of hot blood ran down her chest. Had the blade hit a few inches down, he would have sliced open her heart.

She forced a grin. "Thanks for the weapon."

Kill him. Kill him now or die.

Yes. No! Just knock him out. Whatever you do, do not hurt the Sent One.

Roaring, he leaped at her, and a lethal dance ensued. He struck, she blocked. She struck, he blocked. Didn't take long to learn he had skill. The urge to end his life strengthened, beginning to cloud each of her thoughts. But still, she resisted. Bjorn might know and love this man. If she killed him, she might lose Bjorn. She'd definitely lose what little trust she'd managed to curate.

Can't lose him. Just can't. Not yet. Deciding to use Mr. Rage's skill against him, she purposely allowed him to land a blow. When his dagger sank into her belly, he grinned, thinking he'd won.

As if a little internal body bling would kill her. The fool had left his side unguarded. She twisted, slicing the dagger across his throat.

His eyes widened, the color draining from his cheeks. He released the other blade to clutch at the injury, opening and closing his mouth to no avail. As an immortal, he would heal far too quickly, so, she didn't stop there. Punch, punch—she blackened his eyes. Hopefully, they'd swell closed. Punch—she broke his nose. Punch—she knocked the air from his lungs yet again.

Again, he gasped for breath he couldn't catch. She spun behind him to knee the backs of his legs, sending him crashing face-first to the floor.

Kill him!

"No!" She straddled his waist and raised the dagger, thinking to slam the hilt into his temple the same way Bjorn had once slammed his sword hilt into hers, knocking her out.

Then, she swung—

Chapter Seventeen

Ten Minutes Earlier

"The decision has been made." The pronouncement came from Zacharel.

"Tell me the verdict." Bjorn paced inside the man's brand-new cabin, his sandaled feet practically stomping holes in the floor. Zacharel and his wife, Annabelle, sat nearby. Annabelle reclined on her husband's lap, eating from a bowl of popcorn. Not too long ago, the dark-haired beauty had been locked inside a facility for the criminally insane, all because a demon high lord had murdered her parents and she'd taken the fall.

Before his marriage, Zacharel had an iron fist. Break a rule, and he would break your face. After his marriage, the male had an iron fist still, only it was encased in a silk glove. Break a rule, and he'd break your face, but now, he felt bad about it afterward.

Zacharel huffed a sigh. "I'm sorry, Bjorn, but Fox's execution will proceed as ordered. Before the sun sets, you will remove her head."

Heart beating his ribs bloody, Bjorn ground to an abrupt halt.

His boss wasn't done. "You will remove her head and place it upon a pike outside of this camp. Forevermore, she will serve as a warning. Strike at the Sent Ones, and suffer."

Denial screamed inside his head. Behead the woman he desired? The one he craved? The one he thought he might...need? "Why?" he demanded, though he already knew the answer. His loyalties were being tested.

"I am not privy to that information." The male wrapped his arms around Annabelle, as if he feared she would be taken away and said, "I know you have come to care for the woman, and I truly regret the pain you will soon endure."

"If it's any consolation—" Annabelle began.

"Let me stop you there. It's not," Bjorn snarled, keeping his focus on Zacharel. "Fox is not a threat to us. She regrets her actions and strives to aid us."

"Nevertheless."

One word. A death sentence. Cursing, Bjorn stalked from the cabin. White-hot breath scorched his nostrils and lungs.

"Bjorn," Zacharel called from the doorway. "Do not turn your back on the people who love you, guard your back, and always have your best interests at heart for a woman who uses you for protection and will betray you for money."

How many times have I been blinded by prejudice, as Zacharel is right now?

All around, Warriors continued their work on the cabins. Hammering sounds provided a riotous soundtrack in tune with the pounding of his heartbeat. Anyone foolish enough to get in Bjorn's way got mowed down.

Some part of Fox must have sensed this outcome. She tried to warn Bjorn, tried to get him to see past his hope for the best. Now…

Behead Fox? Never! When he failed this test, and he would, another Sent One would receive the assignment, and Bjorn would face a Tribunal—the judging of his actions and subsequent punishment. Perhaps he'd receive a suspension. When he actively protected Fox from the new assassin, however—and he would—his next punishment would be banishment.

Do I love her? Once he'd thought they would never work long-term, but here, in this moment, he could not imagine a life *without* her. He luxuriated in every aspect of her personality, dreamed and fantasized about her body, and loved spending time with her. The woman had become his safe haven. When they weren't together, he missed her more than a limb. The thought of never holding her again…never breathing in her sweet scent or hearing her quips…

Very well, then. He would do it; he would fall. Anything to keep Fox safe! He cobbled together a plan. Speak with Fox, gain her cooperation. Speak with Thane and Xerxes. He would explain his reasons and beg his friends not to follow him. Though he'd always expected the two to fall with him, he thought he knew how to stop them—remind them that he needed soldiers on the inside, to mislead others about Fox's location and listen for any strategies against him. Finally, he and Fox would flee.

And live happily ever after?

Bjorn entered the cabin he shared with Fox—only to see her pinning down a Sent One, a dagger raised to deliver a deathblow. Shocked horror propelled him closer. He clasped her wrist, stopping her.

"Release the weapon," he commanded, squeezing her wrist tight. Too tight. Later, she would bruise, but he couldn't let it matter. He'd decided to fall for this woman. He'd intended to give up everything he loved to save her life…just so she could murder more Sent Ones.

He didn't…he couldn't… Red dotted his vision, and fire scorched his lungs. Boiling blood rushed to his muscles, causing them to bulge. *Betrayed my trust in the worst possible way.*

"Do it!" he shouted. "Release the weapon before I take it from you."

Fox yelped. Looking shell-shocked, she opened her hand. The dagger whooshed to the floor, landing with a heavy thud. Voice soft but ragged, she stuttered, "I—I wasn't going to kill him, just knock him out. He attacked me."

Though he tasted no lie, he did not believe her. You didn't need to state the truth to negate the taste of a lie; you need only state *a* truth. About anything. In her mind, the "him" and "he" could reference anyone, rather than the male she had pinned.

"No Sent One would dare accost and harm someone in my care," he grated. Distrust must have led her to attack, just as before. Meaning, she could not be trusted. Not now, not ever. *Pang.*

"He did," she insisted. "Aren't my injuries proof?"

"They are proof he fought back when you attacked!"

"I swear to you, he followed me—"

"Enough!" Bjorn pushed her away from the Sent One with more force than intended, and she stumbled to her ass. He hardened his heart and checked the male for a pulse. There! A cool tide of relief rolled over him. The pulse was a little fast, but steady. "He lives."

"I know! I made sure of it."

Another misdirection to prevent him from tasting the lie! "What is your endgame here?" he snapped as he straightened. "Did you think to hide the body? To destroy my army from the inside?"

For a long while, she simply stared up at him, mouth agape. He continued to wrestle with the truth. How he'd trusted and defended this woman. How he'd decided to risk everything just to be with her. To say goodbye to the life he knew, to forge a new future. The pain…

You are a fool!

Finally, she stood and wound her arms around her middle. She lowered her head and drew in her shoulders. All emotion wiped from her features, one after the other. Shock—gone. Worry—gone. Heartache, fear and fury—gone, gone, gone.

Another, sharper pang tore through him. How fragile she suddenly appeared. How breakable. Vulnerable. As if she'd prayed for a knight in shining armor to ride in and save her from undeserved malevolence, but he'd attacked her instead. Another deception!

Rage spread through him like a virus, anguish close on its heels. He directed the rage at Fox just as much as himself. For the first time since his imprisonment and torture, he'd lowered his guard with someone other than Thane and Xerxes. *And this is my reward.*

Should have known better.

His insides shredded, his future a misery-soaked quagmire, he stumbled back, away from Fox. Again and again, his heart punched his ribs, each beat more painful than the last.

Arms outstretched, she stepped in his direction. With a grunt, he batted her hands away.

Abject hurt contorted her features, tears welling in her eyes. Fox, crying… He noticed a gradual softening deep inside and fought harder to turn his heart against her, lest she set him up for another betrayal.

Another. Betrayal. The words echoed in his head. Roaring, he twisted and punched the wall, once, twice. A plank cracked, splinters of wood flying in every direction. His knuckles split, blood trickling. A sting of pain never registered, his adrenaline too jacked. "I risked everything for you," he snarled. "Everything!"

She opened and closed her mouth. The only sound to be heard? The force of their panting breaths.

"Won't defend yourself?" he sneered. "Won't try to convince me—again—that I misunderstood what I saw with my own eyes? Or are you too afraid I'll taste your lies?"

"Don't do this," she whispered. "Please, don't do this. Give me the benefit of the doubt."

"Begging now?" he all but purred. "How delicious." A foul taste coated his tongue. *I castigate her for lies, then tell my own?* He balled his hands into fists.

She flinched, then lapsed into silence. He almost punched a new hole in the wall. He wanted—needed—her to yell at him. Or insult him. Something! Anything to push him over the edge and make him hate her.

Why don't I hate her?

He needed to kill her. Needed to *want* to kill her. As long as she lived, he might be stupid enough to give her a third…fourth…twentieth chance. But even still, he didn't want this. The thought of her headless body pouring its lifeblood into the soot-covered ground nearly destroyed him. When it came to Fox, he'd never been rational. "Not going to say anything else? Very well. I'll speak for us both. You and I? We're done."

Another flinch. Hurt glittered in her eyes, but only for a moment. Like all other emotions, it too got wiped away. Color drained from her cheeks. "I'm such a fool. I thought I'd made progress with you, but you never trusted me, did you? Not once. Not even a little. You were *never* going to trust me. Not fully."

One emotion she hadn't wiped away—bitterness. It honed her words into weapons.

Bjorn swallowed a curse. He wanted his warm, teasing Fox back. The woman who was his undoing. *No, no. Do not soften!* He opened his mouth to snarl, "*You're right*," but the words died on his tongue. Because they were a lie with no truthful inference? Maybe, maybe not. Because, despite her awfulness, he still didn't want her dead.

But he couldn't stand to look at her a second longer. The demon she'd invited inside her heart and mind would never allow them to find peace together, and now the sight of her ripped up his soul, reminding him of what could have been. "I'm going to do what I should have done the day we met. I'm going to kill—" Again, the words died on his tongue. "I will kill—" Damn her! "I will punish you, and the Sent Ones will cheer."

He *would*. He would swing his sword and remove her head. Would burn her body, watching as it ashed. Would never again see her, speak to her, touch or kiss her. Would never again sink inside her, hold her throughout the night, or awaken to find her sheltered in the circle of his embrace.

Bjorn yanked at hanks of his hair, punched the wall, re-breaking his knuckles, and slammed a booted foot into the window, shattering glass. Whether he did his duty or not, misery awaited him. Only misery. *She betrayed me. This is deserved.*

Can I truly kill the woman who introduced me to contentment?

"Y-you're going to kill me," she stated.

Do. Not. Soften. "I will." *Will I?*

Hate myself already. Will hate myself for the rest of time. Sometimes, though, sacrifices must be made.

His eyes stung and watered. Not because of tears. No! He refused to cry. *Betrayed. Deserved.*

No reaction from Fox. She peered up at him, growing colder by the second. No doubt she'd stripped herself of emotion so she wouldn't have to deal with her own wretchedness, her personal defense mechanism. He only wished he had the ability to do the same. Or breathe. He desperately needed to breathe. Why couldn't he inhale? Exhale? *Breathe, damn it! Chest on fire.*

"One day, one day soon, you will look back on this moment with regret," she told him, seemingly calm and steady. "You'll perform an autopsy on our relationship, and find out you are the one who poisoned us. You'll replay this day over and over again and come to realize I held the dagger in a way that allowed me to knock him out with the hilt, not kill him with the blade. You'll ask around and discover I walked away from this man, whoever he is, and he followed me into the cabin without my permission. He believed you'd fallen under my spell, and hoped my death would set you free. You'll apologize to me, because yes, I'll still be alive, but it'll be too late. As of this moment, I've already moved on."

Her words hit him like bombs, and he huffed his breaths. *Having learned a trick or two from Distrust, she seeks to manipulate me.* But he would not be swayed—*I won't!*—his rage only spreading. She thought the more *facts* she shared with him, the more readily he would believe her lies. Wrong! The only thing he knew beyond a doubt? *Believe her now, suffer later.*

"This. Is. Deserved." Eyes narrowed to slits, Bjorn swiped out his arm. He shackled her wrist with his fingers, then dragged her out of the cabin. A cool temp gave way to molten heat. In seconds, sweat glossed his skin.

The constant *bang, bang, bang* as workers built their cabins assaulted his ears. Fresh lumber scented the air, chasing away the awful scent of brimstone and sulfur.

He maneuvered through a cluster of cabins, piles of supplies, and groups of Sent Ones, surprised Fox kept up, not trying to drag her feet or wrench free. No, she kept her gaze straight ahead, those icy hazels free of tears. She even smirked.

Growls rumbled deep inside him, his rage reaching a new plateau. How *dare* she smirk. And damn it, why wasn't she fighting this? From the moment they'd met, she'd been in survivor-mode. Here, now, she acted as though he'd broken her heart.

Key word: acted.

Deserved! He stomped his feet with more force and tightened his grip on Fox. Anyone who caught sight of her recognized her instantly. She received glares, jeers, and curses. No way she could miss her reception; they were loud and proud. New pangs cut through Bjorn's chest. Still, he struggled to breathe.

Someone tossed a small stone at Fox, leaving a gash in her shoulder. Crimson wet her already stained shirt as select Sent Ones laughed. Others cheered.

Bjorn came to an abrupt stop, released Fox to pick up the stone, then hurled it at the person responsible, nailing him between the eyes. The male toppled, already unconscious.

The laughter died down. "Anyone else?" Bjorn bellowed. "You do not harm my prisoner. Understand?"

A commotion across the sea of Sent Ones. Whispers reached his ears, and he detected "the Ever Randy," "furious," and "someone's going to die."

A pathway cleared, and yes, William the Ever Randy marched into view. He was tall and muscled with black hair and blue eyes, and almost too beautiful to gaze upon. Runes etched both of his arms—slightly raised, swirling designs tattooed into his flesh to absorb magic.

During the past year, Bjorn had dealt with William a handful of times. He'd found the male annoyingly irreverent, conceited, and untrusting of anyone outside of his alliance. No one was more self-serving, and here, now, William looked like a man on a mission. Anyone foolish enough to step into his path got tossed to the side.

Had he come to take Fox?

Never! The growls started up again, rumbling deep in Bjorn's chest. *He will have to pry her from my cold, dead fingers. There's no other way I'll allow her to return to her old life, to enjoy a happily ever after, laughing about my gullibility.*

William stopped mere inches away from Bjorn and Fox. Bjorn frowned. The male projected a different energy than usual. It was darker. *Much* darker. And pure evil. Those electric blues gleamed with hatred and fury, emotions he'd never before directed at Bjorn. Why now?

"If you wish to remain in my territory, you will give me the girl," William snarled. "I've already spoken with Lysander and Zacharel, and they agreed I may oversee her care for the remainder of her days. Give her to me. Now."

No. No! William was a playboy who slept with anyone willing. If he seduced Fox...

She would live that happy life. "No," he snapped. Bjorn did not want Fox happy. *Ignore the foul taste in your mouth. Means nothing.* "I respect you, William. I—" He went quiet as a sharp pain registered in his gut. Confused, he glanced down.

Blood. So much blood. It soaked his white robe.

Plop. His intestines splattered over the ground.

William grinned. The bastard held a dagger—a dagger he'd slicked across Bjorn's abdomen. Speaking for Bjorn's ears alone, he said, "I wasn't asking for permission, Sent One. I'm taking her, no matter how many must die in the process."

The audience didn't react in any way, shape or form. Did they not understand what had just happened? Had they somehow missed the stabbing?

Fox didn't seem to notice, either, not until she placed a hand on Bjorn's shoulder to gain his attention. At the second of contact, a switch must have flipped in her mind. She noticed the injury, and she screamed and threw herself at William.

As the two stumbled to the dirt, viciously punching, kicking, and swiping at each other, Bjorn's legs gave out, the pain increasing exponentially. He hit his knees, then toppled over. *So dizzy.* Blood rushed from his limbs, pooling around his vital organs to keep them warm.

Though he fought to remain aware and active, black dots encroached on his vision. His blood turned to acid, and he knew. The blade had been poisoned.

Whatever William had planned, it did not bode well for anyone, not even Fox. Did he hope to use her, perhaps, for her portal-opening skills?

No, no, no. *My prisoner. Mine!* No one else had the right to use or harm her. *Must save her. Must...*

Darkness enveloped Bjorn's mind, dragging him kicking and screaming into a deep, deep sleep.

Chapter Eighteen

Fox fought William's hold, desperate to return to Bjorn, who had passed out on the ground, surrounded by his own intestines. A development she should applaud, considering he planned to exterminate her.

The knowledge still tore her up inside. At least Distrust had gone quiet, petrified of the Ever Randy for some reason. A first.

Would Bjorn pull through? He had to pull through. She loved him and—

Whoa. She sucked in a breath. She loved him?

A tiny glimmer of light chased away the shadows in her mind, the truth suddenly clear. She did. She loved him. Or rather, she *used* to love him. After everything he'd done today, she planned to switch off her emotions every time she thought of him. Or saw him. Or spoke to him. That way, she would never hurt over him again. But…

The hurt proved too strong, and wouldn't go away. It gnawed at her insides. *Lost my lover and best friend today.* And he *was* her best friend, wasn't he? Or he *had been.* She'd enjoyed conversing with him, sleeping with him, and making him smile. Now, tears scalded her eyes.

Okay, so, maybe she'd switch off her emotions tomorrow and go back to her cold, barren existence then. Today, she would wallow in her misery, ensuring she never forgot the consequences of falling in love.

William maintained a tight hold and flashed her to—she gasped, her jaw going slack. *What is this place?* Eerily dark, illuminated by thousands of mini-fire pits. Inside each set of flames—a human soul. The scent of burnt meat saturated the air, stinging her nostrils. She gagged.

Shackled by chains and staked to the ground in a supine position, those souls writhed in pain. Scream after scream assaulted her ears, broken up by the occasional moan. Everyone within her vicinity begged for help.

"What is this place?" she croaked.

He unveiled the evilest grin she'd ever beheld, every inch a prince of darkness. "I call this area a spice rack. During their human lives, these people chose to serve me. Upon their deaths, they became my property. As spirits, they never die and never ash. They *do* feel the heat and agony of the flames. Then, whenever I crave soul food"—he snickered at his own joke—"I pick a tasty one or two."

Soul food. A disgusting reference on so many levels. "You snack on people?" A lump grew in her throat, and she gulped.

"Among other things," he sang.

Fox had spent a little time with William when she and Galen visited the Lords of the Underworld. William of the Dark had irritated and amused her, but he'd never disgusted her like this. Something had changed. He wasn't the same man as before.

"This is where you think you're going to keep me?" She tried to wrench free, but he dug his claws deeper into her wrist. Either that, or his claws had lengthened. She winced as the tips embedded in bone.

When Fox kneed his groin, he willingly released her.

"You little bitch," he snarled, backhanding her across the cheek.

Her head whipped to the side, pain exploding through her brain. Blood coated her tongue, and weakness poured through her. He wore a ring on every finger and one—or all—must have had some sort of toxin. *Losing too much blood too fast. Too weak.*

"I *know* I'm going to keep you here until I decide to make use of your Gatekeeper abilities. You will help me win my war with the Kings of the Underworld and their Sent One allies, or I will magnify your suffering each and every day."

Confirmation: this was *not* William. William *aided* the Kings. Suspicions danced through Fox's mind, followed by rumors she'd heard about William's brother, Lucifer, some type of sorcerer, who used magic to cast illusions and shapeshift into anyone, at any time…

Finally, comprehension dawned. So did horror. "You are Lucifer," she rasped. "The Destroyer, King of Deception, Prince of Darkness, the Dark One, Satan, and the Devil.

"Ding, ding, ding." Right before her eyes, his appearance changed. Dark hair lightened. Blue eyes darkened. Bronze skin became gold. As beautiful as an angel—a lie.

Nauseous, she stumbled back, putting distance between them. Or trying to. She tripped over a set of shackles and crashed to the ground. Lucifer followed her down, clearly intending to chain her there. That evil, evil smile…

The second he moved within range, she kicked him in the stomach. As weak as she was, she caused little damage. Worse, he latched on to her ankle with minimal effort and laughed.

He laughed harder as he spread her legs and kicked the apex of her thighs, sending painful vibrations through her womb. "You kneed me, and I kicked you. Tit for tat. Everything you do to me, I will do to you, only worse."

"Thanks for permission, asshole." Drawing on a reserve of strength, Fox erupted, bucking and kicking until she knocked him down.

They rolled across the ground, and ended up in a flaming prison. Searing pain! Excruciating agony! The flesh on her left side blistered and melted, and stars winked through her vision. He remained unaffected, punch, punch, punching her face. One of her eyes swelled shut. Her lip split, blood filling her mouth. More stars obscured her line of sight.

Come on! Finish him! He took his next swing. At the last second, she threw herself to the side. He hit air, his momentum propelling him forward. Fighting for every breath, each movement a lesson in torment, Fox crawled toward the empty prison and latched on to the chain. As she hoped, he followed, flipping her over, dropping to his knees, and pinning her legs. A total mistake on his part.

She used the chain like a whip—*thanks for the idea, Thane and Xerxes.* The links wound around Lucifer's neck. Yank. She drove him to the ground face-first. Before he righted himself, she hooked the end of the shackle to the chain itself, securing the links to each other, ensuring he couldn't slither free; he'd have to use a key. A key he probably had in his pocket.

Time wasn't her friend. *Go! Now, now, now.* Did she have enough juice to open a portal?

As Fox lumbered to her feet and raced away, she pressed her fingertips together. Sparks ignited. Not as many as usual, but enough to open a portal, taking her somewhere else. Relief bombarded her. Where should she go? No, *to whom* should she go? Easy. Galen, the man who loved and trusted her. No doubt he was out of his mind with worry. She never wanted to see Bjorn again. He'd turned his back on her when she needed him most, choosing to believe the worst of her. But. *There's always a stupid* but. First, she had to see Bjorn again. One last time. She had to warn him about Lucifer.

It was decided, then. She would issue the warning, then she would leave. Forever.

* * * *

Bjorn came to as familiar voices invaded his mind.

"—out of Water now," Thane was saying. "The next time Alana summons him…"

"We knew this day would come," Xerxes replied, worry roughing up his tone. "At each syphoning, Alana has drained more from him. Without the Water, he won't survive the next visit. I've asked around, but no one is willing to share what little Water they have left."

"We must find a way to break Alana's bond to him, then, without harming him. I know we've tried and failed in the past, but we must have missed something, somewhere."

"As long as he stays in Hell, she will not approach him. Nor can she force him to visit her lair."

Footstep sounded. Someone patted his cheek. He blinked open his eyes to find Xerxes beside him. Thane perched at the edge of the bed.

Bjorn cast his gaze this way and that, but his surroundings proved unfamiliar. He wasn't in a cabin in Hell or a cloud in the heavens but…a room the armies of Sent Ones had built for medical emergencies? Sterile environment, with medical equipment scattered throughout.

He lay upon a gurney, inhaling highly oxygenated air. Another patient slept on the other side of the room. Someone he recognized…who, who?

The answer hit him, and he stiffened. The Warrior Fox had tried to kill.

Fox… Memories assaulted him. Her betrayal…William's attack… The pangs started up again, tearing through his chest.

"How long was I out?" he demanded, jolting upright. "Where is Fox?"

His friends ceased pacing and zoomed to his side.

"You were out for roughly twelve hours," Thane told him.

"We don't know where Fox is being held," Xerxes said. "I'm sorry, Bjorn."

Twelve hours. Twelve hours Fox had been with William, the male who'd disemboweled Bjorn. He fisted his hands. Twelve hours with no leads on her location.

Before this, Bjorn would have bet his life the bastard would have died protecting her. Anything to prove he safeguarded the people under his care. Now? After sensing all the evil that radiated from the guy, Bjorn believed he would *enjoy* harming her.

"We interrogated everyone within the vicinity of William's attack," Xerxes said. "We even spoke to the Warrior in your cabin. Apparently, he decided to kill Fox to save you from her influence. He is currently cuffed to his bed. We saved him for you. Everyone else claimed William flashed Fox away as soon as you fell. No one knows where he took her, but he's been spotted inside his home without her. Actually, there's another woman in there."

He will die screaming! Then the rest of Xerxes' speech registered, and Bjorn went cold. Fox had told the truth. What she'd done to the Sent One, she'd done in self-defense. *And I punished her for it.*

Who deserved punishment more? The Sent One who hoped to right a wrong, or Bjorn, who'd betrayed her trust?

She'd told him this would happen. She'd even told him what would happen after he realized the truth, too. How he would want her back, but she'd have zero interest in a reconciliation.

Panic clawed at him. *I wronged her. I wronged her terribly, and now she's gone.* If he'd done it, if he'd gone through with her murder only to find out she'd told the truth... *Would never forgive myself.*

"No one can understand why William stabbed you and absconded with her," Thane said, his brows knitted together.

"I will find out. Whatever the answer, I will punish him." Sickened and frantic, Bjorn threw his legs over the gurney. He had to find her, apologize and beg for forgiveness.

Xerxes cupped his shoulder to try and ease him back down. "You need rest. Tell us what you want done and we'll take care of it."

"No, I must do this on my own." He'd helped create this mess, and he would be the one to fix it.

Thane's eyes widened. "You love her." A statement rather than a question. "She maddens, irritates and annoys you, just as Elin did to me before I admitted my feelings for her. Yet, there is no one else you would rather hold, yes? No one else you'd rather see or speak with. No one else who makes you smile and laugh."

Yes! "I can't love her. Not really," he croaked with a shake of his head. "The second I believed she betrayed me, part of me considered executing her a good idea. A man in love would have trusted his female."

"Not a man still fighting his feelings," Thane said.

"Bjorn." Xerxes patted his shoulder. "I have watched you with this woman. She has changed you for the better. You laugh and you smile. You are excited to start each day. No longer do you dread the morning. You've grown. Today, you backslid. Tomorrow, you'll do better."

"Not tomorrow. Now. I must find her." Then, whether she took Bjorn back or not, he would speak with Zacharel. She'd done the ten dirty, yes, but the punishment for the crime belonged to Distrust, not Fox, who'd already been whipped, poisoned, stabbed, and stoned.

If Zacharel still insisted on Fox's death, Bjorn could demand *suppono*. He sucked in a breath. Yes. Yes! By demanding *suppono*, he would have a legal right to be Fox's stand-in. He could accept punishment on her behalf, ensuring no other Sent One could harm her for the crime…ever. Bjorn would be dead, but Fox would be free.

Perhaps I do love her.

"And William?" Thane asked. "I am surprised he did anything at all. He's been distracted with his own prisoner."

"He should have stayed distracted. For his actions, William dies today." He unfolded to surprisingly steady legs. Judging by the fresh, clean taste in his mouth, his friends had fed him the last drops of Water of Life. A blessing and a curse. If Fox required the Water in order to survive whatever torments William dished… *Pang.*

Bjorn exited the building, heat engulfing him. Sweat beaded and trickled. He marched through the sea of Sent Ones still building their cabins, menace accompanying his every step. Thane and Xerxes flanked his sides. Wise Warriors jumped out of his path as he made his way to William's fortress. A few members of his army spotted him and rushed to join the procession.

"What are we doing?" one of them whispered to another.

"Does it matter? If our leader fights, we fight."

No guards blocked the entrance, and the doors were unlocked. Bjorn stalked inside without pause, entering a large foyer. He noted the layout of the interior—and the obstacles in his way—with a swift visual sweep. Black-and-white-tiled floor, both covered in gold filigree. A mural depicting a battle in Hell probably had a secret passageway hidden somewhere. A side table with crystal vases filled with roses of every color.

No sign of William or the woman he'd been keeping here.

Palming two daggers—he wouldn't use his sword of fire until he'd discovered Fox's location—Bjorn stomped up a winding staircase. Midway, voices caught his attention. One male, one female, both out of breath. He tensed. He didn't recognize the woman's timbre. Still, he increased his pace, drawing nigh.

When he reached the door—closed and locked—he didn't bother knocking. No, he kicked the door down and stomped inside, shouting, "William! Today you pay for your crimes."

In bed, the dark-haired male jolted upright at the same time as the woman beside him—a delicate-looking beauty with a sheet clutched to her chest. Her hair was a rainbow of colors—no, her hair was silvery white. The change baffled him. Her brown skin glittered as if dusted with diamond powder. Her nails grew into black claws. She was a Gothic fairy tale Barbie come to life.

Relief warred with rage. Fox wasn't in bed with the Ever Randy—a relief. Fox wasn't here, period—rage!

Rage won.

"There's a gun in my nightstand," a naked William informed the female. "If anyone looks at you, give them a Sunny Lane special."

With a voice as sweet as sugar, she asked, "You mean a bullet to the face?" A wicked, wicked smile bloomed—a smile she leveled on Bjorn. "Excellent idea."

William surged to his feet, telling Bjorn, "You have three seconds to exit my bedroom, or you will suffer. Three. Two."

Bjorn remained in place, the rage pulsing from him.

"Very well," William snarled. "You suffer."

"Don't taint your growing bond with Axel by killing his friends," the woman called. "Just spank them a little."

Oh, yes. Axel and William. The immoral world was abuzz with news about their recently admitted familial connection.

William ran his tongue over his teeth and returned his focus to Bjorn. "To which crimes are you referencing?" The woman's words had impact, then. William, a prince of darkness, truly cared about Axel, a Sent One.

"As if you don't know!" The other Sent Ones—everyone but Thane and Xerxes, who knew him best—lined up behind him. "Stay back," he snapped at them. "William is mine." Then, he unleashed a war cry.

The others ignored his order to stand down. Either that, or they were too caught up in battle heat to have heard him. They summoned swords of fire and surged forward, attacking the dark prince in unison.

Bjorn hung back. Disobey an order, and suffer. So, he'd let William teach these Warriors a valuable lesson, *then* he would act.

With a growl, William picked up two daggers that rested atop a pile of clothes. He blocked and slashed the blows launched his way. Blocked. Blocked. Slashed. Then, he stabbed a Sent One in the eye. All the while, a rage very similar to Bjorn's emanated from the prince. Lightning flashed under the surface of his skin, wings of smoke rose from his back, and claws extended from his nail beds.

"Tell me what you think I did," William snarled at Bjorn now.

"Do not pretend ignorance." Adrenaline scorched Bjorn from head to toe as the heat of battle overtook *him*. Screw hanging back. He shoved another Sent One out of the way to leap at William, slashing. One blade nicked William's cheek, blood trickling, yet the bastard grinned. The second blade followed, doing the same, and the POS only grinned wider.

Bjorn blocked a counterstrike. William probably expected him to fight like a typical Sent One, but he didn't. No, oh no. He fought like a True Dread, going for the eyes, throat and groin. The exact same way the dark prince fought.

To his surprise, the male landed as many blows as he received.

William blocked a strike, twisted and tossed a dagger at a portrait on the wall. The moment the blade embedded in the image, spikes shot out from the floor. Multiple Sent Ones stepped on those sharp protrusions and toppled, groaning with shock and pain.

Hissing, Bjorn used his wings to avoid further impaling. Though the massive size of his wings coupled with the limited space worked against him, he hovered in the air. The Warriors still standing followed suit.

One of those Warriors made the mistake of turning his focus to the girl in the bed. William grabbed him and cut his throat from ear to ear, then threw the bloody dagger at the portrait. This time, two short swords popped out from a bed poster.

Palming those hilts, William stabbed one, two, three Sent Ones. Bodies dropped. Blood spurted… everywhere.

All this destruction, and for what? Why had William taken Fox? "You—will—pay." Bjorn spun mid-air and flared his wings as far as they could go, a bone hook protruding from the golden feathers.

The male moved quickly, faster than anyone Bjorn had fought before, but not fast enough. One hook sliced William's cheek, while the other sent him flying back. He crashed against a wall.

One of the two female Sent Ones rushed at William. Or tried to. The silvery-haired woman lifted and aimed a gun. *Boom!* The female flopped to the floor.

Two other Sent Ones ran at William, who'd already climbed to his feet. He went low, raking his claws over one, then the other. They, too, flopped to the floor, where they writhed in agony.

Others approached the prince and received the same treatment.

"Go, William!" the woman on the bed called. "You've got this, baby!"

Seemingly empowered by her cheers, William threw an elbow at Bjorn, who'd thrown his body at the other man. "Tell me what you think I did, or I stop playing nice."

"*You* tell me where she is!" Bjorn's words lashed like a cat o' nine tails.

Slash, parry. "She who?"

Slash, slash. "As if you do not know!"

"I don't." William flapped his smoky wings, jumped up and kicked out, nailing Bjorn in the nose. Cartilage snapped, and a stream of blood spurted. William didn't fall to the floor, not right away, but remained in the air to twist and hurl a dagger between another Sent One's eyes.

As the male collapsed, William opened a portal behind his body, ensuring the Sent One slipped through...and reappeared directly *in front of* William.

The only other female Warrior was in the process of swinging her sword at William, and she could not stop her momentum. Her sword slicked through the Sent One, his intestines spilling out.

Realizing what she'd done, she dropped her sword and gaped, horrified. William lobbed the man's body at her, sending her crashing into the far wall.

"That's what you get," called the woman on the bed.

Bjorn was the last man standing. He and William circled each other in the air.

"I'm guessing the *her* in question is Fox the Executioner," the male said.

Hearing her name spoken in such an irreverent tone only added fuel to the flames of Bjorn's fury. "We saw you stab and grab her." Bjorn swung a dagger, then another, William blocking, then parrying.

"Not me." Swing. Parry. "I haven't stabbed a woman. Not today, anyway."

They plowed into furniture, overturning side tables and chairs. Vases shattered, glass shards flying.

Bjorn scowled and grated, "Do you hope to blame Axel, since you look so much alike?"

"No doubt it was Lucifer, who shape-shifted to look like me," William grated right back. "The same way he shape-shifted into Axel to attack me."

"You lie!"

"Often. But think, you fool. All Sent Ones have the ability to taste lies. What do you taste right now?"

He tasted *a* truth, which didn't mean he tasted *the* truth. But even still, Bjorn halted and lowered his daggers. What if Lucifer had taken Fox? *Then I waste precious time here.* Time that Lucifer could use to do what he did best: rape and torture.

The urge to vomit returned. Lucifer showed no mercy; he maimed and murdered with abandon. Age, gender and species never mattered to him.

Gazing at the carnage wrought in this room, Bjorn withered inside. When he caught the white-haired girl's eye, he withered further. She remained at the edge of the bed, now dressed in a T-shirt, glaring murder at him.

"Tell me everything," William snapped, lowering to the floor and yanking on a pair of leathers so forcefully, he ripped the waistband.

Drowning in foreboding, urgency, and panic, but needing their help, he admitted, "I'd done it. I'd captured her. Fox was my prisoner." Pain coated his words. "She ran from me. You—Lucifer appeared, eviscerated Bjorn and vanished with her."

William scrubbed a hand over his face, looking fatigued. "Apologize to Sunny and vow not to kill Fox, and I'll consider helping you get Fox back."

The need to get to Fox grew, overtaking him completely. Frantic, he blurted, "I apologize for frightening you, for damaging your bedroom, and threatening your man."

She narrowed her eyes. "How dare you!? I was *never* frightened."

Bjorn pivoted back to William and said, "I cannot vow that I won't kill Fox. The order for her death came from Clerici himself. But. I will vow not to kill her without first coming to speak with you." *Or at all.* He ground his teeth. "Agreed?"

The male appeared to be fighting to maintain his stern expression and might have even bitten his tongue to stop a laugh. Why laugh? "Very well. Agreed."

"Tell me where Lucifer keeps—" Bjorn's ears twitched. He heard a commotion outside, the noise drifting through a crack in the window. He thought he detected Fox's name. Heart galloping, he rushed over to peer outside. One look, and horror crept icy fingers down his spine. A bloody, wounded Fox was crawling into camp, cursing anyone who attempted to aid her. "Never mind."

Bjorn hurried from the bedroom, determined to reach his woman.

Chapter Nineteen

More frantic by the second, Bjorn shoved his way through a growing crowd of Sent Ones. As if the Most High reached down from the heavens and swept the soldiers apart, they parted like the Red Sea, a path to Fox opening up.

The moment Bjorn spotted her, more shock, rage and horror stabbed him, slashing his insides. His body shook uncontrollably. She still hadn't rallied the strength to stand; she could only crawl. One of her eyes was swollen shut, blood smeared over the rest of her face. The left side of her body had been scorched, including her hair. Every individual strand looked as if the end had been used as a candlewick.

"Fox!" It was then, in that moment, that the truth hit him so forcefully he nearly toppled over. It was a moment of total clarity unlike any he'd had before. He didn't just care for this woman, and he had been fighting his feelings, allowing fear to dictate his actions. But fear lied and destroyed. Fear never led anyone in the right direction. Fear made you a fool and brutally murdered hope. The same reason he'd lashed out at her earlier. A mistake he could never undo. All he could do? Fight to make it right. Because he loved her with every fiber of his being.

My woman. Mine! The truly startling revelation? He loved Fox the Executioner more than he loved his own life, and he would happily die for her if necessary.

No longer would he let fear take the wheel. No longer would he worry about going all-in and losing her. No more wallowing in betrayal and pain. No more resisting change. Whether or not he loved and lost Fox, he would face betrayal and pain because *life* was pain. And why fight change, when the life you currently lived consisted of misery rather than happiness? Bjorn *needed* change.

He needed Fox.

Cannot imagine a future without her. The words infiltrated his mind, all passion and fire, before solidifying in his bones. *I. Love. Her.* He loved her and craved her nearness in ways he'd never loved or craved another. She didn't just make him smile and laugh; she didn't just blow his mind with every kiss and caress; she didn't just encourage and help him. No, she anchored him in the here and now, rendering the horrors of the past insignificant. An abundance of blessings awaited him—because of her.

Desperate to touch and hold her, to beg for forgiveness, he raced closer. Halfway there, he dove and skidded across the ground. At her side, he blurted, "I'm here, vixen, I'm here." Gently, he drew her into his arms. White-hot tears trickled down his cheeks. "What did he do to you?"

Voice weak and thready, she told him, "He planned to chain me in a graveyard of souls he referred to as his spice rack. I declined. We fought. I escaped. Just don't...don't touch me." She wiggled out of his embrace, and he quashed a thousand protests, each one louder than the last. "I'm here to tell you William isn't William but Lucifer. That's it. Now I'm leaving. If you try to stop me...don't try to stop me, Bjorn."

He flinched as though she'd stabbed him. The outcome of a conversation had never been as important as this one. Giving up wasn't an option for him. "I learned the truth a few moments before your arrival. I went to William, the real William, as soon as I awoke. We fought—" *Not important right now.* Bjorn had a narrow window of time—very narrow—to apologize, to beg, to do whatever proved necessary to win her over. "Don't go. Please don't go. I must know..." What, what? "Is Lucifer dead or on your trail?"

"Not dead. Maybe on my trail. Not sure." She rubbed her temples. "I left him chained, but I suspect he'll escape at any moment, if he hasn't already."

"Do you recall where you left him?" If Lucifer was chained, there was no better time to slay him.

"I barely even have the strength to breathe."

Another pang, this one stronger. "I'm so sorry, vixen. I saw you crouched over an unconscious Sent One, a weapon at the ready, but I should have trusted you." He said the words loudly, for one and all to hear. "You've been—"

"Let me stop you there," she snapped. "You and I are not happening. I came here to warn you, nothing else. If you don't want me to leave, you'd better kill me, because *nothing* will stop me."

Window of time—closed, locked and barred. His panic was resurrected, clawing at him once again. "I will pay you to take me to the Realm of Phantasia. Name your price." Though decades would pass for their friends, the war in the Underworld raging without him, he would have Fox.

"No thanks. Not interested." She offered no qualifiers, no room for negotiation.

His panic sharpened. "I'll pay you to take me to Alana, then." He would kill the woman, ensuring she never threatened Fox again. If he died in the process, he died. No more playing things safe. Look where he ended up when he did. "I'll doctor your wounds and guard you while you rest."

"No." Again, she offered no qualifier. Eyes slitting, she dragged her tongue over her teeth. "I can doctor myself. I just need a place to hang out until I have the power to return to Galen."

Pang, pang, pang. "You may stay in our cabin as long as you desire. Please, Fox. If you don't want me there, I won't come inside. I'll remain outside and ensure no one enters without your express permission. I just need to know you're in a safe place."

She cast him a death-glare. When she tottered, about to pass out, he scooped her up and pushed to his feet. Once again, the Sent Ones parted, creating a pathway. The Warriors who had not attended his meetings stared at him with wide eyes and open mouths. He lifted his chin, unashamed.

Thane and Xerxes stood at the forefront, ready to stop anyone who thought to act against him.

How Bjorn thanked the Most High for those two. The worst experience of his life had led to the best friendships, something beautiful growing from something hideous. Exactly what happened with Fox. Ugly situation, exquisite love. It was time to prove his claims with action.

"This is Fox the Executioner, once a fugitive to our people," he called as he marched on. "Like so many of us, she killed innocents while overcome by the heat of battle. Unlike us, she did it while simultaneously dealing with the demon of Distrust. She has since received forty lashes for her crime, with a whip laced with *infirmədē*. She also received a beating from Lucifer." Not to mention mistrust and betrayal from Bjorn. "If the order to kill her is not rescinded—the order must be rescinded." If not, he would fall. He'd let her down once, but never again. He would do anything to keep his vixen safe. "I love her, and I will protect her with my life. Attempt to harm her, and it will be the last thing you ever do."

She sucked in a breath. "Y-you lie. You cannot love me."

"I can. I do. And I will. Forever."

Slowly she exhaled, and he began to hope...but she didn't speak up again.

"I, too, protect Fox with my life," Thane announced then. "A strike against her is a strike against me."

"I protect Fox with my life," Xerxes called, thumping a fist over his heart. "A strike against her is a strike against me."

My most treasured friends. He'd known they would support him, no matter the path he decided to walk, but this...this went above and beyond.

Bjorn directed his next words directly to Fox, at a much softer volume. "I love you, Fox." He didn't try to hide the emotion, didn't blank his expression or put up new guards because he feared she would issue another rejection. If she rejected him, she rejected him. He would deal accordingly. How she might react wouldn't and shouldn't dictate how he proceeded. If he wanted to keep her—and he desperately wanted to keep her—he had to risk everything.

No risk, no reward.

"I love your sense of humor," he continued, still marching. "I love your fearlessness. I love your mind, and I love your body. I love your honesty and loyalty, both a rare and precious prize. I love your strength, and I love your vulnerability. I love your everything, and I hate the way I treated you and made you feel. You built me up, yet I tore you down."

Though she remained silent, tremors rocked her against him. When he reached the cabin, he shouldered his way inside and carried her to their bed. As gently as possible, he laid her upon the mattress and tucked her under the covers. He sprinted to the bathroom, afraid she would tell him to leave if he took too long; he grabbed and wet a towel to gently, tenderly wipe the soot and blood from her face...collar...arms. When no protests rang out, he took the TLC to the next level, and trimmed the ends of her hair. He didn't want her waking up, smelling the stench of burnt hair, and remembering what happened. Again, she issued no protests.

When he noticed one of her cuts had opened up, blood welling, he collected the droplets as gently as possible. He knew what to do with them. Though he would have severed every limb to climb into bed beside her, he remained standing at the side, telling her, "I will go now, but I will be close. If you have any need of me, you have only to shout and I will come running." Pause. "I am so very sorry, vixen. What I did to you...what I considered doing...there is no excuse. If I could go back...if I could kick my own ass...I am so sorry," he repeated.

Looking past him, she admitted, "I do understand why you thought the worst of me. But you were so cruel and cold, willing to part with me and even let me die. That hurt far worse than your accusations or the whipping."

His chest tightened, constricting his airways. "I will regret my words and actions for the rest of my life, but I will make it up to you. Somehow. I will not stop until I take my last breath. You are an incredible woman, and I love you. I didn't show you before, but I will show you from this moment on." He dropped to his knees. "Never again will I allow past hurts to color my perceptions. Never again will I fear the things you make me feel. Never again will I doubt you."

"Easy to say. Harder to do." Though she opened her mouth to say more, she quickly pressed her lips into a thin line, released him, and rolled to her side, showing her back. *Deserved.* "Tired. Going to sleep now."

Heart heavy, he placed two daggers on the nightstand closest to her, wanting her to feel safe. He also added the drops of blood he collected to the bloodline, saying, "Around the house, there is a bloodline. That is what prevented you from portaling. But now that I've added your blood to the mix, your powers will be restored to you fully."

Her eyes widened. He said nothing more, just strode to the porch and took a post in front of the door. Had he lost this battle? Yes. Badly. Would he lose the next one? Probably so. Would he give up? Never! He would work up a game plan. One way or another, he would win back Fox, and have the happily ever after he'd never before expected.

* * * *

Shouts woke Fox. With a gasp, she jackknifed to an upright position. Took her a moment to orient herself. She was in the cabin...after returning to Bjorn...after being abducted by Lucifer... after being accused of a crime she hadn't committed. Tears burned her eyes and blurred her vision. *Ugh! When did I become such a baby?*

The shouting had stopped, at least. Maybe she'd dreamed it?

With a sigh, she flopped backward, reclining on the mound of pillows. Silvery moonlight seeped through the room's only window. Getting back to sleep would be impossible, her mind too active, her emotions too raw. She should go on emotional lockdown but...she kind of wanted to embrace the pain. Maybe then she would wise up and refuse to go back to Bjorn...who she still craved more than air.

He claimed to love her. Her! He claimed to want a second chance with her, and he'd openly acknowledged his feelings in front of his peers, as if proud to be with her. As if a Sent One and a demon-possessed assassin weren't the oddest couple ever.

Should she give him another chance, though? Did he truly love her, or did he simply feel guilty for the way he'd treated her? Could two opposites have a fulfilling life together?

Don't be a fool. He'll never trust you. You'll get hurt again, only worse.

Stupid Distrust! She sprayed a little mental Windex on her brain, and wiped away her every thought. That was when little aches and pains registered in different places on her body. No doubt she had a couple of broken ribs, a bruised liver and kidneys, and a fractured wrist. Thankfully, she'd healed quite a bit.

"You *will* come with me, Bjorn." Alana's voice seeped through the window. "Do not even consider resisting. I'm in a *mood*."

Horror inundated Fox. The shouts. The shouts had come from her. Realization: the bitch *had* come to Hell. She prepared to take Bjorn back to her lair, no doubt to drain his life-force again. And, as angry as Alana sounded, she'd probably take more than before. Would he recover?

Foreboding prickled the back of her neck. *Can't let her leave with him. Not this time.*

Heart thudding, Fox jumped up and raced to the closet. At some point, Bjorn must have returned to the cabin and changed her. No longer did she wear her singed, smoke-scented clothing. A pink tank graced her up top, and a pair of boxers covered her intimate area below. She donned a pair of boots and spun, searching for a weapon, any weapon. There! The daggers Bjorn left on the nightstand. She swiped them up and hurried to the front door—closed.

Bjorn's voice sounded at last. Unlike Alana, he maintained a moderate tone.

"I will not be going with you, Alana. I will not be supplying you with power at the expense of my life. I will not act like your husband—I am not. You forced a bond and now, I want no part of it. I am disgusted by you. You repulse me in every way. No one is uglier on the inside. To be honest, I would rather die than touch you. I am *willing* to die to end our bond."

Bjorn, dead… No, no, no! They weren't on the best of terms right now, but Fox didn't want him dead. She wanted…she wanted…

Argh! She didn't know what she wanted anymore. Before he'd tenderly washed her body, painstakingly trimmed her hair, and pledged to fight for her forgiveness, she'd been ready to cut him from her life. Now the thought of losing him sent her into a panic.

What if they *could* have a fulfilling life together?

Distrust whispered, *You cannot.*

Fox fisted the sheets. For too long, she'd either listened to the fiend or fought to ignore him. Today, she fought back. *You speak your lies to crack the foundation of truth I stand upon, ensuring I will crumble. Bjorn speaks truth, always. If he thinks we can make this work, I choose to trust him.*

Only setting yourself up for pain and failure…

No. I'm setting myself up for love and joy. Alana was going to get the stinky boot. And one day, Distrust would, too. She'd thought to use the phantoms to cleanse Bjorn of the queen's bond. What if she used them to cleanse *her* of Distrust? Or any of the Lords of the Underworld who were interested?

The demon panicked, clawing at her mind.

She grinned. If *she* bonded to someone else, she would survive, avoiding the Gatekeeper death as she'd hoped for so long.

Will Bjorn wish to bond with me?

"It's the girl," Alana hissed, breaking into Fox's thoughts. "You're doing this for her."

"You will stay away from her!" He hadn't moderated his voice this time. No, he'd let his fury ring loud and clear.

Fox nearly melted to the rug as feminine power flooded her. Oh, yes. This man loved her and craved a future with her. He would bond with her. *And I will be his knight in shining armor!*

How to proceed? *With caution! Not at my healthiest. Think!* Should she bust out there and just start whaling on Alana? Then what? Usually, Fox followed a target for days, weeks, before ever making a move; the more she knew about their personalities, habits, likes and dislikes, the better the likelihood of her success. But, at the end of the day, she always had to make do with what she had. So. What did she know about Alana? In other words, what did she have to work with this time around?

Alana was selfish, greedy, and probably a sociopath. She survived off of other people's life-forces. She was the Queen of Shadows—

That! That was the key. The answer slapped Fox silly. Shadows equaled darkness. What if Fox imprisoned Alana in a realm without darkness? If the female weakened in sunlight, Bjorn would weaken, too. But. He would have time to go to Phantasia without Alana's interference.

Do not do this, the demon pleaded. *You're too weak to win. Alana will kill you, and then Bjorn.*

Hardly. But then, he'd say anything to stop her. *Go exorcise yourself.*

As calmly and quietly as possible, Fox opened the front door and leaned into the open frame—a floorboard squeaked, ruining her efforts. Both Bjorn and Alana swung around to face her.

She raised her chin. Not wanting to be distracted, she purposely avoided Bjorn's gaze as she told him, "I'm sorry, baby, but this is going to hurt you." Then she faced the glaring, scowling Alana and smiled coldly. "Hello and goodbye. It hasn't been nice knowing you." That said, she tossed one of the daggers. Aim: Alana's heart.

Chapter Twenty

Fox's dagger whooshed through the air. Time ticked by in slow-motion as Bjorn watched, astounded by the turn of events. The blade sank into Alana's heart, dead center. Thanks to their bond, pain exploded through *his* chest. He saw stars.

Alana screamed and stumbled back. Fox didn't miss a beat. She opened a portal behind the woman. Unfortunately, Alana stopped just before she passed through it...until Fox dove at her, the two flinging out of Hell and into a sunny flatland. They rolled across the ground, throwing punches and elbows. As soon as they stopped, Fox yanked the blade from Alana's body. Black blood spurted from the wound, quickly soaking the queen's torso.

Bright rays of sunshine blistered Alana's skin. And Bjorn's. Weakness poured through him; the same weakness that poured through Alana, though his was much, much worse. She used their bond to steal more of his strength.

While he still had the necessary juice, he shouted telepathically for his friends. *Thane! Xerxes! I need you.* They'd come. He knew it.

Even as his knees threatened to buckle, he tripped to the portal. The two women lumbered to their feet, the fight continuing without pause. More punches and kicks. Daggers and claws slashed. Neither opponent held back, grunts and groans ringing out.

Alana didn't have a tenth of Fox's combat skill. Having always relied on her ability to possess and drain, she'd refused to learn *how* to war. So, she received more blows than she landed, and Bjorn felt every single one. He didn't care. He would happily suffer as long as it led to Alana's defeat.

The problem was, Fox noticed his poor condition and began to hesitate before delivering any shots.

Bjorn rejoiced. *I still have a chance with her!*

Unfortunately, Alana noticed the reason for Fox's hesitation, too, and grated, "The more you hurt me, the more you hurt Bjorn. Right now, he feels as though a thousand little soldiers are marching through his veins, slashing *everything*. Panic must be enveloping his mind in an icy fog…"

Fox grated back, "I'm certain he'll forgive me when I present him with your severed head."

"You fool!" Alana threw a punch and missed. "If I die, he dies."

"Who said I'm going to kill you today?" Going low, Fox swiped out her arm, as if she intended to knock the queen's legs together. Instead, she slicked a dagger across Alana's ankles, nicking the tibial artery. "Maybe I have something else in mind…"

Dizziness nearly toppled him as he bent to withdraw the dagger from the sheath strapped to his calf. *Deep breath in. Hold, hold. Slowly exhale.* Good, that was good. The dizziness faded just enough to steady his aim. He tossed the dagger, and the blade sank into Alana's throat.

Fox screamed a denial as Alana gasped and stumbled back. Now struggling to fill his lungs, Bjorn collapsed. He wheezed, his body wracked by searing agony. *Can't pass out. Must stay awake!* If Fox needed him…

Unleashing a war cry, Fox attacked Alana with more vigor, aggressive as hell and all the sexier for it. Moving quickly. Slashing those daggers. Slice, slice, slice. Blood trickled from the new cuts and gashes as they appeared on his shoulders, abdomen and thighs. The air-less Alana couldn't keep up and tripped over a rock. Unable to halt her momentum, she fell.

Fox dove on top of her. In a one, two motion, she planted a dagger in both of the queen's shoulders, pinning her down. As the bitch bowed her back and screamed, Fox snarled, "I'm going to trap you in this realm of perpetual sunshine until your forced bond with Bjorn is negated."

No. Absolutely not. Alana could not be allowed to live another minute, much less the years he would be forced to spend on Phantasia. Too much risk. If she escaped and summoned her army of Shadow warriors, Fox would be in danger the rest of her life—however long it lasted.

Where were her Shadow warriors *now?* Why weren't they with her, protecting her? For that matter, where had they been during Bjorn's final visit to her lair?

"Let me go!" Alana shouted. "Let me go!"

Fox stood beside her thrashing body. He used the final drop of his strength to crawl to the females. As soon as she saw him up close, Fox released a ragged sound he'd only ever heard from wounded animals.

"Oh, Bjorn. I'm so sorry." Guilt laced her voice, and he hated that.

"You are not to feel shame, vixen. This is not your fault."

"I... I love you. I did my best to avoid harming you." Tears spilled down her cheeks. "Now you're bruised, broken and bleeding."

Oh, yes. She would give him another chance. One he would not take for granted. She loved him. Loved. Him. The knowledge redoubled his certainty—he was doing the right thing. Time and time again, he'd hurt her, but now...now he would help her the only way he knew how. She deserved a happily ever after, and he would do everything in his power to ensure she got it.

"I love you, too, vixen. Always and forever."

Alana went still, though she continued heaving panting breaths. She looked between Bjorn and Fox, rage mottling her cheeks. "Love?" she sneered.

He maneuvered to his haunches, raised his arms, a sword of fire appearing in his hand.

"Wh-what are you doing?" Alana demanded now. "Bjorn, don't do this. You'll kill me, but you'll also kill yourself."

"You are *not* doing this," Fox barked, latching on to his wrist. "Don't do this. Please don't do this!"

I must. No other way. "Tell me where your soldiers are," he demanded of Alana.

"They are on their way here," she told him, and laughed, gleeful. "Your whore will be the first to die!"

A foul taste inundated his tongue. A lie. She'd told a lie. His eyes widened. "They are not coming to your rescue, which means, they are imprisoned or dead." Nothing else would keep her minions away. Unless... "You sold them. You sold them to Lucifer to...what? Buy a ticket to Hell. No. Buy Fox's abduction and murder."

Her gaze skidded elsewhere, anywhere but him, and he knew. She had. She had sold her minions to hurt Fox. Done with her, he raised the sword higher and struck, the fiery blade whooshing through Alana's neck, removing her head.

Now, Fox would live.

As Alana's body went lax, Bjorn's world went dark. The last thought to blast through his mind before he dropped face-first to the ground: *Worth it.*

* * * *

With a scream, Fox threw herself at Bjorn's body to feel for a pulse. It was there, but unbearably weak and concerningly slow.

Thane and Xerxes came rushing through the portal. Crouching around their friend, they exuded panic, horror, and fury.

Thane pressed what looked to be an empty vial at Bjorn's mouth, explaining, "We purchased a single drop of Water of Life from a Sent One named Axel. It cost us the Downfall, but saving Bjorn is worth any price. The drop will buy Bjorn a few minutes...maybe."

"Then I have less than a few minutes to save him," Fox said, doing her best to stay calm. She just, she had to save him. "He needs a new bond. I volunteer. But I need him to awaken and pledge his eternal loyalty to me." His safety wouldn't be guaranteed—the bond might kill her instead of save him, thereby killing him, too—but he would for sure die if they didn't try.

She patted his cheek. When he failed to rouse, she slapped him with every bit of her might...

He fluttered open his eyes, and their gazes met. Yes! His irises were glazed over, and he couldn't focus, but he had awoken and that was all that mattered.

"Hey, baby," she said softly, caressing his jaw. "Alana is dead, and you're dying." No reason to hide the truth. "We must forge a bond between us. You'll be saved—"

"No." He thrashed his head, and she reared back, stunned and hurt, the wound soul-deep, even though a part of her had suspected the rejection.

"T-then I'll find you someone else. Just tell me who you want, and I'll portal to her," she rushed out. She would rather he live without her than die. "Remember, timing is critical."

No, no, no, the demon chanted. He prowled through her mind, his claws sinking deeper into her brain, drawing blood. *A Sent One and a demon-possessed assassin? Bjorn will never forgive you for bonding him to evil.*

Oh, crap. She hadn't thought about what would happen if Bjorn bonded to a demon-possessed woman. Yes, she hoped to remove the fiend. But...what if he grew to resent her for the link?

"Do not want...any other woman...I want you...but if... we... bond...and I die...you die, too." He spoke between panting breaths. "I would rather...die than cause...you harm."

Melting. This. This was love. Any lingering hurts faded, new tears streaming down her cheeks. "We won't die, baby." *Ticktock, ticktock.* Those few minutes were running out fast. "Trust me this time." She took his hand and squeezed, then lifted his arm to flatten his palm against her tear-stained cheek. "Trust me," she repeated. "I know you'll have a bond to someone who is demon-possessed, but we'll find a way to make it work. And I've been thinking. Maybe, once I'm bound to you, Distrust can be removed from me—no, never mind. Then I would need to draw from your immortality to survive, and I won't use you as Alana did." Frustration mounted.

"Want you...to draw from me...want to provide...for you."

Melting faster. The man who hated risks was considering her offer? *Another example of his love for me!* "I want you to know that I forgive you for doubting me. We're still learning each other. I also want you to know I'm going to be changing my entire business model. I'd like to become the official Gatekeeper for the Sent Ones...and take the occasional job killing demons." She'd loved aiding Bjorn and his army, and looked forward to doing it again and again.

"But I won't...risk you," he continued, as if she hadn't spoken.

Fox wilted. Unlike Alana, she wouldn't, couldn't force this bond on him. He had to say the words willingly. But she didn't want to pressure him in any way. So, how was she supposed to proceed?

"You love this woman, and she loves you." Thane's deep voice rang out, more bite than bark. "She wants to save you. Therefore, you will let her."

"You will do this, Bjorn," Xerxes commanded. "Or I will follow you to the hereafter, leaving Thane and Elin heartbroken."

In that moment, Fox forgave the pair for their horrendous treatment of her. They'd always had Bjorn's best interests at heart, and she could not fault them for it.

Would that stop her from forever tormenting them about the whipping? Not even a little.

Bjorn opened his mouth to respond, but the words got lost amid a wheezing cough. A death wheeze. His eyelids slid closed, and his head lolled to the side.

I'm losing him. Fox didn't give Bjorn a chance to decline again. Panicked, she slapped his cheek until he opened his eyes once again. "Your friends have spoken. You are doing this, Bjorn." Then, she sliced the center of her palm, blood welling. "I pledge my life and my future to you, Bjorn the One True Dread."

To her astonishment, and delight, he did not hesitate. "I pledge...my life...and my future...to you...Fox the Executioner." He was still panting, his volume lowering more and more.

Since he didn't have the strength to cut his own palm, Xerxes made the cut for him. Fox twined her fingers with Bjorn's to mix their blood, then placed their bleeding hands over his mouth, ensuring the blood dripped down his throat. She did the same for herself, swallowing the metallic drops.

It wasn't the prettiest or most elegant of ceremonies, but it was quick and unadorned. Her preference. "Is something more supposed to happen?" she asked the boys. Having never bonded before—

"Just wait," Thane said. "As soon as the blood hits—"

Bowing her back, she threw back her head and screamed. The pain! She felt every wound that littered Bjorn's body, and oh, how had he survived this? She thrashed. *Too much, too much.*

The demon quieted, as if he'd been muzzled. *Had* he been muzzled?

Her thoughts dimmed, darkness creeping through her mind. She thought someone swept her into his strong arms and carried her away...thought that same someone laid her upon a soft bed. By then, the pain had begun to recede. She became more aware of her surroundings. Thane had carried her, and Xerxes had carried Bjorn, who now lay beside her. His essence filled her mind and her heart. No, all of him filled all of her. She was no longer Fox. She was Fox and Bjorn. She *felt* his great love for her, and oh, it was pure, precious, and all-consuming.

"His heartbeat grows stronger by the second," Xerxes said, his relief palpable.

"Hers, too," Thane replied.

"They will both recover, and all will be well."

They laughed, making her smile. Fox blinked open her eyes. The cabin Bjorn had built. The master bedroom to be exact, the only door closed. There was no sign of Thane and Xerxes. But, but...*they were just here.*

Bjorn lay at her side, as she'd suspected, and he too blinked open his eyes. As soon as their gazes met, they launched at each other, hugging, kissing, crying.

"I'm so sorry, vixen. I'm so sorry. I hurt you—"

"I expected too much too fast, and I should have—"

"No, no, you did nothing wrong. But I did. I doubted you when you needed me most."

"Why don't we blame Alana for all our problems, hmm?" She curled into him, clinging to this man she adored. "I love you, Bjorn."

"I love you, too, vixen. So much." He caressed his fingertips down the ridges of her spine. "Always and forever."

"Always and forever," she echoed, smiling a genuine smile for the first time since their blow up.

Their relationship might have had a rocky start, and they might have made a crap-ton of mistakes, but through it all, Bjorn had been a source of comfort, strength, amusement, and lust. He would forever be a source of comfort, strength, amusement and lust.

With the Elite at her side, the future would be a wild ride, and she looked forward to every moment.

Epilogue

"Welcome, welcome." Fox stepped back, moving out of the open doorway of her cabin. The one she now shared with Bjorn. Their home. She'd officially moved in, with the full approval of Clerici, Zacharel, Thane and Xerxes. "You're only an hour late."

"We're five minutes late," Galen said.

"No. If you're not ten minutes early, you're five minutes late. But, if you're more than a minute late, you're an hour late. The math checks." Fox batted her lashes, all sugar and spice.

The Sent Ones behind her laughed. They kind of loved her now. She'd sparred with Lucifer, and won, after all, and she'd warned others of his tricks. Was he defeated for good? No. But their chances for success were better now.

Galen and Legion strode inside the cabin, hugged her and focused on Bjorn, who remained at her side. He liked to keep her within his sights. Apparently, when the big guy loved, he *loved*. He guarded her with his life, just as she guarded his.

There were Lords and Ladies of the Underworld here, Pandora, Baden, and his wife Katarina, as well as a multitude of Sent Ones and a handful of Kings. They were mingling like old friends, and Fox loved every second of it.

Look at me. Some kind of glamorous Underworld hostess. "Hey, you," she called, pointing at William the Ever Randy. The real William. "Put down the motorized axe I'm building. It's for Bjorn."

"I accept, thank you," William said unabashed, sliding the axe under his suit jacket.

"You," Galen spat at Bjorn, forcing her attention back to the entryway.

"Yes. Me," Bjorn said with a nod, simply stating a fact.

Fox smothered a smile with her hand. "Bjorn has more than made up for abducting me." She patted her man's muscled chest. "I invited you guys into our home because I'd like you to bury the hatchet, just not in each other."

Legion elbowed Galen and moved in front of him to offer her hand to Bjorn. When he accepted, she flipped him to his back, dropping him to the floor. Then she rubbed her hands together in a job well done and walked deeper into the cabin. "Are there whore-derves? I'm starved."

Fox couldn't hide her smile this time. "My hors d'oeuvres consist of ambrosia-laced whiskey with decadent notes of take it or leave it." She helped Bjorn to his feet.

"Knew she was going to do that," he muttered, wrapping an arm around Fox's waist, and she laughed outright.

"Sure you did, baby." She patted his bulging biceps, maybe gave it a little squeeze, and nibbled on her bottom lip. Could they sneak off for a quickie?

The two men faced off once again.

No. No quickie.

"Thank you for taking care of Fox as a child," Bjorn said next, clearly shocking her mentor. "She told me everything you've done for her over the years, and I am in your debt."

What!?

Galen narrowed his eyes. "Don't think thanking me will save you from my wrath. You made me worry, and for that—"

Fox swiped out her arm and flipped Galen over her head, just as Legion had done to Bjorn. She peered down at the closest thing to a father she'd ever had. "You made me worry over Legion. Bjorn made you worry over me. You're even. Now, let's all kiss and make up and get this welcome-to-the-family party started."

To her surprise, Bjorn helped Galen stand and Galen let him. Neither protested.

"You didn't let me finish. Now, then. As I was saying," Galen continued with a grumble in his tone, "for that, you'll have to deal with Fox for the rest of your life, you poor sucker."

She rolled her eyes, and Bjorn grinned. Actually grinned.

"I do not have to," her man said. "I *get* to."

And that, right there, was one of the reasons she loved him so much. She rose on her tiptoes to kiss his cheek and whisper, "We are going to have the best life, baby."

"This, I know. With you, I can have nothing less." He kissed her then, swift and sure, and she forgot their audience. Until said audience cheered.

As she and Bjorn stopped kissing and started laughing, her heart swelled with contentment. "The party has been fun," she called, "but it's over now. Everyone go. Bjorn and I have things to do."

Everyone else laughed, too, and continued conversing with each other. Fox and Bjorn stood in place, watching their friends interact. Two groups who never should have been friends, now working together to take down the world's greatest evil.

She rested her head on Bjorn's shoulder. "Thank you for gifting me with this." A family of her own.

"My pleasure, love. With you, it's always my pleasure."

THE END

* * * *

Also from 1001 Dark Nights and Gena Showalter, discover The Darkest Captive.

Sign up for the 1001 Dark Nights Newsletter
and be entered to win a Tiffany Key necklace.

There's a contest every month!

Go to www.1001DarkNights.com to subscribe.

**As a bonus, all subscribers can download
FIVE FREE exclusive books!**

Discover 1001 Dark Nights Collection Six

Go to www.1001DarkNights.com to subscribe.

DRAGON CLAIMED by Donna Grant
A Dark Kings Novella

ASHES TO INK by Carrie Ann Ryan
A Montgomery Ink: Colorado Springs Novella

ENSNARED by Elisabeth Naughton
An Eternal Guardians Novella

EVERMORE by Corinne Michaels
A Salvation Series Novella

VENGEANCE by Rebecca Zanetti
A Dark Protectors/Rebels Novella

ELI'S TRIUMPH by Joanna Wylde
A Reapers MC Novella

CIPHER by Larissa Ione
A Demonica Underworld Novella

RESCUING MACIE by Susan Stoker
A Delta Force Heroes Novella

ENCHANTED by Lexi Blake
A Masters and Mercenaries Novella

TAKE THE BRIDE by Carly Phillips
A Knight Brothers Novella

INDULGE ME by J. Kenner
A Stark Ever After Novella

THE KING by Jennifer L. Armentrout
A Wicked Novella

QUIET MAN by Kristen Ashley
A Dream Man Novella

ABANDON by Rachel Van Dyken
A Seaside Pictures Novella

THE OPEN DOOR by Laurelin Paige
A Found Duet Novella

CLOSER by Kylie Scott
A Stage Dive Novella

SOMETHING JUST LIKE THIS by Jennifer Probst
A Stay Novella

BLOOD NIGHT by Heather Graham
A Krewe of Hunters Novella

TWIST OF FATE by Jill Shalvis
A Heartbreaker Bay Novella

MORE THAN PLEASURE YOU by Shayla Black
A More Than Words Novella

WONDER WITH ME by Kristen Proby
A With Me In Seattle Novella

THE DARKEST ASSASSIN by Gena Showalter
A Lords of the Underworld Novella

Also from 1001 Dark Nights:
DAMIEN by J. Kenner

Discover More Gena Showalter

The Darkest Captive: A Lords of the Underworld Novella

For centuries, Galen the Treacherous has been the most hated immortal in the Underworld. With good reason! This bad boy of bad boys has lied, stolen, cheated and killed with abandon. Possessed by the demons of Jealousy and False Hope, he has always lived for a single purpose: destroy *everything*.

Then he met *her*.

Former demon turned human femme fatale — Legion Honey -- sought to kill Galen, but ended up parting with her virginity instead. Afraid of their sizzling connection, she ran away...and ended up trapped in hell, tortured and abused in the worst of ways. Now she's free, and a shell of herself, afraid of her own shadow.

Galen's hunger for Legion has only grown. Now the warrior with nothing to lose must help her rekindle the fire that once burned inside her. But as desires blaze white-hot, will Legion run again? Or will the unlikely pair succumb to love at long last?

The Darkest King

Lords of the Underworld, Book 15
By Gena Showalter,
Coming February 25, 2020

Read on for a special preview from the next book in Gena Showalter's scorching Lords of the Underworld series featuring William the Ever Randy, *The Darkest King*.

A merciless prince feared by all...

Cursed by a vengeful witch, William of the Dark will die if he ever falls in love—murdered by the woman who steals his heart. His lone shot at redemption is a book filled with indecipherable code. Break the code, break the curse. Now, centuries later, he's condemned to a string of one-night stands...until he finds the only woman in the worlds able to set him free.

A rare creature of myth and power...

One of the last living unicorn shifters, Sunday "Sunny" Lane works from the shadows as a cryptanalyst, on the run from assassins and poachers. Then the darkly seductive William abducts her, holding her captive in Hell. The closer they get, the more she hungers for his touch...and the stronger a mystical desire to kill him becomes...

Both forever doomed?

At war with his brother, Lucifer, and determined to become a king of the underworld at long last, William must resist the irreverent beauty who threatens his future. But every day Sunny tempts him more, his hunger for her unmatched. Will he risk his heart—and his life—or will the curse ensure his end?

* * * *

Sipping sugar water from a wineglass all classy-like, Sunday "Sunny" Lane meandered through a shadowy hotel bar teeming with youngish and oldish codebreakers, hackers and hobbyists. Most were humans who'd flown into New York City early that morning to network and party before the world's premiere cryptanalyst conference kicked off tomorrow. Her longtime friend…er, acquaintance Sable remained at her side. The six-foot black beauty came from the same realm and ancient village as Sunny.

They'd come to set honeytraps for any immortals who hunted their kind.

A waiter approached with a bottle of white. "May I refill your drink, ma'am?"

Ma'am? The worst insult known to womankind.

Able to read auras, she easily distinguished immortals from humans. The waiter was human. "No, thanks," she said. "As a self-appointed superhero and proud vigilante, I prefer to stay sober and scumbag-aware." *Asterhole.*

Sunny was born with an innate magic that prevented her from cursing, changing obscenities into flowers. "Daisy" replaced *daisy. Argh! D.a.m.n.* "Hellebore" replaced *h.e.l.l.* "Sage" replaced *s.h.i.t.* "Bluebell" replaced *b.a.s.t.a.r.d.* and *b.i.t.c.h.* "Aster" replaced *a.s.s.*, and "freesia" replaced *f.u.c.k.*

The waiter offered her an unsure smile before rushing off.

"Here's hoping the duality serves us well tonight." Sable clinked her glass of sugar water against Sunny's.

Oh, yes. The duality. Half their nature longed to hunt and kill baddies, whether immortal or human. That part of her—Horror Show Sunny—worked as an assassin. A girl needed a purpose, right? The other half demanded they spread love, joy and peace. She'd dubbed that part Roses and Rainbows Sunny, and worked as a decoder.

The two sides were forever locked in a brutal tug-of-war.

"I posted online to let the world know I'd be here," Sunny said, fingering the medallion that hung at her neck. Her most prized possession, capable of feats few could imagine.

As an extremely rare "mythical" creature, they had to remain armed at all times. Poachers hunted them for sport, and collectors hunted them for pleasure. Little wonder Sunny trusted no one, not even Sable, and never stayed in one location more than a couple weeks. She constantly looked over her shoulder and rarely slept.

"If anyone attacks," Sable began.

"They die screaming."

Crackling with excitement, Sable gulped back the rest of her water and set her glass aside. "Once we've eliminated the poachers and collectors, we won't have to worry about being ambushed every second of every day. We can turn our sights to the underworld royals."

"All nine kings, and every last prince of darkness." Two princes of darkness in particular topped her list. Lucifer the Destroyer, and William the Ever Randy. Even their names filled her with blistering rage. The terrible things Lucifer had done to her people…things he'd done while shouting, "For William!"

The two might be at war now, but they'd been inseparable back then.

Focus up. You're here for a purpose, remember? Right. Sunny scanned the sea of faces. Some attendees ambled from group to group. Some remained in place, talking, laughing and generally clogging the pathways. Others stayed at their table, nursing drinks. Many were relaxed and at ease. Oh, to be so uninvolved, unconcerned and untouched by the world's evil, as oblivious to the surrounding danger as everyone else. Sunny couldn't recall a time she'd ever felt safe.

Somewhere in the bar, glass shattered. Both Sunny and Sable jolted.

Deep breath in, out. Good, that's good.

"I'm so ready to stop running and live without fear," she muttered. She'd buy a house and plant a garden. Adopt a dog and a cat. The oldest, crankiest, ugliest mutt and tom at the pound. She'd go on a date for the first time in years…decades…probably centuries; she just had to find the right guy. Someone willing to put in the work to earn her trust. Then, she'd never again have to suffer through mating season alone. A time of clawing, gnawing, uncontrollable sexual arousal.

The next one kicked off in only two weeks.

"Me, too," Sable said. "I'm ready to stop chaining myself in a locked room so that I won't jump unsuspecting or unwilling males."

"Yes!"

"One day, I'm going to melt those chains, and make them into a butt plug. I'll gift it to Lucifer before I kill him."

Sunny snickered. "I like the way your mind works."

The deeper they ventured into the bar, the more perfumes that clashed. Flicking lights illuminated a sea of unfamiliar faces. Human. Human. Human. Vampire. Witch. Human. Human. Human. Werewolf. Though no one seemed to pay them any undue attention, Sunny kept a wary eye on the immortal trio.

Until husky male laughter snagged her attention.

Warm shivers raced down her spine, and she frowned. What a strange reaction to something so ordinary. Yes, his voice was sexy hot, but she'd heard hotter. Surely!

Sunny scanned the bar—there! Him. Though she couldn't see his face, she knew he was the one. He had thick black hair, broad shoulders and a unique aura. One she couldn't read.

He threw back his head, laughing again, and a new tide of shivers raced down her spine.

"Daisy," she muttered.

The woman on his left leaned in to whisper in his ear. The woman on his right ran a hand all over his back.

He was the meat in a flesh sandwich.

Finally he shifted, presenting Sunny with his profile. She sucked in a ragged breath.

A woman never forgot a face like his. *Hello, William the Ever Randy, brother to Lucifer.* The bluebell.

He looked tailor-made, as if every feature had been chosen from a catalog. *I'll take that face, that hair and those eyes. Oh, and don't forget those muscles.* He had flawless bronzed skin, jet-black hair and eyes like a sapphire-diamond hybrid framed by long, spiky lashes. Broad cheekbones tapered to a strong jaw shadowed with dark stubble. Perfect nose, perfect lips, perfect *everything—to everyone in the world but her.*

"What? What's wrong?" Sage asked, already reaching for the dagger hidden beneath her sleeveless jacket.

Rage sparked, quickly catching fire. "Look." She motioned to William.

Had he heard about their vendetta against his family and come to stop them? Why else would he be here? And why not sneak up on them?

"Speak of the devil," Sable ground out, "and he appears."

Sunny had done her research. She knew William was an infamous mercenary and legendary womanizer who disdained the sanctity of marriage. A few years ago, he'd helped slay a god king. More recently, he'd gotten drunk at a nightclub and shouted, "I consider myself a pleasuretarian. I only eat organic pussy." *Cat.* Only, he hadn't used the word "cat," like she had to do to bypass the stupid, magical filter.

"If rumors are true," she said, "he sleeps with a new woman every night, possesses a fiery temper, sometimes injures his friends for laughs and enjoys killing his enemies as painfully as possible." So much to admire. So much to disdain.

"In that case, I think we should rearrange our list of hits, and take out the royal first, while we've got the chance."

"Agreed. One way or another, William the Ever Randy will die today." *Vengeance will be mine!* "Problem. I can't read his aura. Can you?"

"I…can't," Sable said, and frowned.

Daisy! "Despite tons of research, I failed to learn his true origins or species, so I don't know what strengths to guard against or what weaknesses to exploit."

"Well, no matter. We'll find out." Sable chewed on her bottom lip. "He's beautiful, though, isn't he?"

"He is." *Beautiful beyond imagining.* And oh, the admission grated. Sunny did her best to ignore the flutter in her belly. "He looks like an incubus, ready to lure unsuspecting women into his bed." *Was* he an incubus?

Arrogance and sensuality clung to him like a second skin.

Heart thudding, she dragged her gaze over the rest of him. Mmm, mmm, mmm. Had she ever seen such a perfect example of raw, rugged sex appeal? Such a deliciously large muscle mass? A black shirt molded to his bulging biceps, and black leathers clung to powerful things. On his feet, combat boots.

When he shifted a little more, she saw the writing on his shirt. It read, Check Out the Cypher in My Pants. When he draped on arm around each woman, she spotted the metal cuffs on his wrists and the spiked rings on his fingers. Or rather, the weapons on his fingers. But so what? She had a weapon-ring, too: a tiny gun with brass pinfire rounds.

He threw back his head and laughed a third time. The fires of rage grew into an inferno. "After the terrible things he and his brother did to our people, *innocent* people, he deserves misery."

"Agreed."

With movements as sexy as hellebore, he lifted a glass of whiskey to his lips.

Swallowing a moan, Sunny switched her attention to the females at his table. There were three, and they hung on his every word. Sunny recognized two of them. Their screen names were Jaybird and Cash, and they were cryptanalysts, like her.

Jaybird touched her lips to draw his gaze there. Cash leaned forward, putting her wealth of cleavage on display.

"Dude. They have the art of the flirt nailed, and I kind of want their autographs." Both Horror Show Sunny and Roses and Rainbows Sunny sucked at flirting.

She set her glass on a table and led Sable into a shadowy spot beside a potted plant, so they could plan their attack.

"—yeah, man, it's true," the man near the table was saying to a group of his friends. "I kicked the sage—" Pause. "Sage." He frowned. "Why can't I say *sage*?"

His companions guffawed, as if he were teasing. One even elbowed him in the sternum.

Oops. Sunny and Sable's magic filters prevented *anyone* from cursing in their presence. On the flip side, their magic stopped people from speaking lies, as well.

Gotta take the bad with the good.

"How should we play this?" Sunny tossed a flower petal into her mouth and—oh, hellebore! She'd been eating leaves and petals this entire time, the potted plant almost bare. Bad Sunny! This wasn't snack time. She dropped the remaining foliage and dusted the dirt from her fingers. *Anyway.*

"I think we should go in hot. A real ambush. He won't see it coming, because he doesn't know who or what we are. At least, I doubt he knows. If he did, Hades would be here, too. Last I heard, the king hoped to recruit creatures like us to use our magic against Lucifer."

"You're right. Besides, how would he have learned of our determination to slay him? Everyone we interrogate about the royal families of the underworld, we kill, ensuring word about us and our mission never spreads."

Sable chewed her bottom lip again. "I guess the only question now—how do we ambush him?"

Should they wait around and hope William approached them? What if he didn't? Should they lure him over with a come-hither smile? He might not go for it. His current dates wore fancy dresses; as usual, Sunny and Sable wore unadorned T-shirts and jeans, the perfect blend-in and forget-we-were-ever-here outfit.

Should one of them close the distance and make a move? Like hit on him, letting him believe he was going to score, then lead him to their hotel room?

Yeah. That. It guaranteed contact.

As she explained the idea to Sable, her heart sprinted.

"Perfect. Let's draw straws," Sable said. "Girl with the shorter one has to approach him. The lucky girl waits in the room and shoots him as soon as he enters."

Sunny snorted. "No need to draw. I'll do the grunt work. I can't flirt, but I can turn a man's mind to soup with my personality alone." Anticipation fizzed in her veins. "Just...don't kill him when he gets to the room. Let's interrogate him first. We can finally discover the coordinates to Lucifer's territory."

"Done! Before you go over there and do your mind-soup trick, your appearance needs a little tweak. By the way, I'm gonna need you to teach me how you do that. I'm foaming at the mouth with jealousy." Sable unwound Sunny's braid and combed her fingers through the long waves.

Oh, what Sunny wouldn't give for a trim. But even if she shaved her head, the thick azure mass would grow back in a matter of hours.

Sable nodded, satisfied. "All right, you're ready. Irresistible, and all that crap. Just remember. Your biggest weakness is your expressive face. You have trouble hiding your true emotions."

"Ten-four." Sunny jutted her chin and squared her shoulders. "Here goes nothing."

"You got this." Sable patted her butt before heading for the lobby. Like all of their kind, she walked silently, her footsteps inaudible.

I do. I've got this. Sunny stepped from the shadows…and got hit with a wave of nervousness as people looked her way. What if she didn't have this? Perspiration wet her palms.

No, no. I can do anything.

"—like a computer," a guy sitting at one of the tables was saying. He had a familiar voice. "I'm serious. She can break a code with only a glance. Any code. It's shocking to witness. She's—no way! She's right there!" The speaker pointed at her and waved. "Sunny! Sunny Lane. Hi. I'm Harry. Harry Shorts. Can I buy you a drink?"

More people looked her way. Including William. Their gazes met. Suddenly, she felt as if she'd been smacked with a crowbar. She lost her breath and stutter-stepped.

He studied her face, his attention lingering on each individual feature. *His* features darkened with heat.

The heat of attraction? She licked her lips, the nervousness gaining new ground, beading sweat on her nape.

She scowled. Finding a target sexy? Fine. Whatever. Being fluttered and maybe even kinda sorta aroused by one? No! Unacceptable. Either he exuded some kind of lust dust—*yes, yes, all his fault—or mating season had screwed with her hormones early. Or both!*

Then he turned away, dismissing her, and Sunny skidded to a halt halfway to his table. Sage! He *didn't* want her? She ran her tongue over her teeth. Irritation overshadowed the nervousness. Her heart calmed and her blood cooled, the synapsis in her brain firing again.

The prick is going down. Determined, she glided forward once again. When she reached his table, she stopped, expecting him to notice her arrival. He didn't.

She worked her jaw and—her eyes widened. Oh, wow. He wielded magic, too. A *lot* of magic. Ancient, dark and powerful. The air around him vibrated with it, making her skin tingle.

The women ignored her as well, too wrapped up in William to care about anyone else.

Eventually, William stiffened ever so slightly, and she had to fight a smile. Breaking news! His awareness of her hadn't dulled in the slightest; he just didn't want her to know it.

Too bad, so sad. Deep breath in, out. Mistake! His scent... She closed her eyes and savored, her mouth watering. He smelled like angel food cake laced with crack.

Calm. Steady. No need to act like an uncouth wolf-shifter.

"—my best thinking naked," he was saying to Jaybird and Cash, pretending Sunny wasn't there. "You?"

Enough! "Hi. Hello. Hey," Sunny said, rapping her knuckles against the table. Ugh! *Blowing this already.*

At first, only the women acknowledged her presence. But William continued talking and sipping his whiskey, and they forgot all about her.

She rapped the table again.

Finally, he canted his head in her direction, all languid grace self-assurance. He made a real event of it, too, as if premiering a blockbuster movie. Why bother going to so much trou—*ohhh. That's why.* Up close and personal, his eyes were even more of a showstopper, sparkling with arousal, glinting with a sheen of icy rage and glittering with steely determination.

Electrical currents zapped her nerve endings, and she almost yelped. *Ignore the hint of pleasure. Forge ahead.*

She pasted on her best come-hither smile and waved. *A wave? Seriously? Get it together, Sun. Remember what his family did to yours.*

As she balled her hands into fists, he looked her over slowly, starting at the bottom and working his way up—*singeing* her. When he reached the apex of her thighs, shivers and heat consumed her.

No, no. I will not react. He—and mating season—will not affect me.

His gaze continued moving up, singeing hotter...

He reached her pasted-on smile and unveiled a smirking grin. But...but...why?

"How may I service you, pet?" he asked, slow and deliberate.

She felt the words like a caress. Wait. Pet? Pet! Such an insult to her kind! "In ways you never imagined, handsome," she replied, careful to moderate her tone. She glanced at Jaybird, then Cash. They had to go. Letting her savage, violent side glaze her eyes, she snapped, "Get lost."

William's smirking grin made another appearance.

Jaybird stared at him, exasperated. "Are you going to send her away?"

"No," he said simply.

"Fine. She's all yours. We'll go." With a huff, she stood. Paused. Waiting for him to stop her? When he remained quiet, she flounced off. Cash and the other female followed.

Here's hoping Willy-boy is just as easy to manipulate. "Hello." Ugh. Not this again. "I'm Sunny. My turn-ons include kindness and responsibility. I look twenty-one, but I'm older. Promise!" Nearly ten thousand years old.

A flash of intrigue, there and gone. "I'm William. Lovers call me the Panty Melter. Everyone else calls me the Ever Randy. My turn-ons are living and breathing. I'm older than twenty-one, as well."

Mmm. His voice…like audible sex. If women were "sex kittens," this man was a "sex panther." Meow.

Gah! What are you doing, admiring him? She reminded herself of his many crimes. Long ago, Lucifer and his horde of demons had ridden into her village. They'd raped, pillaged and utterly slaughtered her people. Men, women and children. Her family. Her friends.

Sometimes, when she closed her eyes, she still heard their screams.

The only home she'd ever known had been razed, and the entire scope of her life changed.

There'd been six survivors, Sunny included. No one remembered seeing William, only Lucifer, but Willy must have been involved. Why else would Lucifer's cry, "For William"?

Perhaps the Ever Randy had planned the raid. Perhaps he'd hidden behind a mask. Either way, Sunny had lost *everything.* Even the other survivors. To better the odds of hiding their origins, they decided to split up and reach out only when necessary.

She and Sable were together now only because Sunny had requested assistance.

Fingers snapped in front of her face, yanking her back to the present.

Realization: she'd gotten lost inside her head. Did she *want* to die? Sunny repasted the smile on her face. "Ever Randy, hmm? Does anyone call you ER for short?"

"Only if they wish to die," he replied, his tone dry. Despite the dryness, he thrummed with tension. Did her nearness rattle him?

"So he's cute *and* ferocious. Good job, Sunny." She patted herself on the shoulder, playing her role. "I picked the best slab of beef in the deli."

He winged up one brow. "So I'm a piece of meat to you?"

"Yes, pork chop. Yes. But in my defense, I only think it because I'm right." She leaned over and patted his cheek, the urge to slap him almost impossible to ignore. "You should come with a warning label. Or eyeball condoms."

"Why? Do you plan to stuff your eyes inside my sockets?"

"Maybe?"

"Sorry, but I think I'll pass." He crossed his arms, his shirt pulling taut over deliciously flexed muscles. "No, you know what? I'm feeling daring today. Let's go for it. Gotta try everything once, right?"

A laugh slipped from her. What the hellebore! A prince of darkness would *not* amuse her. "Sorry not sorry I sent your companions away. When I want something, I go for it." Truth!

He moved his gaze over her once again. "And you decided you want me?"

His tone...she thought she detected a hint of certainty *and* uncertainty. How odd. "I spent a whole five minutes planning your seduction. That's six minutes longer than usual."

"That means you're only twenty-four hours behind me," he replied, ignoring her screwed up math.

Did he make a joke...or a statement of fact? Did he just admit to attending the conference to find her?

So. *There's a chance I was wrong.* A chance he knew or suspected who she was, and he'd come to stop her—forever.

Rage flared anew. Soon, it would be appeased...

For now, she forced another smile. The jerk had yet to invite her to join him, or express a desire to leave with her. *Playing hard to get?* Time to take their banter to the next level to give him an excuse to act. "If you were a pizza topping, you'd be hamburger and jalapeno, because you're grade-A beef and hot. I'd be ham and pineapple because I'm salty and sweet." *No. No way I just openly compared us to pizza toppings, as if we're taking a Facebook quiz.*

Okay, so she didn't just suck at flirting. She sucked, period. But wait! He smiled a genuine smile, not one of those smirking grins, as if she'd truly amused him. The sight made her belly quiver.

Only a second later, he jerked as if she'd punched him, his smile vanishing. He tossed back the remains of his drink, his movements powerful, aggressive and seductive. The quivering worsened. *What is he doing to me?*

As he slammed down the glass, a blank mask covered his features. "You may go." He'd blanked his tone, too. "We'll chat later, when it's your turn."

Her turn for what? Interrogation? Maybe he suspected every female codebreaker of being the one hunting his family. And leave him? Hardly. Now that she'd breathed in his magnificent scent, experienced the caress of his voice and the lethal seduction of his gaze, she wanted him dead sooner rather than later. *More dangerous than I realized.*

There had to be a way to override his desire to wait. Oh! Oh! "Your loss, baby. I'm *super* horny." Horny to end his life! "I'm probably dying and only an orgasm will save me. I'd planned to invite you to my room for a couple hours of...you know... thought and reflection." She traced a finger between her breasts and purred, "I heard you say you do your best thinking naked."

His pupils enlarged, spilling over all that pale blue. A sign of sexual yearning. But he didn't null and void his demand.

Daisy! She had one last ace to play. If he still turned her down, she'd hide out, then follow him to his hotel room. "Fine, I'll go. Thankfully, you aren't the only slice of beefcake on the menu. Enjoy the rest of your evening. I know I will." She blew him a kiss and pivoted, revealing her best feature: a rounded aster. Argh! A rounded ass-ter. Freesia! Stupid magic filter. She had a freaking rounded butt, okay?

He sucked in a breath. "Or stay for a few minutes," he croaked.

Relief washed over her, cool and soothing. As hoped, her butt had succeeded where her wit had failed. *One step closer.*

Tremors plagued Sunny as she eased into the chair across from him. He watched her, intent and intense, absentmindedly tracing a finger over the rim of his glass.

Ignore the tingle of awareness. Ignore the crackle of need. Ignore the sizzle of want.

Without looking away from her, he raised an arm and snapped his fingers. A waitress came running, offering him a fresh glass of whiskey. One he polished off in seconds.

Sunny planted her elbows on the table. "So. What should we—"

He slammed the glass onto the table, silencing her. Then he stood and extended a helping hand. "I'd already selected the night's entertainment, and I never rearrange my plans. On the other hand, I'm a giver, incredibly generous, and your life hangs in the balance. So, I will do this for you. I will give you an orgasm." He waved his fingers at her. "Come. Let's go to my room."

"No. Let's go to *my* room," she insisted, smiling a real smile this time. She'd done it! She'd won him over!

He jerked again, but he also gave a stiff nod. "Very well. We'll go to your room, and I'll ensure you survive the night."

About Gena Showalter

Gena Showalter is the *New York Times* and *USA TODAY* bestselling author of the spellbinding Lords of the Underworld, Otherworld Assassins, and Gods of War series, as well as three young adult series—The Forest of Good and Evil, Everlife and the White Rabbit Chronicles--and the highly addictive Original Heartbreakers series.

In addition to being a National Reader's Choice and two time RITA nominee, her romance novels have appeared in Cosmopolitan (Red Hot Read) and Seventeen magazine. She was interviewed on Nightline and has been mentioned in Orange is the New Black. Her books have been translated in multiple languages.

She's hard at work on her next novel, a tale featuring an alpha male with a dark side and the strong woman who brings him to his knees. Check her website often to learn more about Gena, her menagerie of rescue dogs, and all her upcoming books. https://genashowalter.com

Discover 1001 Dark Nights

Go to www.1001DarkNights.com to subscribe.

COLLECTION ONE
FOREVER WICKED by Shayla Black
CRIMSON TWILIGHT by Heather Graham
CAPTURED IN SURRENDER by Liliana Hart
SILENT BITE: A SCANGUARDS WEDDING by Tina Folsom
DUNGEON GAMES by Lexi Blake
AZAGOTH by Larissa Ione
NEED YOU NOW by Lisa Renee Jones
SHOW ME, BABY by Cherise Sinclair
ROPED IN by Lorelei James
TEMPTED BY MIDNIGHT by Lara Adrian
THE FLAME by Christopher Rice
CARESS OF DARKNESS by Julie Kenner

COLLECTION TWO
WICKED WOLF by Carrie Ann Ryan
WHEN IRISH EYES ARE HAUNTING by Heather Graham
EASY WITH YOU by Kristen Proby
MASTER OF FREEDOM by Cherise Sinclair
CARESS OF PLEASURE by Julie Kenner
ADORED by Lexi Blake
HADES by Larissa Ione
RAVAGED by Elisabeth Naughton
DREAM OF YOU by Jennifer L. Armentrout
STRIPPED DOWN by Lorelei James
RAGE/KILLIAN by Alexandra Ivy/Laura Wright
DRAGON KING by Donna Grant
PURE WICKED by Shayla Black
HARD AS STEEL by Laura Kaye
STROKE OF MIDNIGHT by Lara Adrian
ALL HALLOWS EVE by Heather Graham
KISS THE FLAME by Christopher Rice
DARING HER LOVE by Melissa Foster
TEASED by Rebecca Zanetti
THE PROMISE OF SURRENDER by Liliana Hart

COLLECTION THREE
HIDDEN INK by Carrie Ann Ryan
BLOOD ON THE BAYOU by Heather Graham
SEARCHING FOR MINE by Jennifer Probst
DANCE OF DESIRE by Christopher Rice
ROUGH RHYTHM by Tessa Bailey
DEVOTED by Lexi Blake
Z by Larissa Ione
FALLING UNDER YOU by Laurelin Paige
EASY FOR KEEPS by Kristen Proby
UNCHAINED by Elisabeth Naughton
HARD TO SERVE by Laura Kaye
DRAGON FEVER by Donna Grant
KAYDEN/SIMON by Alexandra Ivy/Laura Wright
STRUNG UP by Lorelei James
MIDNIGHT UNTAMED by Lara Adrian
TRICKED by Rebecca Zanetti
DIRTY WICKED by Shayla Black
THE ONLY ONE by Lauren Blakely
SWEET SURRENDER by Liliana Hart

COLLECTION FOUR
ROCK CHICK REAWAKENING by Kristen Ashley
ADORING INK by Carrie Ann Ryan
SWEET RIVALRY by K. Bromberg
SHADE'S LADY by Joanna Wylde
RAZR by Larissa Ione
ARRANGED by Lexi Blake
TANGLED by Rebecca Zanetti
HOLD ME by J. Kenner
SOMEHOW, SOME WAY by Jennifer Probst
TOO CLOSE TO CALL by Tessa Bailey
HUNTED by Elisabeth Naughton
EYES ON YOU by Laura Kaye
BLADE by Alexandra Ivy/Laura Wright
DRAGON BURN by Donna Grant
TRIPPED OUT by Lorelei James
STUD FINDER by Lauren Blakely
MIDNIGHT UNLEASHED by Lara Adrian

HALLOW BE THE HAUNT by Heather Graham
DIRTY FILTHY FIX by Laurelin Paige
THE BED MATE by Kendall Ryan
NIGHT GAMES by CD Reiss
NO RESERVATIONS by Kristen Proby
DAWN OF SURRENDER by Liliana Hart

COLLECTION FIVE
BLAZE ERUPTING by Rebecca Zanetti
ROUGH RIDE by Kristen Ashley
HAWKYN by Larissa Ione
RIDE DIRTY by Laura Kaye
ROME'S CHANCE by Joanna Wylde
THE MARRIAGE ARRANGEMENT by Jennifer Probst
SURRENDER by Elisabeth Naughton
INKED NIGHTS by Carrie Ann Ryan
ENVY by Rachel Van Dyken
PROTECTED by Lexi Blake
THE PRINCE by Jennifer L. Armentrout
PLEASE ME by J. Kenner
WOUND TIGHT by Lorelei James
STRONG by Kylie Scott
DRAGON NIGHT by Donna Grant
TEMPTING BROOKE by Kristen Proby
HAUNTED BE THE HOLIDAYS by Heather Graham
CONTROL by K. Bromberg
HUNKY HEARTBREAKER by Kendall Ryan
THE DARKEST CAPTIVE by Gena Showalter

Also from 1001 Dark Nights:

TAME ME by J. Kenner
THE SURRENDER GATE By Christopher Rice
SERVICING THE TARGET By Cherise Sinclair
TEMPT ME by J. Kenner

On Behalf of 1001 Dark Nights,

Liz Berry and M.J. Rose would like to thank ~

Steve Berry
Doug Scofield
Kim Guidroz
Jillian Stein
InkSlinger PR
Dan Slater
Asha Hossain
Chris Graham
Chelle Olson
Jessica Johns
Dylan Stockton
Richard Blake
and Simon Lipskar

CPSIA information can be obtained
at www.ICGtesting.com
Printed in the USA
LVHW041821270920
667211LV00001B/144